The tide was coming in ...

"That's what happened to my life," Willa said softly, gesturing toward the beach where the sand forts were no longer distinguishable. "It simply washed away."

Nick lifted his gaze. "That's why you decided to come here?"

"I guess we could've gone anywhere. Except—"

Nick leaned closer. There was a fine sheen of sweat on Willa's skin. In the sun's glow, she seemed to glimmer like soft gold. "Except what?"

"I want Bethany to have what I had when I was growing up. My grandmother had this huge rocking chair. When I was a little girl I used to climb up on her lap and she'd rock and whisper stories in my ear as if we were having secrets. She told me I was her special girl. When I had a problem I headed straight for that rocking chair. I want Bethany to have that kind of security, those kinds of memories...."

"She has you."

ABOUT THE AUTHOR

Jackie Weger loves to travel and to share the places she's discovered with her readers. In *Best Behavior* she has taken a new tack, choosing to share with her characters a place she'd traveled to and decided not to leave. Jackie says she loves living in St. Augustine, Florida, the oldest city in the U.S. That love comes through in her vivid description of the beautiful beaches and charming historic landmarks that grace her adopted hometown.

Books by Jackie Weger

HARLEQUIN AMERICAN ROMANCE

HARLEQUIN TEMPTATION

HARLEQUIN SUPERROMANCE

Don't miss any of our special offers. Write to us at the following address for information on our newest releases.

Harlequin Reader Service
901 Fuhrmann Blvd., P.O. Box 1397, Buffalo, NY 14240
Canadian address: P.O. Box 603,
Fort Erie, Ont. L2A 5X3

BEST
BEHAVIOR

JACKIE WEGER

Harlequin Books

TORONTO • NEW YORK • LONDON
AMSTERDAM • PARIS • SYDNEY • HAMBURG
STOCKHOLM • ATHENS • TOKYO • MILAN

For the girls in the family
Mary and Margaret
Nilka and Angelica
Courtney and Melissa
Jennifer and Jacquelyn

Published May 1990

ISBN 0-373-16344-4

Chapter One

The sun shone with an increased sharpness. The humid air was hot, glistening hard and bright upon the city that was considered the oldest in the United States. Willa's cotton dress had begun to stick to her back. She felt moisture beading between her palm and her daughter's, which she held tightly.

It was a few minutes past 9:00 a.m. Already there was bumper-to-bumper traffic on the narrow artery that fed tourists into the attractions of St. Augustine, some of which were said to be more than four hundred years old.

There was, too, on the sidewalks, a wealth of foot traffic. Willa allowed the momentum of the crowds to carry her and her daughter along.

"I want to see the Oldest Wooden Schoolhouse," Bethany said, quoting verbatim from the tourist guide Willa had read to her the night before. "You promised."

"We will, sweetie, but first I have to talk to someone. Afterward, okay?"

"How much afterward?" the child insisted, exploiting appeasement with the instinctive skill of a five-year-old.

After I've gotten our lives in order, Willa wanted to say, but that was no answer for a child.

"Right afterward," she said, and smiled slightly to herself. She had learned her lesson well. Being a psychologist held no weight in the face of motherhood. Objectivity simply did not exist.

Satisfied for the moment, Bethany skipped along at her mother's side.

In front of a beige, Victorian house, Willa tugged Bethany aside, allowing a large and cheerful family to pass.

Fleetingly Willa envied the family its gaiety. Her own emotions were a rampant mixture of fear, apprehension and hope.

For the hundredth-plus time, she wondered if she were doing the right thing. Could a journey borne of so much tragedy and mischance possibly turn out right? So much could go wrong. Or simply, be wrong. She doubted the people she was here to meet would be uncivil, but she had dozens of questions, all of which would have to be answered before she could make a decision that would affect herself and Bethany for the rest of their lives.

The first line in the visitors' guide had stayed with her. "Change is an ingredient from which history is made." Perhaps she was making a bit of history for herself and Bethany. Still, change was scary and she felt like someone grasping for a rope that dangled just out of reach.

Recall of what she perceived as betrayal made Willa's throat tighten. She could not be angry at her mother or Peter for dying. Death had no master. But she had loved and trusted her dad. She had depended upon him for emotional support and he had not been there for her when she needed him most. Even worse had been his insensitivity toward Bethany, a child who had already suffered more losses in her short life than any five-year-old should have to endure.

Bethany deserved to have roots, a continuity of family—a continuity that Peter's family, and what remained of Willa's own family, were not willing to provide.

The child tugged on her mother's hand, dispelling Willa's reverie. "Why are we stopping, Mommy? Are we lost again?"

Willa laughed. "Not this time, sweetie, at least, I hope not." She checked the brass number plate on the door against the business card she'd removed from her purse. "We're right on target. Now I want you on your best behavior, okay?"

"I know—" Bethany groaned. "Be quiet and don't interrupt grown-ups."

"Right," Willa said with false cheer, as much to boost her own courage as to dampen the sense of unease that had plagued her since leaving Kansas. But, right or wrong, she thought, she was now committed.

The entrance hall was dim and only a few degrees cooler than outside. Willa stopped for a moment to allow her eyes to adjust. To her left was the door to a souvenir shop, closed. At the far end of the hall, a velvet rope barred access to an upstairs art gallery. To her right, was an open door. A small sign beside the door announced the offices of Nicholas Cavenaugh, Attorney-at-Law. Willa's heart picked up speed, threatening to drive right into her stomach.

A single thought rushed through her mind: It's not too late to back out. The attorney need never know she'd been here. But even as she considered retreat, her feet carried her forward to the threshold of the office.

A man was seated at the receptionist's desk, hunched over the typewriter in deep concentration as he pecked slowly on the keyboard. His tie was loosened and his shirtsleeves were rolled to the elbows. In profile his features were distinctive: a straight nose balanced by a square jaw, and full lips that hinted at an easy smile. Even before he sensed their presence, Willa saw that his was not a conventionally handsome face. The most striking thing about it was its intensity.

"Hello," she said hesitantly, her voice higher than normal.

He glanced up, then returned his gaze to his work. "The souvenir shop and gallery are closed until the airconditioner is repaired." He voiced the information as if by rote, his irritation obvious.

"We need—" Willa began.

"No public rest rooms here, either, lady," he said without taking his eyes from the text in the typewriter. "Try the Welcome Center in the next block."

She should do just that, Willa thought. Just turn and go—but there was no retracing her path home. She and Bethany had no home, only each other. Besides, the man's curt behavior made her temper flare. She had not driven more than a thousand miles merely to be dismissed.

"I'm Willa Manning, here to see—"

The man's head jerked up.

At least that got a rise out of him, Willa thought. Now he was openly assessing her. The yellow cotton shift she wore was a simple affair, buttoned down the front, belted at the waist and falling modestly below her knees. The trim lines of the dress served to emphasize the length of her legs; the straps of her sandals enhanced her wellshaped ankles. Willa knew she looked nice, but could read neither approval nor welcome in the man's face.

It was going to be disastrous. She could sense it. She had done the wrong thing!

He rose to his feet. "You're early by five days," he said stiffly. He was tall, broad shouldered and lean in the hips. Standing, he dwarfed the desk.

"I know." She gave him a tentative smile. "But, I have a job interview next Monday. The appointments overlap. I was hoping..." She placed a protective hand on Bethany's shoulder. The gesture caused him to shift his gaze. He studied Bethany with the same whole-minded concentration he had been applying to his typing. When his eyes shifted to Willa again, she saw that they were very gray, rimmed with curly dark lashes. "You *are* Nicholas Cavenaugh?" she prompted.

"Didn't I say that?"

"No."

He didn't thrust out a hand to shake so Willa kept hers occupied, one rested on Bethany, one clutched her purse.

"So you're Willa Manning," he said, making the redundant observation as if it left a bad taste in his mouth.

"I'm Bethany," the child announced.

The cautious look in Nicholas Cavenaugh's eyes lifted. He spoke softly. "You're a lovely girl, Bethany, just like your mother, right down to the dimples in your cheeks."

Bethany beamed, but the words flicked across Willa like the lash of a whip. In speaking of Bethany's mother, Cavenaugh had not meant herself. That meant... he must've known Bethany's biological mother!

Willa had a sudden chilling thought. Paternity had never been established. Could Cavenaugh be...? She could not finish the thought. Had she been tricked in some horrible way? She glared at Nicholas Cavenaugh, horror-struck. How much older was he than Bethany's birth mother? Ten years? Fifteen? Scenario after scenario raced through Willa's mind. Not one of them seemed impossible. She had to stop him before he said anything more in front of Bethany.

"Thank you," she said rigidly.

Understanding dawned upon him. "I didn't mean—"

"I know exactly what you meant. You're already breaching our agreement."

"Are you the person Mommy has to see?" Bethany asked.

There was a sense of tension in the way his dark gaze darted from mother to child, but he managed to smile once again at Bethany, Willa noticed.

"I guess I am," he said.

"Are we finished, then? Mommy's taking me to see the Oldest Wooden Schoolhouse."

Nick began to roll down his sleeves. "It's too hot to conduct business in here. What do you say we all go for a walk down to the park? You can play on the swings while I chat with your mother." He looked to see if this was acceptable to Willa.

She nodded. She wanted out of the hot, airless office. She wanted space so that she and Bethany could escape at the first opportunity. She needed to rethink the entire issue.

Bethany was not so easily swayed. Swings and playgrounds were too ordinary to compete with the adventure of school, which she longed to attend. "How long will that take?" she asked.

"Only a few minutes, and there's a doughnut shop on the way...."

"Doughnuts? Do they have chocolate-covered?"

"Hundreds."

Bethany looked at her mother.

"One will do," Willa said.

While the attorney closed his office, she and Bethany waited on the front steps.

It was only a few short blocks to the park. Doggedly Willa avoided every stiff attempt at conversation that the attorney made. At the doughnut shop, she refused his offer of coffee.

With each step toward the park she rued the impulsive streak that prompted her to say and do things that were so at war with her practical instincts. Had she been practical, she would have tried to rebuild their lives in Kansas City. But the letter from the Elliotts, those strangers linked to Bethany by circumstances she had never foreseen, had made her think about new horizons. So she had talked herself into taking a risk.

There was a scar on her soul. She wanted healing. She had felt nothing but relief when she left Kansas City; relief when she had driven away from her father's farm. And, as she had come farther south, she had begun to feel human again. Bethany, too, had seemed to sense a release. She'd chattered away, exhibiting an energy Willa would not have believed without having seen it for herself.

So all right. If Nicholas Cavenaugh's attitude was a foreshadowing of what she might expect from the Elliotts, that wasn't the end of the world. She had embarked in a new direction and would not turn back. But, if need be, she would refuse the job offer in St. Augustine and look more closely at the one farther up the coast.

"That's where we live now," Bethany said around a mouthful of doughnut when they strolled past the motel in which she and her mother had spent the night.

Nick glanced at Willa, raised an eyebrow, then too casually, sipped coffee from his paper cup.

"I took the room for a week," Willa said, breaking her self-imposed silence.

"Until something better comes along?" The sarcasm was light, but there. Willa stiffened. She had a pithy retort ready, but Bethany had big ears and a memory too sharply honed for a five-year-old. Willa held her tongue until they were at the park where Bethany raced to play with other children on the monkey bars.

She and Nicholas Cavenaugh sat opposite each other at one of the vacant picnic tables in the shade of a moss-draped live oak. All of Willa's bottled-up tension and apprehension erupted.

"Listen, Mr. Cavenaugh, nothing—and I mean, nothing!—is to be said around Bethany that will hurt or confuse her in any way. She understands that she's adopted. But it's just a word to her. She hasn't absorbed the exact meaning of the word. She knows nothing whatever about the circumstances surrounding her birth. She isn't yet prepared for that. I won't tolerate any more slips like the one you made earlier."

Her hands were trembling. She put them in her lap lest he notice, and guess how nervous and frightened she felt. She stared hard at the angles and planes of his face, superimposing them over the beloved face of her daughter. Both had dark curly hair. Otherwise, she could find no likeness.

"Point taken," Nick replied smoothly, as if undisturbed by her outburst.

He was a mass of raw nerves inside. Willa Manning had caught him off guard. He had been unprepared for her beauty. The years-old grainy newspaper photograph he had seen of her most certainly did not do her justice. Anger put color on her patrician features and deepened the blue of her eyes until they gleamed almost purple.

Her dark hair was straight, styled so that it capped her head and curved forward at her chin. The slight breeze had wind-whipped it just enough to give her a tousled, sensuous look.

He suspected she knew how appealing she looked with her hair wind-tossed like that. Most women would have already had their hands at their head in an effort to maintain their hairstyle.

He had warned the Elliotts that Willa Manning was an unknown. He had pressed for caution, but Claudine Elliott had been adamant that she would meet her granddaughter. Never mind that the child had been adopted.

Discovering that Susan had borne a daughter had been like a miracle. Claudine had felt that God was giving her a second chance. It had been less than two months now since Susan, who had long been buried as a Jane Doe in a pauper's grave, had been brought home and interred in the Elliott family plot.

Nick was becoming certain the Manning woman was aware of this. Her unannounced early arrival could well have been calculated to take advantage of the Elliotts' grief, which meant he'd have to stay on his professional toes to protect them. He owed John and Claudine that much.

"I want more than 'point taken,'" Willa insisted. "I want your word, I want what we agreed upon. I make the decision about when, *if*, Bethany is to be told who her natural mother was, who the Elliotts are."

"I'm not in the habit of having my integrity questioned, Mrs. Manning. May I remind you that you arrived in my office five days early? You've heard of the telephone, haven't you? You could've alerted me. At any rate, I would not have expected you to have the child with you at our first meeting."

Willa gave him a pitying look. "I could hardly leave her unsupervised and alone in a motel room in a strange town, today or next week." She wanted the focus of the conversation off Bethany. It made her speak sharply. "Tell me something about the Elliotts. What kind of people are they?"

"Nice, caring people, a bit old-fashioned. Wealthy, of course." His smile did not reach his eyes. "But you know that."

Blood drained from Willa's face, making her eyes appear darker and deeper set. "I'm not here for money, for myself or for Bethany. You know that. I refused the offer of travel expenses, of gifts—"

"An adroit move on your part?"

"Do the Elliotts think that?" she raged. "Do you? If so, why search for us? Why forward me this...."

She snapped open her purse, snatched the letter and unfolded it.

"'Please, Mrs. Manning,'" she read with trembling voice,

"'...allow us to see Bethany. Just see her. We want to assure you again that we'll make no challenge to your custody of Bethany, but she's the only link we have to our Susan. We like to think that had Susan lived, she would have brought her daughter home. Bethany is our grandchild. She's of our blood. Please come to St. Augustine. We want to help you with Bethany, any way you'll let us. You can set any rules for the visit you like. We'll abide by them. Just let us see our granddaughter. Our hearts ache...'"

In spite of herself, Willa was moved again by the letter. She glared at Nicholas Cavenaugh. "This is why I've brought Bethany. This letter tore at my heart. But I don't suppose a crass attorney like yourself can understand that."

Refolding the letter, a nasty thought struck Willa. Suppose the letter had been designed to do just what it had done—get herself and Bethany to Florida. Suppose the Elliotts were coconspirators with Cavenaugh? Suppose they knew he was Bethany's natural father? No amount of investigation by her own attorney could have discovered that. She had only questioned the Elliotts' motives and their letter had satisfied that question. It had not occurred to her to question Cavenaugh's. She had thought him little more than the Elliotts' spokesperson, as bipartisan as her own attorney—a go-between.

A thought flashed through her brain. Cavenaugh had had plenty of time to make a phone call while she and Bethany waited for him outside his office. The Elliotts could have already filed for custody of Bethany here in Florida. They could've just been waiting for her to show up! For all she knew, Cavenaugh might have someone lurking nearby to slap her with a subpoena, ordering her into court.

She might have made a gargantuan mistake. It could cost her Bethany!

Well, she wasn't the type to sit idly by while Fate grabbed her by the throat and had its way with her. Cavenaugh might as well know that. In one fluid movement she returned the letter to her purse, slipped away from the table and called to her daughter.

Nick was fast on his feet. "Hey! Wait a minute! Where're you going?"

"I don't like having my integrity questioned, either! You can tell the Elliotts I've changed my mind. Goodbye, Mr. Cavenaugh. You'll forgive me if I don't say it's been a pleasure meeting you."

Stunned, Nick realized that short of wrestling the woman to the ground, he had no means of stopping her. Muttering epithets, he watched Willa and Bethany walk out of the park.

Willa sensed his eyes boring into her back, which made her self-conscious. With Bethany in hand, she hurried away, her gait far stiffer than her usual hip-swaying, long-legged stride.

"I forgot to tell the man 'thank you' for the doughnut," Bethany said.

"I did it for you."

"Now we're going to the schoolhouse, right?"

"Right, but I just have to make one stop at the motel office first."

"And I can see other things, too?"

"Until you get tired."

"I'm five now, I don't get tired."

Willa forced a laugh. "Well, I do."

"That's because you're thirty-six, Mommy. You're old."

Not old enough or wise enough, Willa thought.

She knew too little about the Elliotts, their traits and characters—things she had wanted to know for Bethany's sake. She had been stunned when Cavenaugh's first letter arrived, telling her he had established that the Jane Doe who had borne Bethany was the daughter of John and Claudine Elliott. And she'd been frightened when he asked if she would be willing to meet the Elliotts.

She had taken the letter to her own attorney. He had doubted Willa would lose a challenge against her custody of Bethany, but reminded her that more and more grandparents were suing for visitation rights to their grandchildren—and winning. Considering the unusual circumstances surrounding Bethany's birth and adoption, he had urged Willa to allow a meeting between the biological grandparents and Bethany.

There had been an exchange of information via their respective attorneys. On the Elliotts' part, their response had been to assure Willa that they would honor her wishes concerning Bethany. They emphasized they had no desire to cause any discord in her life or Bethany's.

They wanted to know whether her husband would object to the meeting? What did the other grandparents feel? What about her work? Could she take leave?

She had written that her husband had died more than a year ago; that there were no objections from other family members and she was working only part-time.

She had not told them that her own mother had died in a fire years ago or that her father had recently remarried a woman two years younger than Willa was, or that she had not seen Peter's parents since his funeral. The senior Mannings had never approved of Bethany's adoption. They had wanted a Manning heir out of their only son's loins—not the discard of some young chit found wasting away on a Kansas City street curb.

But all of that was information that could easily be had, Willa realized now. The Elliotts and Cavenaugh knew she alone was responsible for Bethany. It gave them an advantage.

Damn it! She had been too eager to reach out, too quick to respond to Claudine Elliott's emotional plea. But, having suffered grief and loss herself, Willa empathized with Claudine's pain and grief. Six years they had searched for their daughter, only to finally discover Susan dead and buried.

Willa knew what grief was, first at the loss of her mother, and later, after Peter's sudden death. She knew how grief made you want to curl up and avoid life. She knew about the ache that lingered for months. She was over Peter's death now—or as over as she could ever expect to be. She would always miss her mother, always miss Peter, but the emptiness those deaths had left in her life was no longer so overwhelming. And she did have Bethany.

Willa understood, or thought she understood what it would mean to the Elliotts to see Bethany, to get to know her. But if Cavenaugh was any indication of their attitude, then she and Bethany were victims of their duplicity.

Going to court would thrust Bethany into the limelight once again and raise questions in the child's mind. Just now, the answers to those questions might do more harm than good. Bethany was an exceptionally sensitive child, her sense of self too fragile to bear assault.

To think she had decided a meeting on pleasant terms was in Bethany's best interest. Pleasant terms! With Nicholas Cavenaugh as intermediary? What a farce!

"Mommy! Slow down. You're walking too fast."

"Oh! Sorry, sweetheart, my mind was miles away."

"That's dumb," said Bethany, a stickler for exactitude. "If your mind was far away, you wouldn't have one."

Willa laughed. "What are you—gifted, or just persnickety?"

Brown eyes alight, Bethany cast her mother a look of impertinence. "Prob'ly persnickety?"

"Good guess."

Dark curls bouncing, Bethany giggled.

The sound of her daughter's laughter made Willa catch her breath. Peter's death had seemed to regress much of Bethany's hard-won emotional growth. Not a little of that regression had been caused, Willa knew, by Bethany witnessing her own grief. Both of them had been sad and mirthless far too long.

The tone of Claudine Elliott's letter ran through Willa's mind again. Could the woman who wrote that be an underhanded villain? Or was it just Cavenaugh? If he was Bethany's father, would he want that known?

Perhaps, Willa thought, she should pick up the telephone and make the contact with John and Claudine Elliott on her own. It wasn't fair to penalize them on Cavenaugh's account. Appealing as that idea was, she nixed it as being unsound. She, herself, had set the criterion for meeting. To change in midstride might give them the impression that she was a pushover, willing to make concessions.

At the motel she learned she'd have to forfeit a large part of the unused portion of the week's rent she had paid in advance should she check out now. The manager apologized, but said he didn't make the rules.

While part of her mind grappled with the problem of what to do, Willa observed her daughter. It was time for laughter, she decided. The remainder of the day belonged to Bethany.

Chapter Two

Willa sorted through the Polaroid snapshots and picked up the two she liked best. In the first, Bethany posed, displaying her yellow "Diploma" from the Oldest Wooden Schoolhouse. The second was a candid shot; Bethany, ice-cream cone in hand, wide-eyed and smiling, at a street musician. Her expression was pliant and guileless.

Proof positive, Willa thought, that Bethany had begun to emerge from her self-contained cocoon of diffidence and restraint. The realization prompted Willa to bend over and press her lips lightly to the sleeping child's forehead. Lingering a moment, she traced the delicate, perfect eyebrows.

Bethany's hair formed a nimbus around her wan little face. Willa studied the curls. No! she exclaimed to herself. Cavenaugh couldn't be. She was just tilting at windmills. She was assuming complications where there weren't any.

Bethany stirred. Willa moved from the bed to a small table to put the photos in her album. Within the plastic-coated pages was a record of Bethany's short life.

It was still almost unbearable to look at the first entry. Then, Bethany had been known only as Baby Doe. In the

picture her tiny form was obscured by a maze of tubes
and bottles and machinery.

Because she had been on staff at the hospital, she had
been offered the early photographs from Bethany's files.
The nurses had been glad to give her the photos that had
been tacked to their bulletin board. It had been less easy
to approach the couple who had first taken Bethany
home, then discarded her like a defective toy when
Bethany became ill. Even after three years, Willa could
recall the startled look on the woman's face when she had
requested their photographs. The couple's self-centered
cruelty had made her rage inside.

"You do understand, don't you, Mrs. Manning?
There's just no way we can cope with a child who might
be retarded or stunted. And she's forever getting sick.
The medical bills..." The couple had called the state
adoption agency, abandoning an eighteen-month-old
Bethany while she lay in the hospital with pneumonia.

"You want that little girl, don't you?" Peter had said
the night she told him that Bethany was back in the hospital and how cruel it was that she was going into foster
care when she was discharged.

So they had applied to adopt Bethany. Remembering,
Willa smiled. And the first set of adoptive parents had
not been let off so easily.

The entire pediatrics staff was incensed at their behavior. One of the nurses leaked to the press that Baby Doe
was back and had been abandoned for a second time.
The public was outraged. And although she and Peter
had been subjected to microscopic inspection, they had
not been found wanting. When Bethany had left the
hospital, she was released into Willa and Peter's care.

Nothing else in Willa's life compared to the milestone
of signing the final adoption papers for Bethany. Those,

too, along with all the newspaper clips, were in the album. One day she would present it to Bethany, but not yet. It was too much, too soon, for Bethany to absorb.

Bethany was her heart. There was no other way to express it. Sometimes it astonished Willa how strong her maternal instinct was, how fiercely protective she felt about Bethany. She never bothered to analyze the depth of her emotions. They were just there, burrowed deep in her psyche.

Had she been counseling parents in whom she had found the same behavior and emotions, she would have cautioned them not to smother their child, to allow the child to develop and become independent. She supposed it was normal that she could not take her own advice.

The light tapping at the door so startled her, Willa jerked, scattering snapshots. The tapping became insistent. She peered between the curtains.

Nicholas Cavenaugh! She opened the door the length of the safety chain, eyeing him through the narrow gap. She had a frustrating impulse to call him a name. Good sense and decency intervened. "What're you doing here?" she said, the tilt of her chin indicating her willingness to do battle.

"Take the chain off so we can talk properly."

"Not in a million years."

He rocked on his heels. "I'm here to apologize."

"Under duress, no doubt."

Nick's head was still vibrating with Claudine's hysteria and her accusation that he had deliberately, mean spiritedly, cut off all access to her only grandchild. Even John, normally the most taciturn of men, had managed to string twenty-five words together on the subject. If it was money the Manning woman wanted, give it to her! he had insisted. Nick was to protect their interest in the child. Go back and make everything right with Mrs. Manning. Today. Tonight.

"You're right," Nick admitted to Willa. "I've been instructed to cajole, coax and persuade you by any means, to remain in St. Augustine. Barring that, I'm to go off somewhere and cut my throat."

"Mr. and Mrs. Elliott sound like people after my own heart," Willa said sweetly. "Go do it."

"Has anyone ever told you that you have too many opinions, and no talent at all for stifling them?"

"I'm not impressed with you, either. Tell the Elliotts I'm willing to continue as planned, provided they choose someone other than yourself as emissary."

"No way. What's wrong with me? I'm skilled at this sort of thing, sensitive—"

"Mr. Cavenaugh," Willa said in a clipped tone that cut to the bone, "you're about as sensitive as an attack dog."

Nick did a double take. He had spent hard years perfecting his style. Years in which he had learned how to deal with judges most effectively, outargue colleagues in front of juries, outwit recalcitrant insurance companies bent on delay, and to develop what little charm the Lord had seen fit to bestow upon him. He was a man of modest desires and humble needs. Hell... he was one of the best attorneys in St. Johns County. He was not going to take abuse from a woman whose motives he had yet to fully discern. But if he were to accomplish what he came for he'd have to eat crow and pretend to like it.

"I really made that bad of an impression?" he said, sounding certifiably contrite.

"You did."

He massaged the bridge of his nose. "All right. Come out to dinner with me. I'll show you I'm a nice guy. No hard edges. I'm a pussycat once I've eaten."

"We've already had supper. Besides, Bethany's asleep."

"Then open the door and let's talk about this face-to-face like civilized people. I feel like a fool standing out here talking through a one-inch crack."

"Rather you a fool than me a victim of—whatever."

"Now wait a minute!"

"I believe that's your swan song," Willa said, attempting to close the door.

"Hold it!" His fingers curved around the jamb before she got it entirely shut. "I blew it this morning. I wasn't being objective. I'm more than just an attorney in this case—"

"Oh?" Willa's legs suddenly felt like wet rope. "In what way?"

"I'm a close friend of the family."

Again all sorts of conjectures raced through Willa's brain. "How close a friend?"

"Old Elliott senior, John's dad, was my godfather. John Elliott is like an older brother to me...."

Willa took a deep breath and held it. Now he would say it, that he and Susan...

Instead he said, "I've been in on the search for Susan since the very first. I was just as stunned to learn about Bethany as John and Claudine were. And when I saw her today... it took my breath away. I don't know where my head was."

"What about the cracks you made about money?"

"I was being a jerk. Listen, if dinner is out, can we talk about it over breakfast?"

"I need time to think about everything some more."

"You'll have all night. How about this: I've cleared my calendar. I'm free all day tomorrow. Let me show you around, take you and Bethany to the beach—"

"While the Elliotts are watching from some discreet vantage point. No thanks."

"John and Claudine are honorable people. They gave you their word and they'll keep it. You can plan the day. Any questions you have, I'll answer as best I can."

"I have one now. Have the Elliotts filed a custody suit for Bethany here in Florida?"

"No, I give you my word on that. They want to meet her and see her. They want what's best for Bethany, the same as you. Let's you and I get together tomorrow and work out plans for you to meet them."

Willa felt shoved against a wall. She had reservations by the bucketful. Yet—it was important to talk to the Elliotts.

So little of Bethany's genetic background had been discovered. For her daughter's sake, she wanted to chart as much of it as she could determine.

Eventually Bethany's natural curiosity about herself would come to the fore. She would ask those seemingly innocent questions: What was my Dad like? Who do I look like?

Willa wanted to have answers ready.

Too, over and above the issue of paternity, lingered the reason Susan had wandered alone and pregnant from her home to end up undernourished and dying more than a thousand miles from her family. Finding an answer to that, Willa knew, required a delicacy of approach and, more than a single meeting.

Most of all, she wanted to know if John and Claudine Elliott were the kind of people she wanted in Bethany's life.

Could she afford to pass up a source of information just because he had an abrasive attitude? The answer was, no.

"You know I don't want to discuss anything in front of Bethany."

Nick sensed victory. "I promise to be circumspect. How does eight o'clock sound?"

Willa almost laughed. Bethany was a sluggish riser. "Awful. Make it ten."

His fingers tightened on the door. "You won't bolt, will you?"

Willa closed her eyes. She had given the idea hard thought all day. But when she left Kansas, she had decided there would be no turning back. She had no place to bolt to. The only question was how much contact she would be willing to allow between Bethany and the Elliotts. "No, we'll be here."

"Ten o'clock, then." His lean fingers with their well-tended nails slipped from the door.

Willa snapped the lock into place. Before she switched out the light, she cradled Bethany's short, stubby hands in her own and studied them. Were Bethany's delicate, child's hands a juvenile version of Nicholas Cavenaugh's?

I'm getting paranoid, she thought, disgusted, and switched off the light.

Lying in bed with the dark all around her, she considered that Nick could be...*could be*... Yet, without rhyme or reason, she hoped the attorney wasn't Bethany's father.

NICK SAT behind the wheel of his car and felt the fatigue of the past few hours wash over him.

He dreaded the outcome of a meeting between the Elliotts and Willa Manning. John had ignored entirely the investigator's report on Willa—not that there was anything derogatory. John just refused to read between the lines. That Willa Manning was a widow, educated, to be sure, but somewhat financially strapped held not a whit of interest. Was she a good mother to their grandchild? was all they had wanted to know.

Nick had been forced to answer that she appeared to be a devoted mother. Now that he had met with her twice he could also report that she had the unyielding personality of a lioness unafraid of fire, flood or drought.

He ought to be crowned with a halo for agreeing to spend an entire day in her company.

The bright spot on the horizon was the child. Bethany promised to be a charmer. She was the spitting image of Susan, right down to the pixieish curve of her lip when she smiled.

Nick sighed. He had prevailed upon John to be cautious. But the very day that Bethany had been proved without a doubt to be his granddaughter, John had wanted to set up a trust fund. Willa Manning had a gold mine in Bethany. So what if she had thus far refused even so much as a nickel!

He knew strategy when he saw it. Were the Manning woman his client, he'd even admire her business sense.

Actually, had they met under any other circumstances, there were any number of things about her he'd have found admirable—such as the way she held her head, those long, long legs... Of course she wanted another attorney to represent the Elliotts. Discovering him to be immune, she wanted someone she could bat those demure lashes at and use to further her own interests.

Only time would tell if all Willa Manning was after was money. Nick fervently hoped that wasn't the case.

He inhaled deeply.

Ah, Susan, he thought, you had it all. Beauty, brains, money—what made you throw it all away and complicate all of our lives?

With a last glance at the door of number fifteen, Nick drove out of the motel parking lot.

"YOU'RE EARLY!" Willa accused. She had overslept and had yet to apply her makeup.

"Turnabout is fair play," Nick said with just enough cheer in his tone to take out the sting.

He had thought that he was prepared for her good looks this morning and was determined not to let that interfere with his professionalism. But she wore a slip of a knit blouse that buttoned down the front and a pair of Bermuda shorts that still left a lot of leg showing. It was a strain on his willpower to keep his eyes above her neck. "It's going to be a long day, I thought we'd start with breakfast. There's a pancake house around the corner."

"Pancakes?" Bethany was off the bed and beside her mother like a shot. "I love pancakes."

Willa made a grab for Bethany before the child was past her and out the door. "You said I could plan the day," she reminded Nick.

"You can. My suggestion is innocent. I'm in the mood for blueberry waffles and a gallon of coffee."

"Give me a minute," she said, then turned and ordered Bethany to stay put before disappearing into the bathroom.

Nick lounged against a column in the breezeway.

Bethany stared up at him. "I can talk to you now, because you're not a stranger anymore. Mommy said we're goin' to the beach. I have my swimsuit on under my shorts. As soon as we have pancakes, can we go see the

Atlantic Ocean? Will we see a whale? I have a picture book on whales.''

"Not a whale," Nick said. Although the sea creatures did occasionally wash ashore here, dead, he didn't think he should mention it. "Maybe a porpoise."

"I don't know a porpoise. Is it awfully like a whale?''

"They eat fish like whales do," said Nick, which used up his repertoire on whales and porpoises alike.

"Whales don't eat fish. They eat teensy-weensy, little plankton. If you're in the ocean, you can't even see it, even if you wear glasses.

"Did your mother teach you that?''

"Mostly. I'm gifted, y'know. That means I'm extra smart.''

"I believe it," Nick said wryly.

"I'm adopted. Do you now how a baby gets adopted?''

Nick opened his mouth to answer, which was as far as he got.

"You get born in a hospital and all the nurses fall in love with you and want to take you home, but they only let mommies do that because mommies love you best.''

"That's the best way," Nick said, trying to remain noncommittal lest Willa reappear and accuse him of making another faux pas.

"I had a daddy once, but now I don't. He died. And Grandma Dawson died, too, before I was even born. They're in heaven together watching over me. They're my guardian angels now. Do you have a guardian angel?''

"I'm sure I don't," said Nick.

Bethany frowned. "That's sad. Who looks after you and makes sure you're safe when you sleep?''

"Well, I try to muddle along on my own.''

Willa came out of the bathroom, hair tidy, nose powdered, and gathered her purse, keys and tote. She smiled briefly at Nick. "I suppose Bethany's been chattering like a monkey."

"We had an enlightening conversation."

"He doesn't have a guardian angel and he doesn't know anything about whales," announced Bethany.

"I'm sure Mr. Cavenaugh has some redeeming features," Willa replied with such amiable civility that Nick looked at it ten ways to ninety, and still couldn't label it ridicule. "Call me Nick," he volunteered. "'Mr. Cavenaugh' makes me feel like an old man."

"You are old," said Bethany. "Mommy is, too."

"Bethany..." her mother warned, and offered Nick an apologetic glance.

He grinned. "It's okay. We're both tarred by the same brush, I notice."

Willa noted he looked younger when he smiled. Less intense. "Children see us differently than we do ourselves."

Conversation at the pancake house dealt with nothing more pragmatic than the weather and tourist attractions. Willa suspected they each were trying to get the measure of the other, deciding if the day was to be spent trading insults or spent in a friendly, albeit tense fashion.

She was resolute in her attention to proprieties. She insisted upon paying her share of the bill.

Nick balked. "Now look, the idea of today was—"

"That you're going to answer all my questions," Willa said. "That didn't include treating us."

He trailed her out to the car. "Suppose I told you it does dastardly things to my ego for you to be paying your own way while in my company?"

"I'd counter by saying, it won't do any irrefutable harm. From what I've seen, your ego appears in fine condition."

When she twisted to buckle her seat belt, Nick got a glimpse of enticing white flesh where her shirt opened between the buttons. He shook his head, his mouth forming a knowing, ironic smile.

"Something tells me we're going to have a tremendously magnificent day."

Willa slipped on her sunglasses. "I think so, too. Bethany, buckle up."

Nick had absolutely resolved to pick Willa apart piece by piece. But somehow within the next hour he found himself having a good time, until eventually, without ever having made a conscious decision about it, he was admiring the way she handled Bethany, was impressed with her intellect, and much taken with her casual grace.

She was pretty enough to get glances from other men when they stopped to sightsee at various attractions. Willa was beautiful, but Nick sensed she was not truly aware of this. He glared at the men he discovered ogling.

"When are we going to the beach?" Bethany asked.

"Next stop," Nick replied. "Atlantic Ocean coming up." He glanced at Willa. "Do you need to change into your swimsuit? I can stop at the bathhouse..."

"No, I'm fine as I am."

Nick paid their way into the state park before Willa had time to delve into her purse. "I'll let it slide, but only this once," she told him.

"My ego thanks you."

Prudently Willa turned her attention to the scenery. Nick maneuvered the car right onto the beach, driving until he found a parking spot above the high-tide line. "This okay with you?" he asked.

"It's wonderful," she said, and meant it. The tide was out, sandbars had trapped shallow pools in which children splashed and cavorted. Couples and families strolled at the water's edge searching for shells. Beyond the sandbars, waves rushed in, sending up sprays of white water. Before Willa could slip from the car, Bethany was excitedly peeling off her outer garments.

"Go on," Nick suggested. "Take her for a dip. I'll put out the beach towels."

"You don't want to go with us?"

He did, but he thought better of it. "I'll just sit on the beach and keep an eye on you . . . both."

She raised her eyes to his. His mouth relaxed into a smile. His controlled vitality and extraordinary eyes made him a very attractive man. Willa felt unnerved, and tried to allay the feeling with small talk while she removed her sandals. A light blush suffused her cheeks.

If she didn't know better, she'd think the man was flirting with her. But of course he wasn't. She was thinking like some fifteen-year-old adolescent. His interest in her was only on behalf of the Elliotts, unless . . . Maybe he was testing her? Checking out her morals. She glanced at Bethany. Or did he have a more underhanded motive? Willa shivered slightly. The reaction was brief and she controlled it quickly, but she knew Nick had noticed. "We'll be back in a few minutes."

"Take your time." He waved a hand toward the shimmering water. "You're going to regret not wearing a swimsuit."

Bethany pulled on her hand. "Come on, Mommy. Look, there's somebody flying a kite! *Ooooo*, it's going down in the water."

The pools of water trapped by the sandbars were warm and shallow. Bethany threw herself into a pool with a huge splash, pretending to swim, and made a beeline along the shore toward a group of children building a sand fort with buckets and paper cups. She hung back shyly for only a moment. "Forts are supposed to have moats," she said.

"We have to build a tower for the princess, first," one of the little girls told her.

"What princess?" Bethany asked, scooping up sand in an extra cup.

Willa sat on the sand and tilted her head back. The sun felt marvelous, and in a few minutes, hot. Sunscreen! She had forgotten to lather it on. But Bethany couldn't be budged. Willa gave up and with a word of caution to the child not to wander off, hurried back to the car for her tote.

She walked up on Nick as he was stepping out of his slacks. "Oh! I'm sorry." She did an about-face.

He laughed. "Don't panic. I'm only stripping down to my swimsuit."

Willa rummaged in her tote. "I forgot sunscreen."

Nick leaned into the car on the opposite side and folded the slacks atop his shirt over the seat. "You didn't really think a fine upstanding citizen like myself would strip down to his underwear in front of God and everybody, did you?"

"Of course not," Willa managed. She smiled weakly, held up the tube of sunscreen, said, "Got it," then faltered.

The swimsuit he wore was somewhat more than a bikini, but a lot less than a pair of cotton shorts. A whole lot less.

"Want me to rub some lotion on your back and shoulders?"

"No. Really. The sun doesn't bother me," she lied. She usually burned to a crisp in twenty minutes flat. "It's Bethany I'm worried about."

"I'll walk with you. I might as well take a quick dip."

He strolled along at her side as they maneuvered among the sunbathers. Nick was lightly tanned, his shoulders were broad, his hips narrow, his legs long and muscular. Willa was conscious of the hungry eyes of some of the women upon Nick. She wondered if her own eyes had reflected that kind of hunger. She suppressed the thought as inappropriate. Heavens. She had worked in a hospital, been married for ten years. She knew what the male body was all about.

At the water's edge Nick flashed Willa a smile, lifted his hand in an aborted wave, and raced into the deeper surf. She watched him dive into a wave. He surfaced a moment later swimming strongly. She turned away, giving her attention over to lathering Bethany with sunscreen; and after a quick glance at the surf to determine Nick's whereabouts lest she get caught in her fib—she coated herself from ear tip to toe.

When Nick finally came out of the surf, he rummaged in the trunk of the car for a pair of shorts.

Relief swamped Willa. It was one thing to remind herself that she knew about men's bodies; entirely another to sit next to a skimpily clad, magnificently built man on a beach—without becoming a closet voyeur.

"Is it a secret you're smiling at?" Nick observed. "Or something you're willing to share?" He set down a cooler between them. "Soft drinks and croissants," he added, indicating the cooler. "There's a selection: raisin, cheese, cinnamon. Chocolate for Bethany. I wasn't sure what might appeal to your taste."

"Any of them. Thank you. It was thoughtful of you to—"

"I wasn't doing you any special favor. I get on a beach and think, 'food.' Early conditioning, I guess. You didn't answer my question."

"Which one?"

"The source of that little cat smile you displayed a few moments ago."

"Oh." Her mind raced for a respectable reply. "Well, I was reflecting on woman's universal frailties."

"Really. Which one?"

Willa looked into the cardboard box inside the cooler, selecting a croissant. "No single one in particular. These smell delicious."

IT WAS LATE in the afternoon, the beach still crowded. Willa sniffed. The fragrance of suntan oil was thick in the air, the smell of coconut oil somehow lending itself to a feeling of well-being and nostalgia. The tide was coming in. The shallow pools were now waist deep. Bethany and her newfound playmates, forced to retreat, picked up their pails and shovels and moved inland. Undaunted, they began anew.

The beach towel Nick had provided was huge. Willa shared it with him, sitting on one corner with her feet buried in the sand. Watching the sand forts and moats being washed away by the incoming tide prompted a comment that had been lurking in her mind. "That's what happened to my life," she said softly, gesturing toward the beach where sand buildings were no longer distinguishable. "It simply washed away."

Nick lifted his elbow from his eyes and sat up, alert. "That's why you decided to come here?"

"I was invited, remember? But I guess we could've gone anywhere. Except—"

Nick leaned closer. There was a fine sheen of sweat on Willa's skin. In the sun's glow, she seemed to glimmer like soft gold. "Except what?"

"I want Bethany to have what I had when I was growing up. My grandmother had this huge rocking chair. When I was a little girl I used to climb up on her lap and she'd rock and whisper stories in my ear as if we were having secrets. She told me I was her special girl. She died when I was ten. I missed her, but when I had a problem I headed straight for that rocking chair." Willa laughed. "I think her aura stayed with that chair until the house burned down. I want Bethany to have that kind of security, those kinds of memories."

"She has you."

Willa frowned. "I know. But it's not the same." She debated with herself how much to tell. The attitude of Peter's parents was bound to come out sooner or later. Better sooner, she thought. "You might as well know...my husband's parents never approved of our adopting Bethany. We haven't seen or heard from them since Peter's funeral. My mom died years ago, and my dad remarried a woman much younger than himself. He's not into grandparenting. Bethany has never received a birthday card, or a Valentine's Day card, an Easter basket—none of the special little things grandparents do for their grandchildren. I try to make it up to her, but it's not the same." She looked into the distance, her frown deepening. "I hope the Elliotts..."

"You want them to give Bethany things?"

Willa faced him. "I want them to love her, I want her to have grandparents who don't distance themselves. That's what I want."

"That sounds reasonable. But so does a cash settlement."

The look Willa gave Nick would've made a lesser man feel like a worm. "For your information, I have a little money saved. And Bethany receives a social-security check because of Peter's death. It's not much, but between the two we can scrape by until I'm working again. Mention money that way again and meeting the Elliotts is off."

"Consider that the comment was never made."

Willa was not so easily appeased. "I can hear the wariness in your voice. You ought to know that if my mother were alive, I wouldn't be here today. Considering the circumstances, I might've sent Claudine Elliott a photograph now and then, but Bethany wouldn't need them. My mom was wonderful. She always smelled of pie dough and spices. She had a kitchen that was...if I could have taken Bethany back to that..."

"What was it like?"

"Welcoming. Friendly. Lots of windows, tomatoes ripening on the sill. An apple bin, a potato bin, onions and garlic hanging on pegs. Bread cooling on a rack near the ceiling... The smells in my mother's kitchen made you think you'd died and gone to heaven. We had a wood-burning stove we used to sit around in the winter. Dad picked on a guitar, Mom and I sang...Bethany would've loved it. And been loved." Willa looked down at her feet, wiggled her toes and watched the sand trickle between them. "I hate it when people are cruel!"

Needing something to do with her hands, she rolled up her Bermudas, squaring them off to cuffs at her thigh.

Nick expelled a breath. She had sensational legs, wholly unblemished by so much as a freckle. He tore his eyes away. "Maybe I'd better warn you, Claudine Elliott isn't much of a cook."

"I won't be judging her on that."

"But you will be judging?"

"Wouldn't you if you were in my place? Haven't you been judging me?"

"Not judging, no."

"Pooh. You've been probing for my warts all morning. Why don't you just ask me what you want to know?"

"Hold on. I've been trying to be tactful. I promised you my best behavior and that's what you're getting."

"Thank you."

"You have to admit, this is an unusual situation."

Willa breathed deeply and exhaled. "I know. But a part of me aches for Claudine Elliott. To have a child die and not get to say goodbye, not to be there... Do you have children?"

A pained expression creased Nick's brow. "One."

"Boy or girl?"

"Girl."

Willa's expression was suddenly so forlorn, Nick almost put a comforting arm around her. He stopped himself.

Willa's thoughts were chaotic. The attorney had been wholly circumspect throughout the day, businesslike. "Have... have we taken you away from your family today? Your wife?"

"Nope. I've never been married."

"But—" Willa sank back on her palms and stretched out her legs. She couldn't think quite how to phrase what she wanted to ask. "But you have a daughter? Do you see her? Do you have a relationship with her?"

Nick shook his head. "I'd like to. It just never worked out. Maybe one day. But I think it's too late. It's not something I like to talk about."

"Of course. I didn't mean to pry." She felt her heart thudding in her ears and knew she didn't have the courage to push the conversation a single step further. The idea that Nick truly *was* Bethany's father played havoc with her senses. "How...how have the Elliotts handled learning about Susan's death?"

"They were grief stricken, doing better now. It—" He pursed his lips, looked at his watch. "It's getting late."

Willa put a hand on his arm. At her touch, Nick felt the hairs on his neck prickle. "What were you going to say?" she asked. "Please, tell me."

"Finally finding Susan brought six years of misery to an end. Grief is better than not knowing, if that makes any sense. I've watched John and Claudine age during the search. Not a nice thing to see."

"Did you know Susan well?"

"I thought I did."

"You like the Elliotts, then," Willa said, as if she hadn't heard his last remark.

"It goes a little deeper than that."

Willa stood and brushed sand from her hands, her legs, the seat of her shorts, anything to ease the inner confusion he was making her feel.

"I'll see them tomorrow, if it's convenient," she said. "At that park down from the motel."

"In the morning?"

"Afternoon would be better. I have to clean out my car, do some laundry, find an apartment— Would two o'clock be okay?"

"If I can keep Claudine on a rein until then."

"I hope she's all you've made her out to be."

"I haven't said ten words about her."

"It's what you haven't said." She gave him a smile that didn't quite come off. "Thank you for today. I was ... tense. Scared a little, too, if you want to know the truth. Not exactly sure what I ought to do."

"Being unsure is part of the human condition," Nick said lightly. "Why would we call it life if it were a certainty?"

Bethany came running up. "My new friends are leaving."

"So are we," Willa told her, brushing sand from Bethany's arms and legs.

"I'm hungry, Mommy. I'm so hungry I could eat a Happy Meal all by myself." She looked past Willa to Nick, who was changing into his slacks. "Aren't you starved?"

"Don't answer that," Willa cautioned him. "She's being manipulative."

"Those croissants didn't exactly stick to my ribs. I am hungry."

"Good!" Bethany cried. "If we all order Happy Meals, I can have three toys."

"I'll bite," said Nick. "What's a happy meal?"

"You get Happy Meals at McDonald's."

"I'm afraid I've never eaten a Happy Meal."

Bethany gaped. "Not even when you were a little kid?"

"There weren't any McDonald's when I was a little kid. I'm a Dairy Queen fan myself."

"You must really be old," Bethany said.

Nick leaned down and put his lips to her ear. "I'm only almost forty. That's not old."

Bethany scowled. "Forty comes after thirty-six, doesn't it?" She didn't wait for an answer. "Mommy's old and she's thirty-six—"

Willa clamped a hand lightly over Bethany's mouth. "We'll talk about this later."

Bethany wriggled loose. "But I was just figuring—"

"Into the car. Put on your shorts." Willa looked at Nick. "I hope your feelings aren't hurt. She's fascinated with numbers. If she were twenty, she'd find you adorable."

"Oh? What if she were thirty-six?"

"I think I'll shake the sand out of the towel," Willa said, and went to do it.

Chalk one up for me, Nick said to himself, grinning. He sat on the front seat and slipped on his espadrilles. Bethany leaned over and poked him in the back.

"You got me into trouble."

Nick swallowed his laughter. "Sorry. Suppose I treat you to a Happy Meal. Will that make it up to you?"

"Okay. But I might get a spanking anyway."

"Do you get spankings?"

"No. But Mommy thinks about it sometimes."

Willa tossed the towel into the car and got in behind it. Bethany was sitting primly with her hands in her lap. Nick was quiet, his expression so neutral she at once recognized subterfuge. "Are you two joined in a conspiracy of some sort?"

"Only so far as I'm treating you to a Happy Meal," Nick said. "Which, under the circumstances, I expect you to graciously accept."

"Which circumstance is that?"

"The one that says I'm ready for a cane and rocking chair."

"That's convoluted lawyer thinking," Willa replied, then pursed her lips. "All right. Just this once."

From the back seat came a barely audible, "Hurray."

Chapter Three

"I don't see why I have to be all dressed up in Sunday clothes on Saturday!" Bethany complained.

"We're meeting some people, that's why. I want you to look nice and sweet—and clean. I'll introduce you when they get here."

Bethany sorted that out. "Grown-ups. Pooh." She looked longingly at other children scurrying to and fro in the park.

"Can't I just sit in the swings? I won't dig my shoes in the dirt. I promise."

Willa vacillated. She had decided to arrive at the park twenty minutes early on the off chance that the Elliotts might themselves arrive before two o'clock. She considered that their arriving before her might, somehow, put her at a disadvantage. Still, common sense told her it was asking too much of Bethany to keep still in a playground. She gave in.

"Go on, then. But walk, don't run or you'll get sweaty."

Willa kept surveying the nearby parking lots, groups of tourists, and twosomes, watching. She was waiting for the couple to stand out, to identify themselves by making their way toward her. No one did.

She tucked her purse under her elbow and smoothed her skirt. It was too warm even in the shade. She wanted to look her best and had chosen a lightweight tan suit that buttoned high enough that she could wear it without a blouse. But now even the suit's silk lining was clinging to her back.

The minutes dragged. She found herself too nervous to sit. Anxiety was casting all the wrong images on the backdrop of her mind. The Elliotts might be the most horrible of people. Sarcastic. Cold. Vulgar. How could she have even remotely considered subjecting Bethany to that?

If they were good and kind, and gentle people, why had their own daughter run away? She should've ignored their grief, or found a way around it somehow and asked that question.

Brash and reckless, that's what she had been to leave Kansas. Had she given these moments more thought, she never would've packed that first bag, sent those résumés, or contacted Nick Cavenaugh.

"Give me a hint, what distant planet are you on?"

Willa jumped as if she'd stepped on a snake. "Do you always sneak up on people like that?"

Nick held up both hands as if to ward off a blow. "A bit touchy today, aren't you?"

"Are the Elliotts with you?" she demanded, her gaze sweeping the landscape.

"They're on their way. Claudine had to change her clothes twice. She wants to look her best for Bethany. It's a big day for them."

"Yes, I guess it is." Willa took a deep breath. "I hope Bethany likes them. I hope they like her."

"What about you?"

"I don't know. Does it matter?"

Nick took a step back and studied her. Willa was slim and provocative, her deep blue eyes, filled with tension, were large and luminous. She was quite the most desirable woman he had ever met. "You look exquisite, calm and cool." His tone took on a sympathetic note. "You're a nervous wreck, aren't you?"

Nick's compliments sent a flood of warmth through Willa, but she discounted them. Growing up she had been gangly and awkward, always the tallest in her class, the subject of cruel teasing by other students. Her mother had said not to worry, God loved all creatures, large, small, pretty and ugly. Ugly had stuck in Willa's mind. But the teasing had had one lasting effect. Her pride would not allow her to slump at her desk or slink through hallways. She had developed a posture that gave her a poise of which she was wholly unconscious.

"I might be a little nervous," she said. "You really think I look nice?" The words slipped out.

Nick hid his amazement. It was utterly foreign to him that a woman as lovely as Willa would question her looks, much less be oblivious to them. "Take my word for it, you'll do. Ah, here they come." He slipped his hand under Willa's elbow. It was the first time he'd touched her. Her perfume was faint, but alluring. He felt some sort of elemental force jolt his senses. Whoa, he told himself, and glanced at Willa. It seemed she had noticed nothing. All of her attention was focused on the approaching couple.

"Remember," he said softly, "they're a bit different."

Willa froze. "Different? You never mentioned 'different.'" She felt a tug of fear. Was there a strain of madness in the family? A peculiarity that might manifest itself in Bethany. Her thoughts touched on every mental illness she had ever studied or heard of.

She could not take her eyes from the couple as they negotiated the sandy terrain of the park grounds. Though dressed in dark and somber colors, they were the epitome of elegance. Willa's heart began to beat uncomfortably fast, her mouth went dry. "In what way, different?" she whispered.

"I used the wrong word. Delicate or otherworldly, would be closer. Shhhh. Here they are. Claudine, John, this is Willa Manning, and that pink, ruffled vision over there on the swings is Bethany."

"Hello—" Willa said, her smile as stiff as starch.

"Mrs. Manning—" Claudine said, taking Willa's hand in both of her own. "It means so much to us to have you here." Her eyes swept over Willa, not unkindly, then went at once to Bethany and stayed riveted there. "Oh!" she said faintly. "Oh, oh, oh." Then she put her hands to her face and cried. "I'm sorry," she said through her tears. "Truly. I knew this would happen. Forgive me."

Willa fought the urge to put her arms about the woman. John Elliott patted his wife awkwardly on the back. But his eyes, too, were drawn to Bethany.

Willa looked at Nick. "Give them a minute," he mouthed silently.

While the elder couple were absorbed watching Bethany, Willa observed them. She got an inkling of what Nick might have meant about their being otherworldly.

They had a kind of rare dignity defined as much by breeding and background as by money.

Though their clothing was subdued—respectful mourning for their daughter, Willa surmised—it was well cut and expensive. The only jewels on display were gold wedding bands. Both Claudine and John displayed an aristocratic bearing. It was in the manner in which they held heads aligned with spine; posture that took years to perfect. Their grooming was immaculate.

John Elliott was rotund, his seamed face clean shaven, his hair a silver gray. He gave the impression of calm, but Willa noticed the tension at the corners of his eyes and mouth. His skin was sallow, as if he'd been ill.

Though several inches taller than her husband, Claudine's bearing was lessened somewhat by an almost childlike quality in her features. Her wide eyes were wistful and unfathomable, at odds with the severe chignon into which she had shaped her light brown hair. Her complexion was smooth and had a translucence one seldom saw outside of retouched photographs.

There was a resemblance between Bethany and her biological grandmother, Willa decided. There was a sameness in the well-shaped head, the smooth, high forehead, the lift at the corner of the mouth. Claudine was small boned. Bethany had a more rangy, long-legged body—like Nick's? asked a voice buried at the back of Willa's brain.

A small white handkerchief appeared in Claudine's hand. She dabbed at her eyes. "You must think me exceedingly rude," she said to Willa. "Cutting you off like that."

"I understand. Why don't I get Bethany? I'll have to introduce you as Mr. and Mrs. Elliott—"

Claudine gave a sad little nod. "Yes. Nick told us. But that seems so formal. Would you mind if we asked her to call us Claudine and John? For now, anyway?"

Willa hesitated.

"And you, too, of course. We do want to be your friends, Mrs. Manning, don't we, John?" He cleared his throat and nodded.

"Then I suppose I shouldn't stand on formality, either," Willa said. "I'll only be a minute."

Bethany had to be coaxed from the swing, her ribboned barrette reset, her sash retied. "Then can I come right back to the swings," she asked.

"Maybe," Willa said.

Nick and the Elliotts had moved to the picnic table. Claudine was sitting, the men standing nearby. Willa made the introductions between grandparents and grandchild, then took a step back to listen and observe. But the look she wore said she was prepared to snatch Bethany from danger and hurt if any one of the other three people present so much as put a comma in the wrong place.

"You're a beautiful little girl," Claudine said softly, her eyes flashing with delight.

"I'm gifted, too," Bethany told her. "That means I'm extrasmart. I'm adopted too, did you know that?"

Willa winced. For Bethany's sake, she had made adoption sound like an adventure. Bethany often used it as an opening gambit when she met someone new, child or adult. Bethany expected the notion of it to be as fascinating to others as it was to herself. Now Willa wished she had talked of adoption more matter-of-factly, explained it more fully.

Claudine looked startled but recovered quickly. "Well, I believe your mother mentioned it. I'd like to hear all about it, sometime. Would you like to come to supper at my house?"

"I don't like grown-up food. Would you have hot dogs?"

Claudine glanced at Willa. "We could, if your mother approves."

"She will," Bethany replied. "She loves hot dogs. Do you have any little kids for me to play with?"

For a few seconds Claudine's expression was grief stricken, but she hurried past the moment. "We used to, but now we don't. But I know how to play jacks—"

Bethany frowned. "I can't ever catch the ball. I'm clumsy."

"Surely not. It just takes practice."

"No, I'm pure and out clumsy," Bethany insisted. "I was born too little. I have to do exercises so I won't be."

"Cards, then."

"I can play Fish and Old Maid. I always win."

"I'm sure you do," Claudine said, her voice breaking, as if she were about to start crying again.

Willa stepped in then and sent Bethany off to the swings.

Claudine turned to John. "I can't get over it. She looks just like Susan did at that age. Don't you think so, Nick?"

"The resemblance is remarkable," he said, watching Willa out the corner of his eye.

"She's so spirited. I like that." Claudine touched Willa's arm. "Is Bethany ever melancholy?"

Melancholy? Willa thought. It was an odd choice of word. Alarm flashed through her like lightning. "How do you mean—melancholy?" There was such a discordant note in her voice, John caught it. He touched Claudine's arm.

"Not now, dear..." He looked apologetically at Willa. "We've been searching for reasons that Susan..." Shaking his head, his voice trailed off. Willa recognized his discomfort, and his self-irritation at having displayed it.

"You will come to supper, won't you?" Claudine asked.

Willa was at sixes and sevens with herself. She wanted very much to question Claudine about Susan, pinpoint what she meant by melancholy, but she did not want to appear overanxious. John seemed inclined to caution his wife about what to say or not to say. Willa knew very well that once a family member died, he or she often suddenly became draped in all sorts of wonderful attributes. She did want to know the fine things about Bethany's biological mother, but she also needed to know other elements of Susan's personality.

"I'd like that very much," she said.

"Tonight?" Claudine suggested hopefully.

Willa's first impulse was to accept. She caught herself. Now was the time to go slowly. She mustered a slight smile. "We wouldn't be good company tonight. We've been on the go since we arrived—" She indicated Nick. "We're still recuperating from yesterday."

Claudine had difficulty hiding her disappointment. "Tomorrow is Sunday. Come early, spend the day with us."

"We're going to church in the morning, at the Mission of Nombre de Dios. I thought it would be nice to attend church on the site where the first Christian ceremony was held in the New World. And after church, I'm apartment hunting."

"Sunday evening, then," Claudine insisted. "You're staying in a motel and having to eat all of your meals out? Doesn't a home-cooked meal appeal to you? Nick, you'll join us won't you? And drive Willa and Bethany over?"

"It's up to Willa."

She hesitated. "All right."

Claudine beamed. "You'll come as early in the afternoon as you can?"

"Yes, thank you."

"That's settled, then," John said somberly. His gaze drifted back to Bethany.

"May we go say goodbye to her?" Claudine asked.

"Of course," Willa replied. "I'll walk with you."

As the couple turned away, Nick clasped a hand on Willa's arm. He bent his lips to her ear and whispered, "Let them have a moment with Bethany on their own."

The back of Willa's neck suddenly felt prickly and cold. "Why? What are they going to say?" The Elliotts were nearing Bethany. Willa tried to pull away from Nick's grasp.

"Calm down!" he said, voice low. "They're not out to harm or steal her."

"I'm her mother!"

"No one is disputing that. Have I? Has Claudine? Has John?" Because he had known them all of his life, Nick had seen what Willa had not. John and Claudine had been restrained to the point of fear, concerned that an offhand gesture or word would cause Willa or Bethany to reject them. After all they had been through with Susan, it hurt him deeply to see them so reduced. "You don't have to monitor their every word and gesture as if they're criminals."

"Turn me loose."

"Done!"

Willa took a few steps toward the swings, and slowed her pace. Even at a distance she could see that Bethany was doing all the talking. The Elliotts were bent over, listening, enthralled by Bethany's chatter. Willa backed up and sat on the picnic bench. She did not deign to glance at Nick.

John and Claudine left Bethany and angled toward their car. Smiling, Claudine waved. "See you tomorrow," she called.

Willa nodded and lifted her hand in return.

"Now that wasn't so hard, was it?" Nick crooned.

Willa rounded on him. "Don't you ever, ever, come between me and Bethany again!"

"What!"

"You mind your own business."

"She is my business. You've—"

"She is not," Willa warned, on the verge of blurting her suspicions.

Nick shoved his hands into his back pockets and rocked on his heels. "You know, up until two seconds ago I was impressed with your sincerity, your honesty, your—" He'd almost said, beauty. "I mean, over the past three days, you've completely turned me around. So what built a fire under you so suddenly? You angry that John and Claudine didn't arrive bearing gifts? Money? I guess maybe from your perspective, a supper invitation is a little short of expectations."

"That's a vile thing to say. Especially since you know it's not true. We spent all day yesterday in each other's company. Was that for nothing?"

"Today is a new day. Maybe I want more convincing."

"I don't have to prove anything to you."

"I have a lot of dumb clients who say that."

"Lucky me. I'm not one of your clients."

Nick gazed heavenward. "A small favor for which I shall be everlastingly grateful."

"I don't see why John and Claudine put any faith in you, either."

"They have an advantage. They know me."

"They think they know you."

Nick paused and took a breath. "What exactly do you mean by that?"

"Just what I said."

"I'll give you this much—you've completely mastered the art of talking in circles."

He had her figured out now. Of course she knew she was stunning. Pretending to be unaware of it was all an act. And sprinkling all those little snippets of home on the range in conversation yesterday were to stop him from asking more searching questions. Sure. Display a little leg, a bit of décolletage, get a man all wound up and distracted and she could work her con with no interference.

"If you'll excuse me..." Willa said, lifting her chin. She was pumped up with adrenaline by the secret knowledge that she had skated too close to a topic better left unresolved for the moment. She could have ruined everything!

"Oh, by all means, *madame*," he said with a sweeping gesture. "Make your exit."

It was only after she and Bethany were back in the motel room that Willa remembered Nick was to pick them up for dinner the next evening. She wished she had declined his company, said that she would find the Elliotts' home on her own.

The man irritated her, plagued her the same way an infinitesimal splinter did; burrowing under a layer of skin where you couldn't see it, couldn't pluck it out, but you couldn't forget about it, either.

Evidently John and Claudine did not suspect what she suspected, that Nick and their daughter had been more than friends.

What would that alter in the scheme of things? Willa wondered. Bethany was hers. She was allowing these others into Bethany's life on her terms—not their's.

Anyway, why should discovering who Bethany's father was upset her? It was a boon, really—more genetic input.

But it just doesn't feel right, she told herself.

Why not?

Because she was attracted to him herself?

What a stupid thought!

"I don't want to take a nap," protested Bethany.

Willa started. She had been undressing Bethany by rote.

"We're just going to lay across the bed and cool off." She turned the air conditioner on high. It groaned and wheezed, drowning out the sound of the television.

"But I'm not hot."

"Well, I am."

"Then let's go swimming in the pool," Bethany said, all hope.

Stripped down to her slip, Willa settled against the headboard and opened the paper to the rental ads. "Tell you what—later on we'll pick up some hamburgers, and picnic at poolside. You can swim until the sun goes down."

Expelling a martyred sigh, Bethany stretched out on the bed. "How much later?"

"Soon. After I line up some places to look at. You don't want us to live in a dumpy old motel room the rest of our lives, do you?"

"I don't mind. I think it's fun."

It wasn't fun to Willa. It felt as if the small room were closing in on her, the walls echoing with the effort of shrinking.

Eventually Bethany dozed. Willa turned off the television and made a few calls. The most promising and least expensive accommodations refused children and pets. At the forth refusal she got angry.

"What do people like you expect us to do with our kids? Store them in a closet somewhere until they're grown? Live in a tent?"

"Both ideas sound good to me, hon," replied the man.

Willa slammed down the receiver.

Several complexes were open on Sunday. She added them to her list.

She settled down next to Bethany and tried to read the rest of the newspaper. The words ran together and blurred.

"Melancholy" kept running through her mind like a warped record. Why would Claudine use such an odd word? Why not sad, or pouty or sullen? Above all, why even ask a question like that? Nothing was beyond the bounds of possibility. Mental illness, birth defects. Though the possibility couldn't make her love Bethany less, the very idea filled Willa with horror. John had been quick to halt the direction of that conversation.

Genetically Bethany was the sum of both biological parents, and their parents, ad infinitum. Willa knew there were things she might never learn about Bethany's heritage. People were funny—storing away their secrets, guarding them from prying eyes and curiosity with astonishing skill and fervor.

She recalled the tension John's sallow face, the caution he exuded. There was something there, veneered by wariness. Some mystery.

Willa closed her eyes and massaged her temples.

True, Bethany had, at one time, been withdrawn, silent. But for a very good reason. She had been abandoned, left to get well among strangers. Bethany was fine now.

She tossed aside the newspaper and snuggled down next to her daughter.

There was nothing to worry about.

THE ELLIOTTS' HOME was a grand old affair. Shingle siding, turrets and a gambrel roof spoke of a colonial Spanish influence upon its builder. It was two-storied, painted white with dark green trim on the shutters, door facings and railings. The porch showcased an intricately carved front entrance, then swept around one side to a screened door—a more prosaic second entrance. An ancient oak cast shade in which tropical oleander, rhododendron and wood fern thrived.

Willa parked in the narrow driveway behind Nick. For one brief moment she admired the house. Then John and Claudine emerged onto the porch.

"You came in two cars?" Claudine observed, turning the obvious into a question rife with anxiety.

"I didn't want to inconvenience Nick in case we have to leave earlier than he does," Willa replied smoothly, feeling a tiny stab of guilt at the half-truth.

Nick had arrived at the motel stiffly formal and still prickly from their clash the day before and that was more than she could bear. After rushing hither and thither the entire afternoon viewing overpriced and underfurnished apartments, she was in the mood for empathy and kind words.

Nick had given neither. Discovering that she had yet to bathe and dress Bethany, he had muttered a pithy comment about hating to be kept waiting. She had told him to go on ahead. She'd find her own way.

He'd refused, arguing that she was being foolish, accusing her of a stubbornness beyond redemption. He'd said that she was intent on vexing him for no good reason. After that diatribe, there was no way that she could've been persuaded to ride with him.

"That's not what you said, Mommy," Bethany contradicted innocently. "You said you'd walk to China before you'd ride with Nick. China is a long, long way. Remember, you told me about Chinese children eating rice and I should eat it, too, and grow up to be strong."

Willa had the grace to blush.

John scowled. "Nick?"

"Not to worry, Willa and I just had a slight difference of opinion. It's all water under the bridge. We've made up, haven't we?" He gave her a grin, which she interpreted as a smirk. Then he put his hand on the small of her back and propelled her up the steps as if he owned her.

"We have," she said for the Elliotts' benefit. The older couple was trying so hard, she didn't want to ruin the evening for them, or Bethany. But she plotted mental revenge while every fiber of her being was aware of Nick's hand on her back.

"Good," said Claudine, obviously relieved. "It's not healthy to eat on an agitated stomach. Well, come in, come in, we can't stand around on the porch." She took Bethany's hand and led them all into a huge foyer illuminated by a massive crystal chandelier.

Willa used the moment to bestow on Nick a hostile glare that, beneath the sparkling chandelier, lit her eyes to pinpoints of brilliance.

His response was a wicked, half smile. He slid his hand to her waist and squeezed.

Galled, Willa stepped out of his grasp.

"Ooooo," Bethany exclaimed. "I like your house."

Claudine beamed. "We do, too."

Willa was silent. She had been this close to such elegance only once—years ago when she and Peter had toured preserved historical homes during a Christmas season. She could feel Nick's gaze on her, watching her reaction. She was a little bit awed, and if it showed, he could make of that what he would. She tried to move as if she did not feel threatened and out of her depth.

"We seldom use the front parlor," Claudine said, gesturing with her free hand. In passing Willa glimpsed a room of delicate shirred rose satin wallpaper inlaid with dim, frosty mirrors.

There was a great deal of understated wealth on display, even in the spacious family room where Claudine admonished, "Nick, you know where everything is. Do the honors on the drinks. There's Château Lafite in the wine cooler. Pour Willa a glass. A small sherry for me." She smiled down at Bethany. "I found something better than cards to play."

With Willa trailing, Claudine took Bethany near a rounded wall nook opposite a priory table set with gleaming crystal and fresh flowers. The area was heaped with toys: a music box, a tea set, a porcelain-faced doll dressed in satins and lace, an elaborate dollhouse, the tiny furniture piled in an old-fashioned hat box.

Bethany hesitated. "I can play with all of this?"

"You may. I brought it down from the attic just for you. If your mother agrees, you can have them for your very own."

Speechless, eyes pleading, Bethany gaped at her mother.

Willa was torn between saying yes and no. The toys were antiques, and far more expensive than anything she would ever be able to afford to provide for Bethany. She took the middle road. "Why don't you play with them for now and once we're settled, we'll see."

"But, I thought..." Claudine began, then her face crumbled. "Oh, dear, oh dear."

Willa hated herself for trampling upon the other woman's good intentions. "I meant what I said," she told her. "There's just no place to spread out where we're staying."

Claudine shrugged a little hopelessly. "Of course," she said, then bowed out of her embarrassment by kneeling on the floor next to Bethany. "Watch this," she said, stretching to insert a plug into an outlet. The two-storied dollhouse came alive with the glow of tiny lights.

"Neat-o!" Bethany breathed, utterly enchanted.

"It was thoughtful of you to provide toys," Willa said a moment later as Claudine ushered her toward a pair of long sofas.

"It's just... we want to do so much for her," she said in a hushed voice so Bethany wouldn't hear. "Having you both here is like getting a miraculous second chance. I keep forgetting that we mustn't interfere."

Willa warmed to the older woman. She couldn't help it. There didn't seem to be a malicious bone in Claudine's delicate body. She realized now that had there been, their meetings would have been more strident, and no doubt in a courtroom. And considering the Elliotts' wealth and social status, no judge in his right mind would have refused them visitation rights to their grandchild.

Chapter Four

Nick took nerve in hand and made himself comfortable only an arm's length from Willa. For all she noticed him, he might just as well have been invisible. He wasn't used to being entirely ignored. He could scarcely credit it was happening now.

It wasn't. Willa was very much aware of him. He smelled delicious and looked wonderful. He wore white slacks and a black silk shirt. Her heart, very stealthily, was stirring and turning over. But, on analysis, she knew if she let her guard down the situation could become far more complicated than it already was. She had to think with her mind, not her emotions.

"What happened to Clytie?" John asked. His tone had an undercurrent of rebuke.

Claudine was at once aflutter. "She was just going to change her dress. I'll go see about the hors d'oeuvres, myself."

"That doddering old fool is here on sufferance," John replied irritably. "You should remind her."

At that moment, Clytie arrived, rolling a serving cart laden with cheeses, boiled shrimp, mounds of caviar and an assortment of tiny iced cakes and cookies.

"Do I hear my name being taken in vain?" she asked. Her voice was amused, full throated and lilting, belying her advanced years.

Willa turned to look at the new arrival. She was a dignified old woman, hardly larger than a child, and rail-thin, like a little stick insect. Her eyes had the sheen of polished mahogany that glittered with a sort of sardonic intelligence. Her skin was colorless as if its once-rich bronze had been leeched out by age. From earlobe to ankle Clytie was as elegantly clad as Claudine, but there the similarities stopped—Clytie's feet were incongruously shod in a pair of much-worn and tattered sneakers. Size three, Willa guessed.

"Our housekeeper," John said loftily, introducing Willa.

Clytie parked the cart at John's elbow. "I'm not 'your' housekeeper. I'm as much a member of this family as you are—more. Your daddy took me in long before you were born." She turned away from John's sputtering to face Willa. "John is just trying to be la-di-da. Comes from inheriting his money, instead of working for it. He's a pompous old toot."

Out the corner of her eye Willa discovered Nick grinning. She realized the verbal exchange was nothing new—except to her. Clytie was "performing" for her benefit.

"Oh, Clytie—" said Claudine.

Clytie ignored the plea and continued to address Willa. "You might as well know that life in the Elliott household is played out by the rules of God, Heritage, Breeding, and John Elliott. Not necessarily in that order, either. He lives so deep in bygone eras he still thinks it's fashionable to wear spats to play golf." Before John or Claudine could dispute this she asked, "Where's the child—Bethany?"

"Here I am," Bethany said, coming out from behind the dollhouse and sidling up to her mother. She ogled the little sticklike woman. "Are you a grown-up?"

"Why—why it's true..." Clytie began.

Willa tensed.

"She's the spittin' image—"

"Caviar, anyone?" Claudine said quickly, the edge in her voice reaching Clytie, stopping her in midsentence.

"It's not nice to spit," Bethany said primly. The fearful moment of revelation past, Willa pulled herself together.

"Too right," Clytie replied and dashed a look of apology to Willa. "Of course, I'm grown-up," she told Bethany.

The child stared out from beneath a sweep of dark lashes, wanting to be convinced. "All the way?"

Clytie's eyes gleamed. "All the way. But I used to be an elf and lived under toadstools."

Bethany glanced at her mother to see if she should believe such an outlandish tale. Willa shrugged and smiled. It was apparent that Clytie had developed the whimsy to deal with the curiosity that her small stature generated among children.

"You're not an elf now?" Bethany asked.

"Oh, no. It's dreadfully damp living under toadstools. I'm too old for that now. But I have lots of stories about when I was an elf. After supper you can help me with the dishes and I'll tell you one."

"If we ever get supper," muttered John.

THE TABLE HAD BEEN CLEARED of all traces of supper, which had been heavenly. Clytie was a good cook. Willa told her so more than once.

Since wild horses couldn't have kept Bethany from joining Clytie in the kitchen for elf stories, Willa let her go. But with Bethany's absence, she became aware of a sudden constraint in the air. At a loss, she looked from Nick to the Elliotts.

John avoided her eye. Willa couldn't decide if the gesture was self-protecting or intended to soften the acuity of his gaze. Claudine busied herself starting a pot of coffee on the sideboard. The silence ensued for another minute.

Finally Nick pushed back his brandy.

"I think John and Claudine want to know if they have met with your approval, Willa."

She was taken aback. "I—I've never disapproved," she said, mortified to be put on the spot, feeling her temper boil. A moment alone with Nick and she'd throttle him!

Now John was looking directly at her. Claudine had gone quite still, the coffeepot poised in her hand.

"You've both been gracious and kind," she told them. "Bethany is comfortable around you." She was flooded with sudden sympathy—for both of them. "I am, too. Please, don't think of me as a judge or jury. I just want family for Bethany. I'm not perfect. I don't expect you to be." She grinned impishly. "On the other hand, Bethany *is* perfect."

Claudine laughed softly. "We think she's perfect, too, don't we John?"

He nodded. "May we assume that you'll be staying in St. Augustine?" he asked. To Willa, he sounded just a tad pompous.

"I hope to. But that depends on... well, any number of things." If she said economics, like job, money and housing, Nick would probably misconstrue the comment and make all sorts of nasty accusations. So might John Elliott. In the event she needed an escape hatch, she added. "I haven't entirely made up my mind. I'm more in favor of settling here than not. St. Augustine is beautiful, the people friendly. I'm told winters are mild—"

"We understand from Nick that there's nothing to lure you back to Kansas City."

Willa realized two things; that every bit of information exchanged between herself and Nick had been dissected and discussed. She should've expected it. And that John was not interested in listening to logic that sounded as though it came from the chamber of commerce. Her eyes flashed with mild defiance.

"No, there's nothing to lure me back there. My Dad has remarried. Bethany and I were just in his way. I expect we'll be invited back for the occasional holiday, but I doubt we'll go. The house I was raised in burned down, so there's not even nostalgia to entice me. As for my dead husband's parents, I'll be generous and just say they weren't the kind of people who opened their hearts to orphans." There. It was said. Perhaps in the future they wouldn't discuss her behind her back. If they had a future.

Claudine reached out and touched Willa's shoulder. "We didn't realize . . . I'm sorry."

Willa made a small gesture of dismissal. "There's nothing for you to be sorry about. It is just the way things are."

"You're here now. That's the main thing. Tell us, how did the apartment hunting go?"

"Not as well as I'd hoped."

Claudine's expression lightened. "Stay with us. We have plenty of room. We'd love to have—"

"Thank you, no," Willa said emphatically.

"But, Willa, when we asked you to come, we meant for you to live here. We meant for you to be our guest for as long as you wished. You and Bethany. We've set aside an entire suite of rooms upstairs for you...."

Seeing the gathering storm in Willa's expression, Nick intervened. "I think Willa has already demonstrated she's too independent of mind and means for that, Claudine."

"But—" The woman broke off, confused.

Willa wasn't confused. Nick was still devising ways to test her motives. Never mind that he had suddenly come to her rescue. He was only making an astute retreat on Claudine's behalf, his innocent accomplice.

John cleared his throat, took a cigar from his coat pocket and trimmed it. "Nick, join me on the porch for a smoke." He pushed away from the table. "If the ladies will excuse us..."

"Only a few puffs," Claudine warned him. "You know what the doctor said."

The men stepped outside via the side door that exited onto the porch. The coffee now perked, Claudine poured and served. "Cream and sugar?"

"Just cream," Willa said.

Claudine sat across from her. "We've offended you."

Willa exhaled. "Not offended, and I don't want you to take this amiss, but I did feel pressured there, just for a minute or two. I don't want Bethany—" Willa stopped. She had almost voiced an opinion that might be hurtful.

Claudine was listening hard. Her keen intelligence came to the fore. The penny dropped. "You're afraid of what kind of influence we'll have on Bethany. You're wondering what kind of parents John and I were." She swallowed nervously. "You must be wondering what caused Susan to run away from us."

Willa's heart went out to Claudine. She reached across the table and squeezed the other woman's hand.

"I didn't mean to hurt you. I'm trying to play this situation by ear and there are so many pitfalls. Bethany is my whole world. I want what's good and fine for her. I think you want the same thing. If we lived under the same roof, we might unconsciously give her mixed messages. It's tempting to take up your offer, you have so many beautiful things I feel grand just being among them. But I have to be strong for Bethany's sake. I have somehow got to see that she has some stability. We need a place of our own. Besides, I couldn't live by someone else's house rules."

"I understand. It's just . . . we've lost so much. Susan, John's health . . . Happiness. There used to be a joy in this house, Willa. There really did. Oh, I don't mean that everything was perfect." Her deep sigh signaled nostalgia for a time lost forever. "Having Bethany near is like getting a second chance. So few people do, you know. Get a second chance."

Willa found herself drawn to this statuesque woman with her high cheekbones, soft brown hair and eyes that seemed young for middle age. Yet she was woefully conscious of the absolute peculiarity of their situation. True, it was as alien to Claudine as it was to her, but it wouldn't do to falter or capitulate. The house was lovely, Claudine a warm and caring person. John was an odd lot, less easy to know, but that might be because he was so taciturn—his prudence might only be to spare the sensibilities of others.

Yet it was obvious both Elliotts were on their best behavior with her. People could mask a lot behind polite, genteel manners. Her work as a psychologist had taught her that, if nothing else.

"Claudine," Willa said gently, "I want everything to work out as much as you do. We're all of us coming into this with a sense of loss. I feel deeply about giving—if that's the right word—Bethany a set of grandparents. I think grandparents provide a richness of . . . of spirit."

Claudine sipped coffee. Her hand trembled ever so slightly. "We don't know why Susan went away," she said sadly. "We don't. We loved her. John and I despaired of ever having a child. I keep thinking perhaps we were too old, not modern enough. Susan used to say we were old-fashioned. I never worked and deferred to John on decisions. He and Susan had some dreadful rows, but they always seemed to work them out. She adored John, she really did." Claudine lifted her head and met Willa's eyes. "But I'm thinking John isn't coming off so well with you."

Willa smiled. "I don't fault him one bit for being reserved. After all, we are strangers."

"That's not it. John is always that way. He's a wonderful man, but he makes me so mad sometimes! Clytie is right. John has never properly come into the twentieth century. Oh, dear, I know I'm coming off sounding like a witch. In so many ways John is a remarkable man, but I want to be open with you. I want you to know the good things about us. But I don't want you to think we're hiding anything. We're not. I'm not."

"I appreciate your bluntness," Willa said. "I won't take what you say wrong—I promise."

Claudine nodded. "Unlike you, I'm not a psychologist, but I do think John was unduly influenced by his mother."

Willa had her coffee cup almost to her mouth. She replaced it in the saucer. An Oedipus complex, she wondered? "In what way?"

"Oh—Natalie was concerned with her image, what others in her social set thought of her, that sort of thing."

Willa knew the type. It was one thing to put one's best foot forward, so to speak, but quite another to insist upon a facade that created confusion within the family. Especially in children, who needed to be taught the difference between fantasy and reality.

"John is that way to a certain extent. Except the social set of his parents' day no longer exists. He misses the leisurely train trips, the boating parties—you know, all the greats used to visit here: Hemingway, Mark Twain, Henry James, Sinclair Lewis used St. Augustine to launch his writing career, Ralph Waldo Emerson came to town to recuperate from a bout with tuberculosis. Marjorie Rawlings had a house across the bay. Of course, St. Augustine would never have become such a wonderful winter retreat if it hadn't been for the vision of Henry Flagler. When the hotel he built closed, it seemed to quietly shut the door on a magical era. And John, well he seemed to close his mind to . . . anything contemporary."

"Are you saying he shut out Susan?"

"Not her, no. But he had the idea that she should go from his house to a husband's. It was hard. For me, too. I've always wanted to work, but he just doesn't understand. His mother never worked. What he can't see is that Natalie didn't want to. Her goal in life was to be the center of attention. When she wasn't, she took to her bed, pouting for days on end. Susan learned from Natalie how to manipulate. Had John's father outlived his wife, I think things would have been different in this house. Much different."

"He didn't tolerate Natalie's pouts?"

"Pouts. Pooh! Once she took to her bed, refusing to come down to supper. John's father flew up those stairs, yanked her out of bed, literally dressed her himself and carried her down. Her hair was awry, her corset improperly laced, her slip hanging, the seams of her stockings every which way.'' Claudine's grin lit up her face. ''I'm afraid I laughed. She never forgave me. Still, from then until the day her husband died, she came down to supper.''

''And after he died?''

Claudine grimaced. ''Three years of misery. To tell the truth, I thought she was going to outlive me, but she died in her sleep, as tidy as you please.''

''How did Susan take her grandparents' deaths?''

''At first not well at all, but by then she was entering her teens. Moody! Goodness. She acted as if no one outside herself existed.

''But after John's parents passed away, I felt such freedom! John did, too. He never said, but I knew. We went out more. We did things. We had fun.''

''Did Susan go out with you?''

''No...but then she was Natalie all over again. Are personalities hereditary, you think?''

''I don't know if anything specific has been proven, but there is a school of thought now that environment doesn't play as large a part in development that we once thought.'' Willa frowned pensively. Claudine had given her a lot to think about.

''I've said something that upset you,'' Claudine said worriedly. ''I can see it. Your eyes are so expressive.''

''No, really. My mind was leapfrogging, going on to something else.'' And because Willa had to make good on that, she said: ''Tell me something of Nick.''

''Oh, Nick. He's been so good to us through all of this, protective of us and dedicated to finding Susan. He's given us so much of his time. We've put such a burden on him. That Susan would go off like she did was as much a shock to him as us. He was so fond of her.''

You may not know the half of it, Willa thought.

''He always had hopes of finding Susan alive.'' Claudine lifted the coffee spoon, began making patterns on the tablecloth. ''At first I did, too, but later... A mother knows. While we were searching I sometimes had this visceral ache... I knew in my heart that Susan was gone from us forever. I think I've been grieving for years. John is still at odds with himself about it. I guess you've noticed speaking of Susan makes him uncomfortable. We brought her back and buried her in the family plot and that seemed to finish my grieving. Learning of Susan's death, the way she died—starvation, which seems so impossible in this day and age—has made him ill all over again.''

''It's hard to lose somebody you love,'' Willa said.

Claudine agreed. They sat a few minutes in sympathetic silence, each pursuing her own thoughts. It was Claudine who broke the silence.

''You can't know what joy it brought us to discover Susan had had a child. That there was a part of her—'' Her voice broke.

''Claudine, I understand. That's one of the reasons I'm here.''

The older woman inhaled and exhaled slowly, regrouping her emotions. ''You were working at the hospital when Susan was brought in?''

''Yes, but I never saw her. It was all over the hospital that a Jane Doe had given birth and died, leaving the child an orphan. I looked in on the baby. All of the staff did. Bethany was so tiny... I have pictures, if you'd like to see them.''

Claudine brightened. ''Oh, I would.''

"The earlier ones are a little bit scary, but you'll be able to appreciate how far Bethany has come. She was so emaciated, so premature, she wasn't expected to live."

Claudine became still. "Had Susan been on drugs? Was Bethany born addicted? John refused to let me see the autopsy report. One hears—"

"No, thank God."

Claudine echoed her words, then went on, "I do want to see them."

"I have the album in the car. I'll get it."

"While you do that, I'll see how Bethany is getting along in the kitchen. I know we had to talk privately, but I hate giving up even a minute with her."

"LESS THAN TWO POUNDS! I read that in the news clippings Nick had copied for us, but I never imagined she had to live her first few months hooked up to machines...poor darling. Poor tiny thing. Oh, those horrid people who adopted her only to abandon her again. How could they do such a thing to a helpless baby!"

"They didn't want the trouble, or the expense. Sometimes people like them slip through the system. The woman didn't want a baby so much as she wanted a doll, some perfect little creature she could put on display."

"Bethany is perfect!"

Willa laughed. "You and I think so."

Claudine turned a page. "Who is this? This man holding Bethany."

"Peter, my husband. He was a biophysicist."

"Nick said he died of a stroke." Claudine stared down at the photo. "So young and handsome! With so much to live for..."

"It was pretty awful for a while," Willa said quietly. "It still is sometimes."

Claudine closed the album and hugged it to her slender chest. "I'm glad you came into Bethany's life, Willa. I'm glad it's you. You're a good mother, much better than I ever was." Her voice softened, became tense. "But I'm going to make myself the best grandmother a child could want."

Willa leaned back in the chair. "I think you will, Claudine. To tell you the truth, I've been really frightened of... well, any number of things."

Claudine's lovely eyes flashed with amusement. "You thought we were going to be ogres. Admit it."

Willa smiled herself out of that one. "Your letter to me was too gracious for me to consider anything of the kind."

Somewhere in the depths of the house a clock struck eight. Willa started. "I have to be going. Bethany's bedtime is just around the corner. We have to get an early start in the morning."

"Will you come again tomorrow night? Nick always has supper with us on Monday nights. It's informal, a buffet, Sunday leftovers usually."

Nick, again. Willa's thoughts raced. She wondered if Nick was being used as armor in some way she couldn't discern. But Claudine's openness was no facade. Willa was certain of that. John had not yet truly reached out to Bethany. It could be that John was not yet certain of her own motives, that Nick was urging caution. If that were the case, then Nick had placed her in the untenable position of having to win John's approval. But to what end? Either he loved Bethany on her own merits, or he didn't. Bethany was not up for approval or inspection.

On the other side of the coin, she did not expect instant affection from John and Claudine on Bethany's behalf. Loving was a growing process and there were five years to make up for. Still ...

"Willa?"

"I'm sorry. My mind wandered for a moment."

"Was it because of Nick? I know you two haven't got on. He can sometimes be abrupt. He hasn't said anything rude again, has he?"

Willa fibbed. "No, of course not. He's been as kind as you've asked him to be. And very good with Bethany. But let me call you about tomorrow night. I'm not sure I'll be free."

"But what could you be doing in the evening?"

"Getting ready for a new job, finding a nursery school for Bethany, laundry." More apartment hunting, Willa thought, but she didn't want to bring that up again.

"But you'll try to make it? You won't forget to call?"

"I won't forget."

"May I keep the album overnight to show John, then? And, Clytie, too. Am I asking too much?"

Willa felt a tug of dismay. All of Bethany's short life was recorded there, the good and the bad. There were no copies and it had never been out of her possession before. It was starting to sink in that Claudine was Bethany's grandmother, that she wanted a role in Bethany's life, and that she wanted to share what she had learned about Bethany with the others in her family. There was no harm in that. It could be a very good thing. She gave up the album into Claudine's keeping.

A few moments later she and Bethany were taking their leave. Nick trailed them down the steps. "I'll follow you back to the motel. Make sure you get there safe and sound."

A twinge of resentment pricked Willa. He was putting on his nice-guy act for John and Claudine's benefit. She wanted no part of it. "No, you won't. I'm perfectly capable of getting myself anywhere."

"That's not the issue. I want to see you safely home." He came closer, as if by depleting the physical gap between them he could banish whatever grievances she had against him.

She got into her car, beside Bethany, and yanked the door closed. It took ten minutes to drive the narrow, quiet streets back to the motel. Willa pulled into her assigned parking slot and Nick double-parked his car behind hers. She waved him on his way. He didn't take the hint. She stepped over to him before he could get out of the car.

"All right. I'm here safe and sound. Go."

"We're not going to have a cat fight about this, are we?"

Willa gave him a smile that would have warned off a lesser man. "We might."

"Well, I'm old-fashioned. Let's do it behind closed doors."

"You're not setting one foot in my room."

"Where's Bethany?"

"Asleep."

"You open the door, I'll carry her in for you."

"No! Get this into your brain—if by chance you have one. I don't need your protection. I don't want you looking over my shoulder, spying on me—"

"You have a touch of paranoia, don't you? Or is that a guilty conscience making itself known? You acquitted yourself well tonight, not a flaw or a slip, but if you think

John and Claudine are easy marks, you'd better rethink your game."

"You know what?" Willa said, breathless, because she was trying not to yell. "Earlier, when you made those kinds of remarks, I was hurt, insulted, but not anymore. Now I know you're small-minded, arrogant, and no doubt have some little something you want to keep secret yourself."

Nick shook his head. Willa had come out with little digs like that more than once. But if she wasn't going to explain them, he was certainly not going to go mining for them with his own ego as pick and shovel. However, he didn't see any reason not to give tit for tat. "I have to hand it to you, you have more bravado than any ten women I've ever met."

"I'm sure I do, considering the kinds of women you're likely to associate with."

Nick felt a surge of an odd kind of exhilaration. Willa's face was pink, her violet eyes flashing, but she was throwing words at him on a level that was rife with undercurrents. Man-woman undercurrents.

"Oh, my," he said. "I have stirred you up, haven't I?"

Willa caught the change in his tone at once. It changed the whole slant of things. It spoke of laughter in bedrooms and places Willa would not want to go, but might love to hear about. Nick wasn't fighting fair. If she wasn't so angry she knew she might now be reduced to tears.

"In the space of ten minutes," she said in a slow, icy cadence, "you have managed to ruin a perfectly nice evening. Why on earth did you follow me over here just to fight? If you don't leave by the time I count to five, I'm going to start screaming 'thief'—or worse."

"Shame on you," Nick said after a lugubrious sigh. He gazed up at her, his eyes alight with a reckless gleam. "Ah, well, I really didn't expect a good-night kiss."

"What?"

"It just slipped out," he said quickly. "Don't give it another thought. Good night." He turned the key in the ignition and without another glance, drove off.

Willa stared after him. She kept on staring until Bethany stirred and began to whimper.

A kiss? She unlocked the motel door and went back to gather her daughter into her arms. The man was entirely off his rocker.

Somewhere along about dawn, Willa awakened out of a dream that had her heart racing and her mouth dry. For a few seconds the lingering image of Nicholas Cavenaugh was vivid in her mind's eye.

She got up and felt her way in the dark to the stiff-backed chair at the tiny table. Dreaming of Nick seemed somehow disloyal to Peter. But that was silly.

Peter was gone. Her mother was gone. Dad was off limits. She had to get through life on her own. There was no one to call and no one to help and she was alone.

Her noble gesture of uniting Bethany with her biological grandparents now seemed emptier than the night. She must be crazy. The Elliotts were foreign to her in every way. She was trusting them on instinct, thinking she'd find security in numbers.

That was dumb. She didn't even feel secure enough to make it to morning, much less the rest of her life.

She could remain sitting all night feeling helpless or she could do something. She had to fill up the night, fill her brain with something besides fear and insecurity.

She draped the lampshade with a towel and switched it on. Then she retrieved pen and paper provided by the motel and began to make a list.

Susan—emaciated and starved. Anorexic?

Natalie—grandmother to Susan. Spent most of the last years of her life in her room. Agoraphobic?

Claudine—never worked but wanted to. Timid?

John—ruled by his mother. Man of few words. Introvert?

John, Sr.—action oriented. Bully or extrovert?

Nick—arrogant, egotistical, devoted to Elliotts. Fond of Susan. How fond?

Willa looked at her list and knew she was going to have to find the answers. Not surface answers, but what it all meant. It begged the question: Was Susan emotionally disturbed? Why?

She folded the list and hid it at the very bottom of her purse. Her eyes were growing heavy. She lay back down and punched up her pillow.

It was the perfidy of human nature that her dreams once again were all of Nick.

HIS TWO-ROOM HOUSE was often described as a cracker box on stilts. Nick didn't care. It nestled at the edge of the Atlantic in a tangled mass of maypop, four o'clocks, wild blackberry and palm shrubs behind sand dunes thick with sea oats. Small green lizards left tracks in the shady sand beneath the house and wrens nested in the rafters. Herring gulls visited him every morning hoping for an air-tossed handout. And Brown pelicans never failed to entertain him as they flew in orderly lines low over the water, breaking the monotony of the horizon.

He lounged in a shabby wicker chair gone soft with age, his bare feet propped on the porch railing. The aroma of his coffee was mellow in the salt air. The sun was coming up. The first glow of pale light shimmered on the horizon. Below the dunes the tide raced in, pounding the beach with four-foot waves topped with lacy white foam. The sound of the surf accompanied his thoughts.

Nick often mused that if he had good enough eyesight he'd be able to sit on his porch and see the coasts of Africa, Morocco and farther inland to Algeria where he had spent his youth with his parents. Later, after they had sent him back to the States to school, he'd only spent his summers with them. Now that was reversed. They came to visit him whenever they could take time from patching up war-torn soldiers or delivering babies in some poor Third World country.

But it wasn't thoughts of his parents that had him up at dawn this morning. It was Willa Manning.

He was angry with himself and couldn't shake it. He'd been bullying Willa and that wasn't his way. He didn't waste toughness in minor personal interchanges. So what the hell was the matter with him? He was picking on her for no good reason and shredding his pride in the process. It made him feel small. Not to mention he wasn't making good sense. She wasn't after Elliott money. He had established that. So, damn it. He had to stop accusing her. He was beginning to sound like a record warped by heat.

The best thing to do was bow out, stay out of her way. Let her establish herself with John and Claudine.

Willa's independence didn't sit well with John, but that was John's problem.

Nick had a few problems of his own. Not the least of which was that the six-year search for Susan had all but eliminated his personal life.

His law practice hadn't suffered, but that was because he'd given the Elliotts his evenings and weekends, save those he held back for the work he did with the Big Brother organization.

It had been months since he'd taken his boat out. Sailing got him off the fast track, put him back in touch with himself. Nature had a way of humbling a man. If there was any single thing he knew about himself, it was that he needed a dish of humble pie now and again.

The sun had fully risen, the glare off the water sharp.

Reluctantly Nick pulled himself out of the wicker chair and went to cook his breakfast. It was one of the few domestic chores he enjoyed. Afterward, he tossed food scraps to the gulls hovering in the air off the porch. The dirty dishes he left for his housekeeper who came three mornings a week.

As for Willa . . . He expelled a long, controlled sigh. It was time for him to step back, distance himself a little. Distance himself from her. She brought out something in him he didn't want to put a label on. He recalled the way other men had stared at her on the beach. He hadn't liked that.

Okay, he'd admit it. He'd felt possessive. He was absorbed in her—dangerously absorbed—and she seemed the kind of woman who would know it.

If only there were no memories, he thought, no previous experience to interfere with the natural flow of emotions. But there were memories. He'd learned not to trust that part of himself that craved the love of a woman.

A man could get hurt, get his heart handed back to him looking like ground meat.

Live and let live, that was the ticket.

He was certain that living by that philosophy would save him inestimable grief.

Chapter Five

"Clytie was born in an apple orchard, not in a hospital like me. The first thing she saw when she opened her eyes was a toadstool. That's why she thought she was an elf. An' when she didn't grow very big, she was sure of it. But one long, *desperate* day she started thinking and acting like a woman, so right then she knew she was all grown up. It was the *saddest* day in her life."

Willa laughed. Sitting cherublike across from her, Bethany was putting as much drama into her repetition as Clytie must have done when first relating the tale. "That's a lovely story."

"It's not a story. It's the truth! When Clytie was little, her whole family *perished* from the flu. Perished means died, like Daddy and Grandma."

The elderly couple at the next table looked over. They gave Willa a smile of commiseration, as if they, too, had once been given lessons in vocabulary by a precocious child. She told Bethany to lower her voice.

"Don't you want to hear this?"

"I do, but maybe everybody else in McDonald's doesn't. Brother! Will I be glad when we have our own kitchen again."

"I won't. I *lu-u-u-v* McDonald's."

"I know you do. Enjoy it while you can."

"Can I finish telling you about Clytie now?"

"I'm all ears, but don't talk with your mouth full."

Bethany swallowed. "Everybody perished." Another bite of egg, another swallow. "They were fruit pickers and too poor to buy medicine. The flu just swept them away. First it got the baby who didn't even have a name yet, then it got Bo Bo, who was eleven, then Mama, then Papa, until there was only Clytie. She was all alone and just cried and cried because she was too little and didn't know what to do." Bethany glanced up at her mother to see if Willa was suitably sympathetic.

Cued, Willa responded. "That's terrible," she whispered. "Poor Clytie."

"Oh, not to worry," she chimed airily. "John senior came along, looked in the car, saw Clytie was an orphan and took her home. She had food to eat and clothes to wear and she got to go to school. She's lived happily ever since."

"She has? Good for Clytie," Willa said with feeling. "That's what I want for us. Happily ever after. Which we won't get unless I make it to my interview on time. Or I'll be crying and crying because I won't know what to do."

Bethany frowned. "You said you were finished with crying, Mommy. I don't like it when you cry. It makes me feel bad all over."

"I didn't mean it literally, sweetie. Finish your breakfast. You have your crayons and coloring book?"

"Right here in my book bag."

"When we get there—"

Put upon, Bethany sighed. "I know. Color in my coloring book and be as quiet as a mouse. Don't ask to go to the bathroom, don't ask for a drink of water and don't ask to play with the typewriter if there is one. You told me a thousand times.''

"I can't help it. I'm only a mother.''

Bethany rolled her eyes heavenward.

In the car, Willa retrieved her road map from her purse. The list she had made at dawn caught her eye. She lifted her gaze and watched in the rearview mirror as Bethany buckled herself in with the seat belt. The child's small, heart-shaped face was a study in concentration.

Whoever her ancestors, whatever their problems, Willa mused, Bethany was bright, open, and becoming healthier and happier by the day. Her appetite was improving, too, her arms and legs were filling out, she hadn't had an earache or stomach upset since they had left Kansas. Bethany looked up, Willa said: "Ready?''

The child nodded. "Maybe I could get a job in the hospital, too.''

"Your day will come, believe me.''

"I mean now. I could talk to little kids in the hospital about being sick. I know a lot about being sick.''

"You feel okay, don't you?''

"Yes,'' Bethany said and, as she was wont to do, skipped to another topic. "If I hang upside down on the monkey bars, will my brains fall out my ears?''

"No.''

"Next time we go to the park, I want to hang upside down. Like a bat. A bat is a vampire.'' Bethany leaned forward. "Listen, Mommy, how can you tell if a vampire has been in your tomato juice?''

Willa gave forth with an exaggerated moan. "I don't want to know.''

The child giggled. "There will be two teensy-weensy tooth marks on the can.''

THE HOSPITAL COMPLEX was new, its buildings beige with red tiled roofs to affect a Moorish look. Between buildings were garden courtyards alive with flowers, shrubs and ponds. The parking lot was full, which indicated to Willa that the hospital was probably running at one-hundred percent occupancy. Which meant that, sight unseen, she had no doubt picked one of the best hospitals in the area. Good. She needed a little something going her way for a change.

In Personnel she had barely a moment to settle Bethany before the receptionist ushered her into the inner office.

The director, a thin, chic woman with large friendly eyes behind gold-rimmed glasses, greeted her warmly with an outthrust hand. Her name was Joanne Green. "I've been looking forward to meeting you, Willa. Your résumé was impressive. Do sit."

"I want to thank you for allowing me to bring my daughter along. I didn't want to just dump her in a nursery without checking it out first, and I'm afraid I don't know anyone here well enough to—"

Joanne Green waved her hand dismissively. "That kind of thought and concern is what we want of our staff." She smiled. "Anyway, hospital staffs are made up of mostly women. We all have children. And if you don't find a school or nursery that suits, give me call, I may be able to help. Who knows, perhaps one day we'll have an on-site nursery for the children of our staff."

"That would be grand."

The personnel director grinned. "All we need is some thankful patron to make a substantial donation and earmark it. Coffee?"

Willa indicated, no. "I've only moments ago finished breakfast."

"You're not a smoker, are you? I'm sorry to have to ask, but we've discovered applicants fib on that a lot these days."

"No, I'm not."

"Hurray for that. Well, as I told you over the phone, your job slot is a new position. At the moment, we have a volunteer psychologist doing grief and separation counseling for our patients. The service has been so popular... well, maybe that's not the right word, but anyway, we did offer her the job—"

"She refused it?"

"It was economics. She already has a job, is fully vested in her pension plan and has only ten years to go until retirement. We couldn't sway her."

Willa smiled. "I'm glad."

The personnel director grinned. "Now that I've met you, I think I am, too. Your résumé said that you'd been doing most of your work in pediatrics. Here, you'd have to cover pediatrics and adult. Will that cause you any dismay?"

"I've worked with adults, I just specialized in pediatrics."

"Yes, I saw that." The director fingered Willa's résumé. "What I'm driving at is that I see your own husband died not so long ago."

Willa inhaled. "I think Peter's death has helped me to be more sensitive. Before, I understood how death affected the family as a unit, what the void would mean. I knew how to alert survivors of what to expect. But after he died, I realized there was more to it." She exhaled softly. "Much more. My mother had died some years earlier, so I'd already experienced for myself the grieving process. I had expected that with Peter's death..." She shrugged helplessly.

"Take your time."

"I'm all right. I was just trying to think how best to explain.... It was his toothbrush that got to me. I'd already cleaned out his closet, his dresser, packed away his favorite cup, but...one day I was cleaning the bathroom...and there was his toothbrush. Peter hated changing toothbrushes. That was when his dying caught up with me. No more husband with his quirky little habits."

"That realization made you better at your job?"

"It made me realize there was going to be that lost odd moment when a survivor was going to think the world had stopped spinning. I was only working part-time by then, but I approached my supervisor with the idea that the hospital should sponsor an on-going support group for survivors. I was moderator for the child and young adult group."

"We would love to add that kind of a program to our services. You evaluated and counseled pediatric patients before and after surgery?"

"Not only then, but also if the child had a long-term illness or recovery period."

"What about the parents, relatives of patients?"

"Except for the support group, I was involved with relatives only to the extent of what was beneficial for the patient. However, if I determined there was an on-going situation or problem among family members, I referred them to our psychiatric staff. They took it from there."

"Emergencies?"

"We had a few. Especially when a patient was traumatized. It was my job to diffuse and stabilize the situation or the patient. Again that sometimes meant bringing in the staff psychiatrist. I know when I'm out of my depth. On the other hand, sometimes all it took was to put an arm around the patient, or the parent.''

"Did you ever run into problems?''

Willa smiled. "In a hospital? Hasn't everyone?''

The director returned the smile. "We're getting along so well . . . don't make me have to write down that you were evasive.''

"I got tossed off cases twice. Once because the religious preference of a patient precluded the service I provided, another time because a patient's father didn't believe in psychiatric mumbo jumbo.''

"I take it that's a direct quote.''

"Almost. I edited out the epithets.''

"One more thing. How well do you get along with doctors and nurses?''

Willa was ready for that one. "In front of the patient and relatives I defer to the medical team without fail.''

"Ah.'' A grin hovered at the edge of the director's mouth. "What about out of the patient's hearing?''

"I'm not histrionic, but I usually have my say.''

"And get things done your way?''

"Mrs. Green,'' Willa said with a sense of admiration for the woman, "you're exceptionally skilled at interviewing.''

The woman leaned back and laughed. "Since you're the expert, I humbly accept the compliment. So let's get down to basics. Your job slot and the salary that goes with it is made possible by a matching grant from the state. That means you'll have to write a report once a month and at year's end. You don't by any chance know how to write up a grant proposal do you?''

"As it happens, I do. My husband was a biophysicist at Kansas University Med Center. He was paid a stipend to teach, but most of his income came from research grants. I wrote them up for him."

"Hallelujah! Then you know the importance of having your department's grant proposal on my desk by deadline every year."

Willa nodded. "No grant, half pay."

"Wonderful. Now the only thing left is to schedule you for orientation, give you a tour and introduce you around." The director checked her calendar. "How does the last week in August sound? That way you're on payroll September first."

Willa's heart dropped into her stomach. She couldn't make it without a paycheck from now to September. That was three months! "Mrs. Green . . . I'm sorry. But I need work now. I thought—"

Joanne Green's expression went blank for a moment, then she winced. "Don't tell me I didn't mention a starting date?"

Willa swallowed. "I'm afraid you didn't, and I just assumed . . ."

"Oh, dear. Let me think a minute. Maybe I can come up with something."

"Don't feel bad," Willa told her. "It's my fault. I should've asked when the job started. Actually I have another job offer from a clinic in Jacksonville that I was holding in reserve."

"Don't even think about it. We want you." She reached for the telephone. "Let me make a call or two . . ."

Willa did not want to sit idly by listening to a one-sided conversation that no doubt would end in more disappointment. She excused herself and went to wait in the outer office.

Bethany was not sitting and coloring quietly. She was leaning on a corner of the receptionist's desk, trading knock-knock jokes.

"She's disturbed you," Willa said to the young woman. "I'm sorry."

"She didn't. I spoke to her first, she rattled off your instructions, and I guess from there we got carried away."

"I haven't asked to play with the typewriter, or for water, or to go to the bathroom," Bethany said on her own behalf. "And I really have to go. Bad, too."

Willa took her to the washroom. "I ought to read you your rights, that's what I ought to do to you, young lady."

"You said: 'Be polite.' I was being polite."

The inconsistencies that we mother's teach! Willa thought. "Okay, you're off the hook this time."

The director was standing on the threshold of her office when they returned. She waved Willa back into her office. "I found you something temporary at the mental-health center. They've got one counselor out on maternity leave and another resigning." Smiling, she handed Willa a slip of paper with a name and instructions on how to get to the center.

"I really appreciate you going out of your way—"

The director's eyes lit with amusement. "Don't thank me. They do excellent work at the center, but you'll be overworked, underpaid, on call, and have to make do with overcrowded offices. I explained that you start work for us on September first, that you're just on loan. Oh, here." She gave Willa a sealed envelope. "These will save you and the health center time. It's confirmation of your qualifications and references." She blushed faintly. "We do check them, you know."

Willa realized the woman was skirting hospital policy by offering the mental-health center her records, going out on a limb on her behalf. She pocketed the envelope. "Once I'm settled, I'll give you a call."

"Do, we'll have lunch. My treat."

"Dutch," Willa said.

"Agreed," said the director.

The job at the mental-health center turned out to be all, and less, than Joanne Green had said. The job was not only temporary, but part-time; a twenty-five-hour-a-week job with a forty-hour-a-week caseload. When the supervisor of the center mentioned the salary Willa paled. On the plus side, she was told she could start work the following Monday. She told herself that a piece of a job was better than no job. If push came to shove, she'd find a second job. After all, it was only for three months.

The basic requirement to sustain life was food, water, air, Bethany's education, and shelter. She'd just have to set her sights lower on the shelter part until she was financially fit.

That decided, to Bethany's joy and delight, they spent the early part of the afternoon checking out day-care centers and preschools. The best of the lot was the most expensive. But it served the students year-round, and had classes in art, music, Spanish and computer use. Best of all it went from preschool through third grade so that Bethany was assured of having some continuity.

The remainder of the afternoon they shopped for apartments. Less was hard to find. The last place she looked at was a furnished, one-bedroom duplex. The sofa sagged, the sinks were chipped, but it was clean and had a postage-stamp-size backyard. It was only three hundred and seventy-five dollars a month. Willa told the man she'd take it.

"I get first and last month's rent in advance," he told her. "Plus one month rent as security deposit."

Willa blanched. "But...but—that comes to more than eleven hundred dollars!"

"An' you pay electric," he said.

"I'm sorry. I've changed my mind."

Her mood as gloomy as the swift-flying summer-storm clouds that blackened the sky, Willa drove back to the motel. She called Claudine as promised.

"...Bethany's education is more important," she said. "We can live anywhere for three months. As long as it has a bed, a bath and a stove. I'll just have to keep looking."

"Nick lives on the island, maybe he knows of something."

"I'd just as soon not bother him," Willa said coolly.

Claudine was silent for a few seconds. "Well, come to supper. We'll put our heads together. I—I may know of a place, I need to talk to John about it. But as a last resort you could always reconsider our house."

"Claudine, thank you. It's tempting, but no. I just have to find something that doesn't require so much cash up-front."

"You are coming to supper?"

Willa looked over at the bed. The disorder and hurly-burly pace of their lives was catching up with Bethany. She was still soundly asleep. "I've dragged Bethany from pillar to post today. She's really tired."

"Oh, Willa, we're so looking forward to seeing her. She's brought something peaceful into our lives. John slept better last night than he has since...since Susan left us."

Willa bit her lip. She was hearing about a side of John she had yet to see for herself. And the professional in her wanted to say that it wasn't Bethany's responsibility to make John happy. A child did not have to justify his existence by meeting a parent or grandparent's needs. A lifelong pressure of that sort would make any child rebel—eventually.

Speculation begged the question: Did Susan run from her parents? From Nick? Or from herself—from something within herself?

Willa felt a delicate stabbing of combined curiosity and aloneness. Claudine was easy to talk to; and talking, even arguing with Nick was stimulating—much better than spending the evening in a crowded box of a room that offered no view and a cloudy television.

"Willa?"

"I'm here. We'll come to supper, Claudine, but I want to let Bethany get her sleep out. Otherwise she'll be a grouch all evening."

"We'll expect you when you get here, how's that?"

"Terrific."

Bethany slept on. Willa soaked in a tub of scented water, her neck resting on a folded towel, her eyes closed, her thoughts as unfocused as the steam that misted the window and mirror.

It had been many long months since she had felt anyone touch her, many long months since she had experienced any form of physical tenderness. She had turned away from the more primitive needs that arose occasionally in her consciousness.

But now, enveloped in the warm bathwater she recalled Nick's hand on the small of her back. Recalled, too, the suspicious skip her heart had given at that contact. Treacherously her mind toyed with images of kisses and caresses; of Nick bestowing explicit attentions, visualizing... She caught herself. Heavens! She was being ridiculous. The man was as difficult as could be. All she wanted from him was information: Was he, or was he not, Bethany's father? Besides, he was probably up to his armpits in women.

"Mommy."

Willa pulled away from her thoughts. "Hi, sweetie. Did you have a good sleep."

Bethany sniffled. "I wet the bed."

"Oh, sweetheart," she consoled, "that's okay. You were tired and when you're tired accidents happen. We'll get some clean sheets from the office and change the bed." Willa got out of the tub to comfort her daughter. She slipped into her robe and gave Bethany a hug. "Here, climb in the tub, honey. I'll wash your back."

"If you ask for sheets, then the people in the office will know! They'll make fun of me."

"People who make fun of others are cruel. But we won't tell them why."

"What if they ask?"

"Then I'll tell them a little white lie and say I spilled a soft drink on the bed or something."

"It's okay to tell a white lie?"

"Sometimes—yes. If you do it so you won't hurt someone's feelings. It's called tact." Willa watched her daughter digest this information. She could almost see her sorting it, compartmentalizing it, making it fit. "Feel better?"

"I guess."

"We're going to see John and Claudine again tonight."

"Clytie and Nick, too?"

"Probably."

"What about the dollhouse and the music box?"

"I'm sure." She helped Bethany out of her underwear and into the tub. For a moment she covertly studied the line of Bethany's jaw, the shape of her nose, the dainty, narrow body. She tried to see it ten, fifteen years into the future. What came to her was a strong, well-defined face, and a long-limbed looseness like that which Nicholas Cavenaugh seemed to possess naturally.

That image didn't erase itself until more than an hour later when she and Bethany were welcomed effusively by Claudine.

"I was worried you wouldn't make it before the storm broke."

Bethany made a beeline to the nook where the toys were stored. There was no one else in the exquisite room. The house itself was mausoleum quiet. Willa felt constrained to lower her voice.

"Have we arrived too early, too late?" she asked.

"John's at a meeting, he should be home any minute. He doesn't know what retirement means. Clytie has her reading club on Monday nights."

Willa followed Claudine through the family room into a cozy nook off the kitchen that opened onto a glassed-in room filled with all manner of greenery, blooming potted plants and hanging lamps. "This used to be a butler's pantry. John's father had it extended and added the Florida room. What with the clouds, it's a little dreary now, but it's my favorite room in the house. It gets the morning sun."

"It's lovely," Willa said with a sigh, sinking into a chair plump with pale yellow cushions. She had a bird's-eye view into the kitchen, a room that was obviously Clytie's domain; stepladders and footstools hugged the sinks and cabinets to accommodate her short stature.

"You've had an exhausting day, haven't you," Claudine stated. "Would a glass of chilled wine suit?"

"It would," Willa replied, then: "Nick's not here?" slipped out before she could bite her tongue.

"He's working late. His air conditioner was off all last week. His secretary refused to work until he got it fixed. He said they're trying to catch up on paperwork."

To her disgust, Willa found that she was disappointed by Nick's absence.

"He'll stop by for coffee and dessert, though."

A swell of anticipation swept through Willa. It was purely physical, she decided. Something having to do with her biorhythm. She'd ignore it; it would go away.

Claudine cranked a bank of windows open. "There. I like to listen to the rain, don't you?"

"It's soothing," Willa said of the steady rustle of the drizzle. She accepted the wine, took a sip and set it aside. "Claudine, are you a native of St. Augustine?"

"Oh, no. I was born and raised in South Carolina. John senior and my father were great friends. Both enjoyed horse racing, or maybe I should say gambling. They met at a race somewhere along the circuit, liked one another and shared a box at the Kentucky Derby every year after that. One year they decided to make a family gathering of it and that's how I met John."

"Love at first sight?" Willa prodded affably.

Claudine laughed. "No, but he was courtly. I admired that. And, away from his mother, he was fun. And then...I don't know why I'm telling you all this, but in this one great giddy moment we made love—on a horse blanket of all things..." Claudine's face flushed. "Goodness! I'm telling you things I've never even mentioned to my closest friend!"

Willa smiled. "I'm enjoying listening. It's a lovely story."

"Maybe that's what it is, you're a good listener. But in my heyday, allowing one's self to be compromised was . . . well—sordid."

"What you did was natural."

"It does seem so in hindsight, but we didn't have hindsight then. Anyway, John insisted we marry. I agreed. Our fathers were delighted. Had I known we were to spend our married life in this house, with his parents, with Natalie . . . well, I guess I can't second-guess my decision now." She looked up, a sudden discomfiture apparent. "I keep forgetting you're a psychologist. You're not analysing me are you?"

"I'm probably trying to," Willa said with a smile. "But, I want to know about you, I want to know about Bethany's heritage. I like listening to you. I'm fascinated."

"Pooh, there's nothing fascinating about me." But her face glowed.

Willa took another sip of wine, using the pause to find a priority in her questions. "Are your parents still living?"

"My father died soon after John and I were married."

"Oh, I'm sorry. Had he been ill?"

"No, he went for a gallop on an ill-tempered horse and got thrown, broke his neck."

"How awful."

Claudine's eyes glazed for a moment. "It was and it wasn't." She smiled wistfully. "Father always said he wanted to go out with his era. He said the fifties and sixties were going to bring changes like we'd never seen. He was right."

"I guess John senior missed his good friend."

"He did, but he didn't go into any great decline. John senior had an affinity for people. Young people. He was always interested. Change didn't bother him. He thrived on it. There was a lot of excitement in this house until the day he died."

Willa couldn't find any but a direct way to ask. "How did he die?"

Claudine chuckled softly. "Oh, dear. I don't mean to laugh. But John senior was always one for pomp and splendor—a little bit of sin goes a long way, he often said. He also expected to be forgiven. He must've been. He died sitting backbone straight in the fourth pew in the Presbyterian church on a lovely Palm Sunday. When the service was over, we all got up to leave. John senior didn't.

"Natural causes, the doctor said. Natalie accepted all of the condolences and then got furious. She had to put away her new Easter ensemble and wear somber colors. She seldom left the house after he died, though. She made herself a little nest in her room and there she stayed. None of us could coax her out. Not even my mother, who could usually get a rise out of Natalie."

"Oh? Is your mother still living?"

"I'll say. Mother lives in a retirement village in Miami. I've tried to get her to live with us, but she refuses. She has her friends, bingo, cruises—her life after Father, she calls it."

"Then Bethany has a great-grandmother, too," Willa said, liking the idea.

"Oh, it would thrill Mother to meet Bethany." Claudine seemed to withdraw into herself for a moment. "She and Susan never got on. But then, Mother and Natalie were never good friends. She called Natalie the 'spineless wonder,' which didn't endear her to John, either. But I like my mother. After Father died, she made her decision as to how she wanted to live and stayed with it. When I was pregnant with Susan, Mother broke her arm. I couldn't go, so Clytie went down to lend a hand. They got on famously, so now Clytie spends a month with her every year.''

Mentally Willa mused on the list folded tightly at the bottom of her purse. Any genetic problems that Bethany might encounter in the foreseeable future kept coming back to Natalie and Susan—and Nick. Willa sat on those unhappy thoughts for a few seconds. Presently she said. ''Speaking of Clytie—she told Bethany a tale about John's father finding her in a car and bringing her home.''

''That was the truth,'' Claudine insisted in the same tone Bethany had used earlier. ''He did. It was in 1921, near the end of the influenza epidemic of 1918. Clytie's parents were migrant workers. They had worked their way north and were homebound to someplace in central Florida. Clytie doesn't remember exactly where. The father became ill. He drove onto a side street here in the city, parked the truck. I guess they had all been ill. They died, all of them, except Clytie, right there in the truck. John's father was walking to the courthouse. He heard Clytie crying, investigated. Of course, it wasn't the done thing, just to pick a child up off the street and raise her— especially a colored child—but, John senior did just that.''

Willa responded ruefully. ''And Clytie has lived happily ever after?''

''Hah! With Natalie in the house—that's the fairy tale part. But oddly, Natalie never made a disparaging remark about Clytie. When the occasion arose, she could be compassionate. John senior never adopted Clytie, but he did legally have her last name changed to Elliott when she was eighteen. He said she was an Elliott by osmosis. He saw to her education at the Convent of St. Joseph. Later she went north to college. Graduated summa cum laude, too. There's nothing small about Clytie's brain. She worked for the Red Cross in World War II—''

"And now she keeps house?" Willa blurted.

"Keeps?" Claudine laughed. "Clytie rules it. We can't keep housekeepers. She wants things done just so. During the month she spends with Mother, I bring in a battalion to wash windows, shampoo carpets and turn mattresses, otherwise she'd be doing it herself."

"But John introduced her as—"

"It's his idea that everything and everybody has a place. He's been trying to 'place' Clytie his whole life. She's neither sibling nor servant. He's sixty-six, Clytie's seventy-eight. Wait until she gets mad at him about something. She reminds him that she changed his diapers out of the goodness of her heart. He can't bear it. On the other hand, when she's not here, he worries dreadfully. When she's with Mother, he finds some excuse or other to call her. Where did she put this? He can't find his store of shaving cakes . . . little things.

"To tell you the truth, I think John has always worried about Clytie's influence on me. When she was younger, she'd go off on any adventures that struck her fancy. But, I've never had the courage to just pack my bag and go. Anyway, Clytie always came back. That's the part I noticed. Oh, but I must be boring you to tears!"

Willa protested to no avail. Claudine glanced at her watch. "I'd better start spooning up supper. John will be home any minute."

Willa peeked around the kitchen corner to check on Bethany. The child was stretched out on the floor, engrossed in a fantasy with the Lilliputian figurines in the dollhouse.

To Claudine she said, "I'll help you. I miss having my own kitchen."

"I accept, but be careful. Clytie's got so many step stools and risers in here, the place is a hazard." Claudine stood in front of the microwave. "Clytie set the timer. I haven't heard it go off, have you?"

"No, but we can check it."

"You know how?"

Willa looked sideways at Claudine. "Don't you?" The woman shook her head.

"Claudine, what do you do all day?"

"I—look after John mostly. Read, sew, shop—worry. Not very fulfilling from your lookout, is it?"

"Forgive me for asking, but don't you ever get bored?"

"I just try not to think about it. Anyway, what would a woman my age do?"

"Goodness. You're hardly on the brink of oblivion. Lots of things."

"Name one."

"Rebel?"

"John would have a fit." She gave Willa an impish look from beneath her lashes. "What would it pay do you think?"

No sooner had they stopped laughing than John came into the house and stood on the threshold of the kitchen. He hovered there as if he thought entering a domain controlled by the women of his household would offend his male sensibilities.

"Willa," he said by way of greeting.

"John," she said, giving him back his own brevity.

Claudine met his direct gaze. She shook her head, and a look of perplexity washed over John's face.

Willa eyed them curiously. A message had been exchanged and she had no doubt that its topic had been herself, which meant that for all her openness, Claudine was still holding back. Or perhaps her spontaneity had been calculated.

Then Claudine was rushing to her husband, helping him shrug out of his raincoat. "Do decant a red wine, darling. Clytie's made a wonderful beef stew and there's French bread in the warmer. For dessert, key-lime pie—your favorite." She linked her arm through his and led him in the direction of the glass-topped table in the Florida room.

"Where's Nick?" he asked.

"He'll be along."

"Not like him to miss Monday night."

Their voices dropped to a murmur, low and emotional.

Willa slumped against a counter, feeling miserable and frustrated. She had a piece of a job, no place to live, no place to go back to, and a five-year-old who was getting saucier by the hour because their lives were so unstructured. To top it off, she now had an intuitive fear that the evening was going to be long and awkward.

She reminded herself that normally she was in control of her life, no matter what the circumstance. But then, her world had never been rocked as it was rocked now. Resolutely Willa pushed aside the negative emotions invading her, refusing to feel sorry for herself. Everything would work out. It had to.

Claudine bustled back into the kitchen. Together they dished up stew, bread, salad, pie and arranged it on the table. A moment later they were all seated. Bethany immediately sank so deeply into the soft cushioned chair that her chin rested on the glass tabletop.

"Won't do," said John, eyeing her predicament. He insisted both Bethany and her food be shifted to his end of the table. Willa bit back her protest. John was making an effort to reach out to Bethany. She watched to see where it would lead.

He took the child onto his lap, but when he lifted a spoonful of stew to her mouth, Bethany balked.

"I can feed myself. I'm not a baby, y'know."

"Eat, then," he said. "Last one to clean his plate is a toad."

Bethany rolled her eyes. "That's a trick to get me to eat stew. I already know about the starving children all over the world. Mommy tells me even when I leave one little bean on my plate."

"Well, one little bean won't go far."

"Yes it would, if you planted it. It would grow into a bushful of beans and *that* would feed a family," she told him proudly, enjoying airing her knowledge. "But not after it's cooked. You have to plant a raw bean. Grampa Dawson told me. He's a farmer. Only I'm not supposed to call him Grampa."

Willa felt her stomach seize up.

John looked startled. "Why not?"

"He's got a new wife and she says Grampa sounds too old."

"Every little girl should have a grampa, young, old, or in between," John said with feeling, stepping entirely out of his usual reserved mode.

He glowered at Willa over the child's head as if Willa were the one at fault. She could make no defense, except to meet his gaze candidly. But at that precise moment her dislike for her stepmother hardened. Would she ever find it in her heart to forgive her own father for accepting without protest, his wife's declaration that "Since Bethany's only adopted, you're not really a grandfather."

With a clarity she had never before probed, Willa understood now that it was her mother who had been the strength of their family. It was Mom who had made the decisions on the farm: when to plow, when to sow, when to harvest. It had been her mother who had encouraged her to participate in 4-H, to try for top honors, to apply for scholarships, to go to college, become independent.

So, of course, Dad did what Nelda suggested. He had always followed his wife's lead. He knew no other way. He was the kind of man who had to be pointed in the direction he needed to go. Perhaps Nelda was realizing she had not married the bargain she thought she had.

But if Mom was looking down from heaven at this very moment, Willa suspected she would approve wholeheartedly of Bethany, Claudine and John.

"Little kids can't always have what they want," Bethany said with her usual perspicacity.

John gingerly touched her silken hair. "You know a lot, don't you?"

"I'm advanced. That means I'm extrasmart." She twisted in his lap to look up at him through solemn eyes. "Do you like me?"

"Yes, I do."

"I like you, too."

John's face went pink.

"So if you're not going to eat your pie," continued Bethany, "I will."

John laughed, but quietly. "But I am going to eat my pie. It's my favorite."

Bethany pulled a face. "Oh, shoot."

Observing, grandfather and granddaughter, Willa's throat tightened. In actuality, Bethany's features were a lot like Claudine's, but now she noticed Bethany and John shared a similarity in mannerisms. It was in the tilt of the head, the often studious expression, the lift of the brow.

Certainly Bethany had inherited her quick-wittedness, her intelligence, and her unnerving forthrightness from the Elliotts. The picture the three made was exactly as Willa had imagined. Bethany deserved their adoration and love. Apart from her mother's imagined approval, Bethany needed to be protected, too; from the unknown, from whatever had driven her birth mother from this home. Willa felt a stab of guilt that she had been prying into their lives. More guilt because she meant to continue prying. But perhaps the fault lay not with John and Claudine at all.

Perhaps it lay entirely with Nick. A coldness settled over her heart like a hoarfrost. An image of Nick with Susan Elliott leaped into her mind with such vividness she stiffened. She didn't want it to be true and she didn't dare explore the reason she felt that way.

As if her thoughts had conjured him up, they heard a car door slam above the sound of the rain. Footsteps on the porch, a cursory knock on the side door and Nick, with his easy grace and cool gray eyes, emerged into the softly lighted Florida room.

Chapter Six

"Rough day?" John asked Nick.

"One of my worst," he said, bending to kiss Claudine on the cheek. In passing he said something to Bethany, which she found funny. Claudine began to cluck and fuss; ordering Nick to sit, pouring coffee, arranging a place setting with napkin, silver; she served him a generous slice of pie.

The fuss and clattering curtailed conversation for a few moments. The others didn't catch it, but Willa noticed Nick was ignoring her. Why? Did he consider her a disruption and a threat to his relationship with the Elliotts? Of course. Reserved though the Elliotts might be, they were sharp-eyed and intelligent. In the same way she had begun to note a likeness in feature and manner between the Elliotts and Bethany, the elder couple were bound to begin noticing traits Nick and Bethany shared; the long legs for instance, the shape of the eyebrow—which Willa had convinced herself were genetically compatible.

Using her coffee as camouflage, she lifted the cup to her lips and observed Nick above its rim.

His eyes looked tired. Beard stubble shadowed his face, but this did not dilute his good looks. If anything, the dark stubble delineated the strong jawbone, enhancing the uneven planes and angles of his face that made one take a second look. Tired though his eyes were, they still had the power to mesmerize. They were enigmatic, appraising and bold; fringed with thick black lashes. Few women would want to resist those eyes, Willa decided. Except herself. Thank God, she had the ability to see beyond a person's looks.

As she was lowering her eyes, Nick looked up. Their gazes met and held for a brief moment. Nick's expression was intense, message-carrying, and primal. She caught her breath, discovered herself trembling. It was as if she had been required to match his intensity. A heightened reaction swept through her. She was struck at once by the irrationality of her feelings. Feelings she had only seconds ago denied.

Fully understanding that an intimate communication had passed between them without benefit of words, Nick felt as if he had been punched in the gut. With courtroom learned skill he turned away, engaging John in an inane conversation about a mutual acquaintance.

When John and Claudine picked up the topic, Nick directed his thoughts back toward Willa.

He knew she was a hazard! Damn it. He'd promised himself to back off. Before he left the office, he had picked up the phone to call Claudine, say he was tied up with a client. He couldn't make himself dial the number. Willa had drawn him to her presence like a fish to bait.

He was hooked. In the gullet. There she sat, opposite him, reeling him in with the feline grace of her posture, with the exquisite structure of her body, with the beauty of her ivory skin, dark hair and those vivid, candid, blue eyes.

He wanted to take hold of her hand, lead her out of this house, go with her somewhere so that they could be alone. He wanted to exchange thoughts and confidences, make amusing remarks to hear her laughter; he wanted to possess her. Longing stirred within him and he felt heat rise into his face and he swallowed, trying to concentrate on Claudine's words.

"We've been waiting until you arrived," she was saying. "John and I want your help to convince Willa of something."

"Convince me of what?" Willa asked, looking from one to the other as she went to wipe Bethany's hands.

"Can I go back and play with the dollhouse now?"

"You may," her mother said pointedly.

Bethany grimaced. "May I?"

"Yes."

"It's about a place for you to live," Claudine explained as Bethany shot off into the family room.

Willa underwent a moment of anxiety. "I won't live in your house—"

"No, no. We know better than to suggest that again. We have a separate cottage in the back. It used to be a carriage house, a stable before that. Tell her, Nick."

He bent his head. "Tell her what?"

"Well, that you lived there for years and years and had your privacy. That we didn't interfere in your life."

Years and years? Willa thought, knees going weak and slipping back into her chair. While Susan was growing up in this house? Growing into a provocative young woman?

"That's true, you didn't," Nick said, keeping his tone carefully neutral.

"It has two entrances, Willa. One onto the alley and one into our backyard. No one has lived out there since Nick left, but I'm sure with a good scrub, some fresh paint—"

But Willa was looking at Nick. "How long ago did you move?"

"Six years or so."

Six years. Susan had run away six years ago. The time frame was right. Willa's throat clotted with emotion. Did she want to live where Bethany might have been conceived? It was the last thing she wanted.

John spoke. "We'd like it if you moved in, Willa. You'd be close enough that we could get to know one another better. We like the idea of you and Bethany being nearby. You don't have to think of it as a permanent solution to your housing problem. We'd understand if you ever decided to move. But it would give you an opportunity to settle yourselves for the summer. Claudine tells me you're concerned that living out of suitcases at the motel might have an unhealthy influence on Bethany. Once the heavy tourist season is done, you'd be more likely to locate reasonably priced housing. Meanwhile..." An almost pleading smile accompanied his shrug.

It was a major speech for John, provoked entirely by his desire to assure her welfare, and Bethany's, Willa knew. Yet he was being very careful about any suggestion that might be subject to the slightest misinterpretation. She warmed to him as she had not done before.

She swallowed, shaking her head. "It's too generous of you—"

Claudine nudged her husband. He spoke. "I'd charge you rent."

"But not much," Claudine put in quickly. "The place isn't worth much. Take her to see it, Nick, please, before she refuses." Claudine pushed back her chair. "And take your time about it. Show her everything. I'll just go keep Bethany company."

"And I'll have my after-dinner smoke," John said, moving off after his wife.

Only the table separated Willa from Nick. She felt stranded, glued to the chair. She waited for him to make the first move.

"Cat got your tongue?" he asked.

"I'm waiting for you to say something nasty."

"Why would I do that?"

"Why?" she repeated, lowering her voice. "You've left no doubt that you consider me a gold digger, and you've missed few opportunities to make snide comments—"

"I changed my mind."

Willa drew back, trying to read the expression on his face, but couldn't. All she knew was that his change of attitude was highly significant. With an interior shiver of alarm and suspicion she said: "Just like that?"

"Seems like it."

"You're playing a game with me. To what end?"

"Believe me, it's no game." His expression was almost solemn.

"You say that as if you're delivering a punch line to a joke."

He pursed his lips. "No jokes. I'm not in the mood to laugh."

"Funny is the last thing I had in mind. I don't know how to take you."

Any way you will, he thought. "You want to see the cottage or not?"

"I think I'm obliged to."

"Before you refuse it? You could've put the skids on their hope on the spot, not prolong it."

Flushed with a twinge of inspired anger, Willa stood, pushed her chair back under the table. "Claudine and John are warm and caring people. More thoughtful and kind than any two people I've ever met. You were right about them being throwbacks to another era. They're vulnerable in so many little ways it's impossible to count them." Hearing herself, Willa realized that whether or not she had meant to, she had very quickly become attached to both Elliotts. "So tell me," she prodded Nick with a continuing trace of anger. "How often do you let John and Claudine down easy, or refuse them anything, for that matter?"

Nick gave a sliver of self-deprecating laughter, as he too, stood. "Well said. Let's go."

She trailed behind him through the kitchen and out the back door onto a lattice-framed porch. The rear door itself was monumental, as if designed to allow in halves of oxen and trunks of trees. The screen door was no less huge. Willa told herself she'd have to caution Bethany never to slam it. The entire house would vibrate.

Nick went into a washroom and switched on outside lights that pushed back the black, drizzling darkness.

The backyard was a long, narrow enclosure surrounded on three sides by high walls of coquina stone. In the far corner was the carriage house. Keeping an arm's length of distance, Willa followed Nick down a flagstone path.

"Maybe I'd better round up an umbrella."

"It's only misting. I won't melt." Beyond the light Willa sensed the presence of a garden; she smelled rain-dampened shrubs and flowers.

There was a wooden awning above the entrance. Nick retrieved the key from the lintel above the door, unlocked it, reached inside to switch on lights, then stepped back, and waved Willa forward.

Musty air greeted her, but Willa hardly noticed. The dark, dim recesses at ceiling level made the vaulted ceiling seem higher than it was, she knew. Still . . . it was a wonderful room, running the length of the entire cottage. At the far end was a small kitchen area separated from the rest of the space by a wide counter that could easily do duty as a table. The ceiling in the kitchen space was low, creating the impression of an alcove. To her left was a narrow, but finely carved staircase of mahogany that led to a second level; Willa climbed the steps. Bed frames, mattresses, chests of various sorts were shoved under the eaves. A door stood open at the near end. She peered inside. The bathroom. Tiny, with only a shower, she noted, but it was appointed with a huge basin and finely wrought brass fixtures.

She turned back to the solid railing and looked down. The upstairs was like a wide balcony. She could do wonders with the place. She could see herself living here. Being happy here. She tried to hide her enthusiasm from Nick and failed.

"There's another bathroom down here behind the kitchen," he called up to her. "It used to be the tack room."

"I can't believe this used to be a stable!" she said when she rejoined him. "If you could see the miserable places I've been looking at—in my price range, I mean." She sat on one of the stools at the counter, her expression suddenly relaxed. "I can't wait to get out of that motel room. It's claustrophobic."

Nick rocked on his heels. "I take it that means you'll be moving in."

"You don't approve, do you?" she said, remembering that he had lived here. That Susan had no doubt visited him—their love nest. Her joy evaporated.

"I don't have a say in the matter."

"But if you did?"

"I don't," he said, his voice hardening. "So my opinion is moot."

"I don't think I want your opinion anyway. How long did you live out here?"

"From the time I was eighteen—off and on."

No one had mentioned his parents. Willa wondered if he'd been another orphan like Clytie, rescued by John's father. "Where did you live before that?"

"What's your interest?" he asked, suddenly wary that to answer would be exposing himself, his feelings.

"Just curious," she said airily.

He shifted his weight, moved toward the door. "Anything else you want to see?"

"No, I've seen enough."

Whether or not she wanted to live here, Willa knew she would. She'd agree to John's terms, provided they were a fair market value, not charity.

In that moment of understanding, as she and Nick returned to the house, Willa knew that even if she discovered it true beyond doubt that Nick was Bethany's father, she would never reveal that knowledge to the Elliotts. They trusted Nick, and loved him. To learn that he had betrayed them with their daughter would destroy them.

She resolved then and there to avoid by gesture or expression to reveal her suspicions to John and Claudine. She would have to make an effort, in their presence at least, to be pleasant and friendly to Nick.

Engrossed so in her thoughts, her foot slipped off the flagstone path. Her heel sank into wet dirt. She yelped and pitched sideways. Nick's hand shot out and closed around her waist.

"Are you all right?"

"Yes. Clumsy me. I caught my heel."

"Anything sprained, bruised?" he asked solicitously, lightly taking hold of her upper arms. Her body felt wonderful under his hands. It made him feel that he was being transfused with some substance almost as vital as blood.

Nick smelled very good, very male; faintly of a spicy after-shave. He was too close, inescapably real and potent. Willa's head was spinning, her emotions a rush of contradictions. She wanted what his nearness promised; yet she didn't.

"I'm fine," she said, pulling her heel from the muck and trying to draw away. His hands tightened their grip. He seemed inordinately interested in the shape of her face.

"Willa..."

The heavy scent of moisture-laden air hung around them like an invisible fog. The evening breeze rustled the trees, bestirring rain droplets.

"We're getting wet," she said, her tone off-putting. Nick felt all at once hamstrung; as if a small rock were lodged at the bottom of his stomach. He must've misread the signal they had exchanged earlier. He dropped his hands before he made the unthinking, feckless gesture of taking her wholly into his arms and smothering her with kisses.

He managed a light laugh. "I don't know what it is about you. I always seem to behave like an idiot."

"Being concerned about a person isn't behaving like an idiot," Willa said smoothly, pretending that nothing monumental was happening between them.

"Concerned?" he scoffed softly, then realized what she was up to. "Right. Just think of me as your handy Boy Scout, doing my good deed for the day."

"Now you are being foolish," Willa said, and escaped, taking good long strides so that every step landed firmly on a flagstone.

Nick stared after her, liking the way her hips moved beneath the silk skirt. He shook his head. Boy, had he stepped in it. Except for that one awful time, women had been casual elements in his life, just passing through. But he knew Willa was different. Worse, he felt uneasy having thought about her body, and his mother had warned him what that meant.

"You'll know when it's love, not lust, Nick. You'll want to put her on a pedestal, no matter how earthy, funny or whatever. She'll be special. You'll know. Just wait and see."

Hooked! And being played with, he thought glumly.

"It's FABULOUS," Willa said with genuine enthusiasm. "I could've looked for months and not found anything so charming."

John actually beamed. "It's settled then, you'll move in."

"Not so fast," she admonished. For the next five minutes, while Claudine and Nick looked on, she and John engaged in gentle disagreement concerning terms.

"But it's a guest house," John kept saying. "One doesn't charge one's guests rent."

"I wouldn't have looked at it if you had not agreed to accepting rent," Willa countered. "I expect you to keep your word." The comment backed John into a gentleman's corner. Caught, he paled slightly. Willa continued. "Anyway, two hundred dollars a month is barely a token. I accept because I'll only be working part-time during the summer. But once I'm at the hospital, we'll talk about the rent again. I know I'm getting the place skinflint cheap. Besides, every other place I looked at wanted first and last month's rent plus deposit, plus utilities."

"Carpetbaggers, the lot of them!" John snorted.

Willa counted out the cash and pushed it toward him. "What's my new address? I have a few things packed and stored at my stepmother's. I'd like to have her send them."

John looked at the money as if it were a coiled snake about to strike. He glanced at Claudine for help, but her expression said she had no intention of stepping on Willa's streak of independence. He appealed to Nick, but Nick shook his head.

"And just to keep it official, I'd like a receipt," Willa added cheerfully. John flushed all the way up to his receding hairline.

With a deep sigh of resignation, John found a piece of paper and wrote out the receipt.

"Drinks all around to celebrate," Claudine said, jubilant.

"None for me, thanks," Nick said. "I've got to hit the road. Another long day facing me tomorrow."

John walked him out. Willa pocketed the scrap of paper, waited a few moments for politeness sake and then she and Bethany, too, took their leave.

"I'll come early tomorrow to begin setting the cottage to rights," she told Claudine. "I'm so excited I doubt I'll sleep a wink."

"We'll go up into the attic. There are all sorts of things up there you might find useful."

"More toys?" Bethany asked.

"A doll carriage, I think."

"You little beggar," Willa chastised. "Stop asking for things. You have to earn them."

"Why can't people give me something because they like me?"

"They can, but you have to let them think of it first."

"Suppose they don't?"

Willa surrendered decently. "We'll discuss this on the way home."

Claudine took Bethany's hand. "I'll trade you the carriage for something."

Bethany eyed her warily. "What?"

"Your time. You could help me weed my flowers."

"Okay. That's easy. You won't forget?"

"I wouldn't dare," Claudine said with an easy smile. "I want you to be happy here, and your mother, too."

"I will be," Willa said graciously. But within her soul she wasn't so certain. Nick had lived there and her imagination would run wild if she let it. He was a wedge inserting himself into her life. He was something for which she wasn't prepared.

He was still on her mind when she awoke at dawn the following morning, anxious to get an early start on the cottage.

Bethany refused to stir. Willa whispered "breakfast at McDonald's" into her ear over and over, which finally brought her groggily awake.

Later, sipping her coffee Willa thought of Nick: Fact one: She liked him. Fact two: To deny it was to be foolish. Fact Three: To cope with it in whatever way possible was a necessity.

Coping was her specialty. At least she had that in her favor. She was sure that Nick didn't have a clue as to her feelings.

And, as distasteful as she now found it, she would continue to probe into Susan's life with her parents; with Nick.

Which reminded her. She knew nothing of Nick's background beyond the fact he was an attorney and had been John senior's godson. She'd have to figure a way to get that information, too. But delicately.

Clytie was bound to be a veritable font of information. Perhaps today she'd manage a moment alone with her and find an opening.

Chapter Seven

"Clytie...please, come down off that ladder," Willa implored. "I really don't mind if there's a whole raft of spiders living up there."

Broom in hand, Clytie took another swipe at the cobwebs before she gazed down at Willa. "Don't go making a mountain out of a molehill," she scoffed. "I've spent my whole life climbing something or another."

"If you fall and break your leg, it'll ruin my day."

"I'll keep that in mind. Go occupy yourself with that stuff piled in the middle of the living room."

Willa complied, but not before she muttered: "Bossy old thing."

Clytie swung the broom down, precisely but gently, and caught Willa on the back. "One thing about these old places—sound carries."

Willa laughed. "Then I'll tell you to your face: You're a sly old creature and I'd hate for you to get hurt. Get down or I'll order you out of my house for which I have paid the rent, and have the receipt to prove it."

"John's doings, not mine," snorted Clytie, not a bit intimidated. She kept her perch atop the ladder.

"Willa," Claudine called, leaning over the upstairs balcony. "Come see if you like what I've done with Bethany's bed."

Willa skirted the heap of boxes piled on the floor—all of which were the result of an early-morning forage into Claudine's attic. The boxes had been hauled into the cottage over Willa's protests. "If you can't find a use for any of this stuff," Claudine had insisted, "why, we'll just put it back."

Willa had wanted to do all the work herself. Unfortunately her appeals fell on deaf ears. Claudine and Clytie were determined to see her comfortably settled within the day. They were having a grand time. Truthfully, Willa told herself, she didn't have the heart to interfere with their obvious joy.

"Well? What do you say?" Claudine asked, gesturing toward the corner space Willa had chosen as Bethany's own. The bed was a creation of pink eyelet ruffles; the pillow sham matched, and the comforter was turned back to reveal pink sheets. Claudine had picture-framed the bed with clever use of the same eyelet fabric tacked to the slanted ceiling.

"It's beautifully done," Willa said admiringly. "Bethany is going to adore it." But the eyelet looked suspiciously new. Willa spied the crumpled cellophane and picked it up. The price sticker was still attached. The ensemble had cost more than the rent she had paid John last night. Dismay overtook her.

"Claudine, you went out and bought this didn't you? I don't mind making use of things you've relegated to your attic. But this is too much. It makes me feel awful."

Claudine's expression took on a battered look. "I did buy it . . . years ago."

"But—it looks new. It even smells new."

"I bought it for Susan. She never even opened it." Claudine sat on the foot of the bed. The distant memory reached across the years to rouse emotions. And for a few seconds she looked positively stricken.

Willa pulled up a three-legged stool and sat down. "What happened? Was the color wrong?" she asked softly, sensing that something was buried beneath the months and years.

"She hated me," Claudine whispered. "Sometimes I felt it as a force. It was just . . . overpowering."

With an interior shiver of alarm, Willa reached out and closed her hand firmly over the older woman's. She wanted to tell her it was all right. That the past was just that and didn't matter in the scheme of things now. She didn't want to hurt this woman who was growing so dear to her. But Claudine was speaking of her own daughter, the girl who had given birth to Bethany, and she couldn't let it go.

"What happened?" Willa asked in hushed tones.

"John was devoted to Susan, but I saw things in her that frightened me. She was angry and moody out of all proportion. At least, I thought so. At first I put her behavior down to puberty, later I excused it as that time of the month. But it was more than that. And yet, she was brilliant.

"If Nick left his law books lying around, Susan holed up in her room and read them. Let me tell you, those two had some heated discussions. Nick said she took the role of devil's advocate so well, it helped him pass the bar exam."

Left his books lying around? That had to mean Nick had actually lived with the Elliotts.

"I swear to you," Claudine murmured, "that we did nothing, nothing to earn Susan's contempt. On her sixteenth birthday, John drove her into Jacksonville to buy a record she just had to have. He indulged her dreadfully, I'm afraid. While they were gone, Clytie and I redid her room as a birthday surprise. The bedclothes we gave Bethany were meant to go with the new decor. I suppose we should've asked her first.... Oh! She was furious. We had tampered with her space. She said we were tedious, outdated..." She pulled her thoughts away from her inner landscape to focus on Willa. "I always thought: When Susan's grown, we'll be close. One day she'll marry, have children and that will help us understand each other." She tried to smile, but it didn't come off. "I feel like I never got to be a mother. Now I'm getting a second chance with you, with Bethany. Is that so farfetched? I don't want to make any mistakes. But I have, haven't I?"

Willa's eyes stung. "No, you haven't. You're good and kind, Claudine. Whatever was the matter with Susan, it wasn't your fault."

"Then why did she leave us?"

Willa squeezed the hand she held gently. "We may never know. Stop blaming yourself. It isn't healthy."

"But I worry so that Bethany might be affected. Do you think—"

Willa had those same fears, but now was not the time to reveal them. "Bethany has her bad days. She's more self-contained than any five-year-old has a right to be, but she's a loving child."

"But she's so smart, and intelligence seems to come with its own demons. It scares me."

"All of that wonderful intelligence could've come from you, you know."

Claudine looked startled. "Pooh. What do I know?"

"Much more than you give yourself credit for," Willa said emphatically, closing her hand more firmly around Claudine's for a moment. Then she opened her fingers, allowing the older woman's hand to slowly slide away.

Suddenly exhibiting embarrassment, Claudine moved off the bed, smoothing the wrinkles. "What about the linens? If...if you think them inappropriate for Bethany, of course I'll take them away."

"It's plenty appropriate. Truly. It can stay, just as you've fixed it."

"Claudine! Claudine!"

"Speaking of the imp," Willa said.

Bethany burst upon them, her fists closed tightly around wads of greenery. She waved them in front of Claudine.

"I forgot. Which is the flowers and which is the weeds?"

"These are the flowers," Claudine said, touching the small left fist.

"But these other ones have yellow buds!"

"Those are dandelion weeds. Some people call them lion's tooth."

Bethany thrust the handful of weeds behind her back. "Okay, I'll go put these others back in the ground."

"Why don't I come help you?" Claudine suggested. "Then we'll have a look at that carriage. It needs a good washing down."

"With the hose? And the nozzle that makes water go in a spray?"

"Oh, I'm sure, with the hose," answered Claudine, casting a smile at Willa.

Bethany got to the top of the stairs and turned back to Claudine. "Are you crying?"

"No, I had an eyelash in my eye."

"Huh! That's what Mommy always says. But it's a real lie, not a nice fib so you don't hurt somebody's feelings."

Claudine managed a small chuckle. "You caught me. I was sad for a minute. I feel better now."

"That's all right. When I'm sad, I cry, too." Then she noticed her bed. "Ooooo. It's grand!"

"You can admire it to your heart's content later," Willa told her. "Get back to work. And next time, wipe your feet. You've tracked mud."

"I'm little, I can't think of everything."

Willa bestowed on her one of those looks only a mother is capable of; and any child can interpret. Bethany clattered down the steps before she was sent to bed or stood in a corner.

"You're so good with her," Claudine said.

Willa swung her eyes back to her companion. "I try. It takes all the patience I can muster sometimes."

Claudine took a somewhat ragged breath. "I'll be so glad when you tell her—about John and me, who we are. Sometimes I feel like I'm about to burst. I want to tell our friends . . . take her places, show her off."

"I know you do," Willa said. "When the time is right, I'll tell her."

"Will it be soon, you think?"

"I hope so." For all of our sakes, she thought.

After Claudine withdrew, Willa continued to sit quietly by herself. So Susan had been an unhappy person. And Claudine had mentioned Susan and Nick in the same breath—linking them more firmly in Willa's mind. And there was nothing she could do about it. Or would do about it. Except use the information, once she had proof, to plot Bethany's paternal medical background.

But secretly, she hoped that Bethany's father's identity would never have to be revealed.

Clytie's head popped up above the stair landing. "Did you know I was seventy-eight and cocking my head at seventy-nine?" she asked.

"I think Claudine told me," Willa replied absently, reluctant to give up her retrospection.

"Then how come you and Claudine have left an old lady like me to do all the dirty work!"

Willa laughed outright. "You just want a warm body to push around. I was just coming."

For the next several hours they worked side by side, rolling out carpets upon the now polished and gleaming wood floor, unpacking boxes, filling cabinets and drawers with dishes and cutlery and pots. Now and again, Claudine pried herself away from Bethany and turned up with items she insisted she had no use for: linens and towels that no longer fit her color scheme, a silver service for four that had never been out of its velvet box—a long-ago wedding gift. When she marched in with an elaborate silver-and-brass coffee service, Willa put a stop to it.

"Enough, Claudine! Take it back."

"Don't blame you," put in Clytie. "The reason it's been in storage is all those curlicues are miserable to polish."

"Well, all right," said Claudine. "Is there anything else I can do? I've oiled the wheels of the carriage for Bethany. We thought we'd try it out on the sidewalk in front of the house."

"If we said, yes, grab the mop, you'd curl up and cry," Clytie chided. "You want to play. Go play."

Claudine went.

Willa stretched and rubbed the small of her back. "I'm beat," she said and moved over to the window.

The late-afternoon sun cast a glaze over everything. There seemed to be no breeze at all. Willa marveled that inside the cottage remained so cool.

"It's the coquina rock," Clytie told her. She came to stand by Willa in time to see Bethany and Claudine disappearing around the side of the house; Bethany proudly pushing the old-fashioned carriage. The silver service had been unceremoniously dumped on the porch steps.

Clytie's brows drew forward. "It's good you came," she said. "Claudine's happy now. Having Bethany here has changed her whole outlook."

"These past few years can't have been easy for her," Willa said, stepping smoothly into the opening presented her.

"They weren't—for any of us."

Willa kept on staring out the window. "What did you think of Susan? How did you get along with her?"

Clytie scoffed. "I'll tell you about Susan. She was beautiful, but didn't believe it of herself. When she wanted something, she saw you, when she didn't, you didn't exist. She was out with the sun and in with the rain. If you stood back and watched, you could almost predict her moods. Of course, John and Claudine were never that objective. Still, I never thought she'd run off and end up... the way she did."

Willa looked sharply at the tiny old woman. "Out with the sun, in with the rain. That's an odd way of putting it."

"That's only on retrospection. We've had six years to ask ourselves what we missed, what we did wrong—"

"Maybe nothing, Clytie. In my line of work, I've met people who did everything right and still things didn't work out like they had hoped. I've counseled—or tried to—people who did nothing but wrong and came out on top."

"Well, spare me the fickle finger of Fate! I don't like the odds."

"Me, either. Can we call it a day? I'm pooped. I still have to check out of the motel and haul the rest of our things over."

"Suits me. I've got a date tonight."

"You do?"

"Sure. Don't look so surprised. Men love little old things like me. Makes 'em feel big and strong." She did a quick two-step and wriggled her bony hips. "We're going dirty dancing. Patrick Swaze, look out!"

Willa laughed. "I'm envious. I haven't been dancing in years."

"That's the trouble with you younger generations, always serious. You never take time to have fun." She looked at Willa coyly. "Now me, I know how to have fun—and then some."

"Shame on you."

Clytie grinned. "The shame's on your generation. Folks my age only have respectable diseases."

"Oh, dear."

It was Clytie's turn to laugh. "You want to have a good time. You only have to take Nick up on it. I saw the way he was eyeing you the other night. He's smitten."

The smile froze on Willa's lips. "You're mistaken."

Clytie picked up the broom and waltzed with it out the door. Four of five flagstones down the path, she stopped and looked back over her shoulder. "No, I'm not."

Willa felt a small twinge of defeat. Her strategy had been knocked out of whack. No way could she pick Clytie's brain about Nick and his parents now. Clytie would think she was asking for all the wrong reasons.

She'd have to put all of her questions to Nick himself, and somehow manage to avoid sounding like a snoop. It wouldn't do to have him thinking she was the least bit interested in him as a man, either. Because she wasn't.

Yes, she was.

Her brain and body insisted on it.

THE NEXT FEW DAYS melted away. The cottage become "home." The telephone was installed, groceries bought; keepsakes and clothes arrived from Kansas. Bethany went to nursery school and Willa went to work.

True to their word, the Elliotts observed her privacy. Bethany observed no one's. To Willa's dismay, and Claudine's delight, she went in and out of both house and cottage with impunity. Unknowingly Bethany held her grandparents in love's bondage. Claudine was always finding bits of ribbon for doll dressings; amid halfhearted protests, John was roped into cutting out paper dolls.

The threads of family were being loomed and woven. Willa had no idea what the tapestry would be like when finished, but at the moment all was well.

As she dried supper dishes and put them away, she realized she was beginning to have a sense of boundaries, a sense of where she fit. And if she didn't quite have a full sense of security, well that would come with her first paycheck.

The fly in the ointment was Nick. She had not seen him in over a week. He had begged off Monday night supper with the Elliotts with some vague excuse or another.

She missed him, which she told herself, was absolute malarkey. Her imagination was doing her in. He was good-looking. It was purely physical, she decided.

Besides, why should he call on her? His job had been to bring herself and the Elliotts together. He had done that. There was no reason whatsoever for him to pursue a relationship with her. And possibly good reason not to.

Willa took the turmoil of questions to bed with her each night. Nick had once slept in this very same bed. Had Susan? Willa's active mind spun with all the probabilities.

Of course Nick would never call on her. Not while she lived in the cottage.

HE KNOCKED and waited. He didn't hear anything and thought she might be out. But, no. Her car was parked in the little nook under the tree where he used to park his own. She was up at the house, then. He was about to go and check when the door opened. For a long moment neither of them said anything.

"Hello," he said finally, feeling overheated.

Willa couldn't think of any legitimate way to refuse him entry. "What brings you down dark alleys and cobblestoned streets in the thick of night?" she said, deciding to wing it, and stepping back so that he could enter.

"It's only a few minutes past nine."

"I'm a working woman now, remember?"

"Of course. I won't stay." He thrust a paper-wrapped box at her. "Housewarming gift."

"I— Thank you. Would coffee suit?" she heard herself asking. "I was just going to make myself a cup." She put the package on the counter. "I'll just plug in the pot."

He was willing to accept arsenic-laced tea or worse—Kool-Aid—if it meant having a few moments with her. "Coffee sounds good. Bethany asleep?"

She nodded.

He stood looking at the cottage. Rose-shaded lamps were lit, and curtains at the windows of a darker hue were drawn for the night. Baskets of plants resided on a butler's table behind the sofa. An escritoire against one wall held framed photographs. A lone white petunia drooped in a water glass on the counter, plucked by Bethany, he was certain. It was homey. Far more than when he had lived here. "You've done wonders with the place," he said admiringly. "It never looked so good when I lived in it."

Willa's eyes darted momentarily to the living room. "Claudine ransacked her attic." With a touch of awe that she had yet to overcome, she added, "Look at that rug. It's an Aubusson."

"Faded a bit, though," Nick said, glancing at the pale rose border.

"That gives it charm."

"Oh."

"Classical male response," Willa said, and found herself smiling at him. "The lamps are my doing. So you have a tableau of a two-thousand-dollar rug balanced against a pair of two-dollar lamps. Claudine and I spent Saturday going to garage sales. Well, that's not exactly true. She drove and sat in the car while Bethany and I rooted through all offerings."

"So that's where you were. I called."

"Did you?" Willa felt the deep-down beat of her heart speeding up. She had to think a minute for something more to say. "What did you want—when you called?"

"Oh, nothing important." He watched her get cups from the cupboard, set out cream and sugar. He wondered if she was as sexual as she appeared, wondered if he'd ever find out; he wondered if he had misread the signals between them. He wondered if he'd made a stupid mistake, coming here like this.

"Open the box," he suggested after she had arranged and rearranged the cups and saucers for want of something to do with her hands. His intuition told him she was nervous. She had nothing on him there. So was he.

She hesitated. "I feel a little odd. Accepting a gift from you. It doesn't seem—"

"It's not new," he injected quickly. "I've had it for years."

Willa's mouth widened the promise of a smile just a fraction. "You have an attic, too?"

It was extraordinary, he thought, how her features seemed to change from moment to moment. She was smiling and yet, she looked almost afraid.

The gift was a detailed and perfectly wrought wood sculpture of a mother and child. It created the illusion of a child being bathed in a lagoon or a rippling brook with the waterfall just out of sight of the viewer. Both mother and child were nude. The wood was two-toned as if it had been bent and blended into shape. Willa's hands moved gracefully over the wood, seeming to communicate with it. Nick's generosity undid her. "It's beautiful."

"The wood is zirocote. It's native to Belize."

"You've been there?"

"I've been to a lot of out-of-the-way places. My parents used to take me."

Willa carried the sculpture to the butler's table and rearranged the baskets of plants so that they did not overpower it. She turned back to Nick. "Should I take the plants away or leave them?"

"You've set it exactly right." Without thinking, or perhaps because he had been thinking of this moment day and night, he crossed the room, reached out and pulled her toward him. To Willa he appeared very intent, very determined.

She wanted to demand to know just what he thought he was doing. And then, without her will, her eyes closed. His mouth covered hers, his arms held her fast. His kiss was soft, questing, and instinctively she responded. See? said a faraway interior voice. It's all physical.

And standing there, in his arms, in the middle of the living room with the pink-shaded lamps and her daughter asleep upstairs, and perhaps his daughter, too, Willa realized that she was going to love again.

The world did not shake. She heard no bells or clashing cymbals or thundering marches. She didn't hear any of those things because she knew, she just knew, she was going to end up with a badly broken heart. Even so it took every ounce of strength she owned to move out of his arms.

"I've made a fool of myself again," Nick said, his voice throaty with unrequited desire. The kiss had said it all. He was plunging into something far more entangling than a casual liaison.

"The coffee's bubbling over," Willa said.

"We're going to have to talk about this," he said, needing to get his emotions and feelings into the open; he didn't like game playing. He wanted to know where she stood.

"Talk?" she repeated, stalling, pouring the coffee, sliding his across the counter and keeping the counter as a buffer between them. "We're practically strangers. I know nothing about you except—"

"What do you want to know?" he said, filled with exasperation. He saw right through her performance, but couldn't fathom its reason. She was looking at him without connecting with him, as if to protect herself in some fashion, while deciding whether or not to get into the conversation. Was she trying to find the best way to make use of his feelings, or trying to find the strength to declare her own feelings.

Finally, after a tentative sip of coffee she said: "Everything," and the tension between them broke into manageable pieces.

HE HAD BEEN BORN in St. Augustine, Willa learned. His parents were a doctor/nurse team that then and now treated the suffering in the world's troubled areas. At present they were working under the umbrella of the United States International Medical Corp and were in Afghanistan.

Margot and Nathan Cavenaugh had met John senior and Natalie when the Cavenaughs had arrived in St. Augustine in 1949 for rest and recuperation. The medical couple had just completed a stint in Africa where they had worked during and after World War II. The Cavenaughs fell in love with the climate of the restful resort that abounded in historical reminders of Spain's lost empire.

Though the senior Elliotts were some years older than Nick's parents, the foursome became fast friends. When it became obvious that Margot Cavenaugh was expecting a baby, the Elliotts encouraged her to remain in St. Augustine until after the birth. Before the Cavenaughs returned to Africa, Nick was christened and John senior stood as godfather.

Until he was twelve, Nick traveled with his parents to whatever backwater their work took them to. But when his parents joined the Paris-based organization, *Médecins sans Frontière* and were sent into neglected and warring corners of the world without regard to the reigning government or rebel approval, they deemed it unsafe for their son. Nick was sent to live with his godfather and to attend school. Whenever possible he had spent summer vacations with his parents, often working with them in some war-torn or disaster-struck country.

"Now every year or so they vacation with me," he concluded. "Is that enough of the Cavenaugh family tree, or shall I invent an eccentric great-aunt or some illustrious—"

Somewhere during his telling they had moved to the sofa. Willa got up to refresh their coffees. "Why didn't you become a doctor like your father?"

"That's an easy one. By the time I was seventeen I'd seen enough malaria, tuberculosis, and amputations to last me a lifetime. And selfish though it may seem, I like the little luxuries in life—toilet paper, toothpaste and water out of a spigot. Only once were my parents ever given a house with running water—and then the rebels blew up the pumping station."

"Your parents sound fascinating."

Nick shoved his mouth into a lopsided grin. "What about me?" he asked, only half joking.

She gave him her loveliest smile. It took the edge off her tone. "Oh, you're fascinating, too. Tell me," she continued in the same breath as if the topics were somehow related. "Why did you move out of this cottage?"

He laughed. "For one of the simplest reasons known to man and the IRS. I was beginning to prosper. I bought myself a boat and a beach house—investing in myself instead of giving it all to Uncle Sam."

It was as if she had not heard him. "For that matter, when did you move in here?"

"My godfather and I used to escape out here during the times Natalie pushed him to his limits. She wasn't the easiest woman in the world to be around. When I was eighteen, I wanted to get out on my own. This was as far as I got. But it suited me.''

"Did Susan ever visit you out here?"

There was a curious, slow something in Willa's glance that made Nick stare back. "Why do you ask?"

"No reason."

"She may have done from time to time."

"I suppose she was like a sister to you?"

For a brief moment his mind seemed to be somewhere else, secret and apart. "She was a pest," he said, wanting to leave it at that, but he sensed Willa expected more. He glanced up at the darkened sleeping alcove and lowered his voice. "Considering how Susan fits in your life, I can understand your curiosity, Willa. But, Susan is dead. Some things are just better left unsaid."

"I see."

The simple comment was an end piece. It carried not one bit of hostility, yet it was the most barren, unyielding sound Nick had ever heard. He sighed heavily. "No doubt about it. I've overstayed my welcome."

"You weren't invited in the first place."

He tried a joke. "I guess that means you don't want to hear how I worked my way through college?"

"It's getting late," she responded softly.

In the space of a couple of heartbeats Nick found himself outside the cottage and staring at a door firmly closed against his hopes and desires.

He held up his hands and stared at them in the moonlight. He had touched her, held her against the long, stirred-up length of himself; he had pressed his lips against the sweet-smelling shell of her ear and been tempted to whisper words that once said could never in a lifetime be retracted.

He had believed it for years, and now it was confirmed. If a man just wanted to do the right thing by a woman, just wanted to fall a little bit in love—watch out! His heart got handed back to him looking like chopped meat.

On the other side of the firmly closed door Willa slumped and let dismay wash over her.

She had been horrible. Absolutely horrible. She had allowed her personal feelings to interfere. She was trained never to register shock or dismay or anger at shocking or dismaying or angry revelations or near revelations. But she had done. And Nick had clammed up. Her own fault. If only he had told her about Susan. Trusted her enough. Wasn't love trust?

She was a forgiving person. She'd have—

She scanned her thoughts, brought them into focus.... Trust? Love?

But there's no future to it, she argued with herself as she turned off lights and went upstairs to sleep in the bed that had once been Nick's.

She dreamed about him anyway.

Chapter Eight

The elderly woman's skin was tinged with shadows. Her hands were liver spotted and twisted with arthritis. She regarded Willa with a look of extraordinary gravity. "I know it's right, but I don't like doing this, Mrs. Manning."

"I know you don't, Mrs. Wheatly," Willa soothed. "But it is the only way to help your son."

Mrs. Wheatly tugged the strap of her purse more securely on to her fragile arm. "I just don't want the judge to think I'm doing it because Billy won't work."

"He won't think that. He understands that people sometimes become too ill to help themselves."

"So, then a member of the family has to step in?"

"Exactly." Willa helped Mrs. Wheatly into her car. Walking an emotionally distraught family member through the process of a court-ordered hospitalization for a dear one was part of her job, Willa knew. But it was so awful.

Billy Wheatly was a diagnosed schizophrenic. He was a slender, fragile, almost androgynous-looking man of thirty-eight; quiet and sweet natured as long as he took his medication. But three weeks ago he had stopped taking his medication and the disease had run its atypical course. He slept all day, roamed all night and forgot to eat. He had threatened to maim his mother's cat and burn down the house. To get any rest in safety, Mrs. Wheatly had had to lock herself and her cat in her bedroom. But two days earlier Billy had knocked the door off its hinges and Mrs. Wheatly had called for help.

"What will the doctors do to Billy?" his mother asked in a quavering voice.

"They'll get him back on his medicine and see to it that he eats. It's called stabilization."

"Then he can come home again? I'll be all alone while he's in the hospital."

Loneliness was as much a disease as schizophrenia, Willa thought. "I could call you every couple of days to see how you're doing, would that help? And, please—call me Willa."

"Yes," Mrs. Wheatly said. "Oh, yes. That would be nice. And what a lovely name you have."

The harried probate court clerk looked up at Willa and smiled. "What, you again? That's two days in a row. Want a job here?"

"Thanks, but no thanks," Willa said and introduced Mrs. Wheatly and her problem.

A court reporter Willa had met on an earlier trip burst into the office, her brow wrinkled with worry. She signaled the clerk to pick up the telephone. "Line two," she whispered. "It's Judge Henley's wife. I told her I'd reserved the space, but that you were the one in charge of food."

"Mrs. Henley," the clerk said into the telephone while offering Willa a look of apology. "No... How are we going to do that? But...no barbecue...no pizza... What about— How can we—? But how do we bake a birthday cake with no eggs? Yes, I understand. The doctor said—

And you'll be here— We'll do our—'' She looked at the receiver for a moment then cradled it with a bang.

"Problems?" Willa said, not really wanting to know, but aware that a bit of sympathy displayed often smoothed and hurried along the paperwork she required.

"We're planning Judge Henley's annual birthday luncheon. That was his wife telling me Judge Henley's doctor has put him on a low-cholesterol diet. We have to plan around that. Cripes! Everything in the world Judge Henley likes is loaded with the stuff. I mean, what's left?"

"Carrot sticks," said the court reporter with a snort of disgust.

The clerk rolled her eyes. "We're in big trouble." She gave Willa a wry smile. "Are there any openings at the health center? I may be job hunting within the month."

"A part-time slot will be opening up in August," Willa said, offering up her own position with a smile.

"I'll keep it in mind. Meanwhile..." She looked over at the patiently waiting Mrs. Wheatly.

An hour later Willa returned a sad and subdued Mrs. Wheatly to her home.

"Should I wake Billy and tell him to get dressed?" she wanted to know.

"No...don't do that. Wait for the health-department liaison. He'll wake Billy for you and help him to dress."

"Then, they'll take him."

Willa patted the wrinkled, gnarled, old hand. "He'll be back soon and you can have your card games, and afternoon teas just like always."

Mrs. Wheatly expelled a gut-level sigh. "Do you have children, Willa?"

"One. A little girl."

"For your sake and hers, I hope she grows up to be strong and healthy in every way."

"I hope so, too," Willa said fervently.

On her way to her next home visit, Willa mentally reviewed the case.

The client was a referral from HRS, Health and Rehab Services, which she had learned in the State of Florida meant the welfare department. The mother had been accused of not feeding her son properly. Willa was to evaluate the mental status of the mother and child. Willa knew the evaluation she turned in would weigh heavily at the court hearing to decide if the child should be placed in a foster home.

Though it was her job to be objective, Willa was certain the woman would see her as an adversary. The mother was a working, single parent with a nine-year-old son. Willa identified with that.

Against all reason and objectivity, by the time she found the small concrete-block house on a sandy lane, tucked neatly beneath the shady leaves of two-hundred-year-old trees, Willa was firmly on the woman's side.

If anyone threatened to take Bethany from her, she'd fight tooth and nail. She had already faced that threat—though in her case it had been couched in much more civilized terms—grandparents' rights.

A moment's apprehension raced through her at how badly everything could have gone, for herself, for Bethany. She had risked a lot.

And there was yet more risk to contemplate. How, she wondered, was Bethany going to react to learning exactly what being adopted meant? That Claudine and John were her grandparents? Willa realized with sudden clarity that Bethany would have to be told soon. The strain of keeping the secret was telling on them all.

Taking a deep breath, Willa erased personal thoughts and knocked on Keta Worthington's front door. The knock was answered immediately. Willa introduced herself.

"I know Roddy is supposed to be here," Keta Worthington said, defiant in expression, stance and voice, "but he's on an outing with his Big Brother."

"You have two children?" Willa asked, surprised.

"Big Brother, the organization. I signed Roddy up. It would've broken his heart if I had kept him home this afternoon."

Willa gave the woman her best smile. "I can see Roddy another time."

Keta's brown hair tumbled to her shoulders. She had a sharp, arresting face and penetrating eyes. Those eyes still regarded Willa suspiciously. "You're not going to count it against me?"

"No, I'm not. I think it's a good thing and it shows you care a lot about your son."

Keta unlatched the screen and allowed Willa into her home. "You mind sitting in the kitchen? I'm cooking. We might be having company for dinner."

"I don't mind a bit. Kitchens are my favorite places." There was something wonderful in the oven. Willa could smell it.

Without asking if Willa wanted any, Keta set out glasses, poured herbal tea over ice and topped them with mint sprigs. She passed one to Willa.

"Whatever it is you're cooking smells wonderful," Willa said. "I have the intuition that Roddy is very well fed. So tell me, how'd you get into this mess?"

"My Nosy Parker of a neighbor. Damn her. She's always trying to ply Roddy with sugar-packed cookies, soft drinks and I don't know what all. We're vegetarians. Or at least, we are as far as we can take it. I mean, we don't eat beef or pork or chicken. Nosy Parker just can't accept that. Looks like the State of Florida can't, either.''

Willa took a sip of the tea. It was delicious. ''Tell me about being vegetarian, how you came to be that way.''

''That's easy. I was raised on a farm. I had to help my dad butcher and scrap hogs every winter. The smell of raw, ungutted hog dipped in boiling water would put anyone off eating pork. If Dad wanted chicken for supper, Mom would wring its neck and let it flop headless around the kitchen yard until it drained. I raised a pair of lambs for 4-H once. They didn't win any ribbons, so Dad butchered them. That was the second worst day of my life.''

''What was the first?''

''Being notified by HRS that my rights as a mother are in jeopardy!'' Her hands dropped to her sides. ''Mrs. Manning, I'm scared. I'm angry, too. What right does the state have to tell me how to raise my son?''

It wasn't a question Willa felt qualified to answer. ''Would Roddy eat meat?''

Keta Worthington laughed. ''Growing boys will eat anything! But commercial meats are so loaded with preservatives and hormones... Listen, Mrs. Manning, when Roddy becomes a teenager I don't expect I'll have much say in what he eats or anything else. I'm just trying to give him a head start. I don't make an issue of what I cook or what we eat. When Roddy's Big Brother takes him fishing and if Roddy catches any, I fry those fish. Sometimes we go crabbing. I make gumbo. I make homemade breads and cakes. It's just I use honey and molasses for sweeteners, whole wheat or rice flours, soft cheeses made without rennet, vegetable shortenings. We have a garden. Roddy is healthy. I'm healthy.''

"You plead your case very well," Willa said.

"I guess I ought to tell you, I'm not taking any chances. I've hired an attorney to represent us—or at least me, at the hearing."

"Good for you."

Keta Worthington stared at Willa, then she smiled, a slow, creeping smile that made her face lovely. "You're new at this aren't you?"

"Very," Willa said, and sniffed. "What exactly do you have in that oven?"

"Quiche, made with egg whites, spinach, spring onions, a few spices, soft cheese, and I rolled my own crust." She removed it from the oven and set it to cool on a counter pad. Then she began to chop vegetables: tomatoes, onions, mushrooms, green and red peppers. She hesitated on a pod of garlic, but pressed it and tossed it into the bowl. She squeezed a lemon, stirring the juice into a spoon of white wine, olive oil, a dribble of vinegar, a dribble of honey, and poured that over the vegetables.

"That's a magnificent salad," Willa said.

"It's my specialty."

"You had to think about the garlic?"

"Like I said, we may have company for supper."

"A special guy."

Keta blushed faintly. "I wish. But probably not. Will you be at the hearing?"

"I'll try to be, if it doesn't conflict with anything else they have me doing. There is one other thing. Roddy has to submit to a physical."

The other woman's face hardened. "Who pays?"

"The County will pay."

"All right." She looked past Willa's shoulder out the window. "You know, this is all about choices. We have the right to choose what we want to eat, how we cook it—how we want to live. How we want to raise our children. I wish I'd never bought this house! If I'd known what lived next door... Roddy takes out her trash, rakes her yard..."

"She's elderly?"

"Older than Moses."

"Maybe she's lonely," Willa said, recalling Mrs. Wheatly.

Keta slumped into a chair opposite Willa. "I know she is. But she has to respect my values the same as I respect hers. And not try to change me or interfere with how I'm raising my son."

"Where's Roddy's father?"

"In Minnesota, working in a feedlot. We never married. He wanted me to have an abortion and I wouldn't. He doesn't care a whit about me or Roddy. Never has."

"Mom! Mom!"

The youth burst into the kitchen. "We put a new fuel pump in the boat. We're gonna—" Noticing Willa, he skidded to halt. "Oh. Sorry."

Roddy Worthington was slender, all knobby knees and elbows with a dusting of freckles across the bridge of his nose. He was also covered in grease. Willa smiled and gathered up her purse and briefcase. "I'm a friend of your mother's," she said. "I was just leaving."

"I'll walk you to your car."

Willa stood frozen in a cave of silence. Nick was standing on the kitchen threshold. He was wearing rubber-soled shoes, paint-stained khakis rolled to the knee, a shirt with the sleeves torn out and tied at the waist. He looked like a magnificent advertisement of a beachcomber.

Willa's mind was in motion, registering chaos and re-membering his kiss. It seemed only hours instead of days since she and Nick had clung to each other and felt a oneness of body and soul. But now his half-lidded eyes were opaque and unreadable. Her voice rose a little. "You're the Big Brother?"

"That's me."

And the probable dinner companion, Willa guessed. There was a stab in her heart.

"You two know each other?" Keta Worthington said, her tone saying she was considering the implications of this.

Willa stumbled over an explanation. "Nick did a bit of...of legal work for me. I'll call you about...that doctor's appointment. I can see myself out."

Nick stepped smoothly to her side, slipping his arm about her waist. "Hit the showers, Rod old man," he called back over his shoulder.

Once outside the house, he gave Willa his undivided attention. "How've you been?"

"Fine."

"How's Bethany?"

"She's fine, too."

"You've been avoiding me. You weren't at dinner Monday night. Claudine said you offered some excuse or another."

"I work. You just saw me at work. Bethany has to go to nursery school. I can't stay up until all hours on week nights. Anyway, the last time...I mean, we didn't ex-actly part friends."

"I went home feeling wonderfully friendly."

He was close. He smelled of sun and surf and machine oil. It was a heady combination. "You never mentioned you were a Big Brother."

"I'm modest."

"You're the attorney she's hired, aren't you?"

"Right."

"You're going to have dinner with them?"

"Right again."

Willa felt a twinge of jealousy. "That's nice. Even admirable. Most attorneys don't get so involved with their clients."

"Oh, I don't know, some do."

When Nick did not add to the explanation, she knew he knew what she was trying to find out. So she didn't hide it.

"Is Keta Worthington special to you?"

"Roddy is special to me. After dinner he and I do dishes, play a game of checkers or cards, then I tuck him in." He opened the car door and gallantly waved her inside. Willa put the key in the ignition, the engine hummed. Nick propped his arm on the roof and leaned down. "I'm very good at tucking in. Could I stop by your place and demonstrate my technique?"

Willa had to bite her lip to keep from saying yes. She drew herself up as stiffly as she could and glared at him. "You are one of the most incredibly obtuse men I've ever met."

"I take it that's no."

"At least you're not deaf."

"Save Sunday for me. You and Bethany. It's your turn to pack a picnic."

"I'm busy Sunday."

"Like hell. Wouldn't you rather have fun? Wear shorts. We'll go sailing. Ten o'clock."

He bent closer. Color stole slowly up Willa's face.

"I'd attempt a kiss, but I'm afraid you'd run over my foot. And Nosy Parker is peeking out from behind her curtains."

"You're an odd man," Willa said smartly, but her mouth widened in just a fraction of a smile.

"That smile of yours could turn a man's head. But you know that don't you?"

"Move away from the car, Nick. I'm leaving. I'll be late picking up Bethany."

"Everything in its place, all nice and tidy, that's you."

"There are worse ways to be. Go eat your veggies."

He laughed. "Oh, my, do I detect a touch of the green plague?"

"You do not. I've never even said that I like you!"

"Psychologists aren't the only ones trained to read body language. We study reams of it in law school. How to Pick a Jury 101."

He tapped the roof of the car and retreated.

Willa gunned the engine, the tires kicked out sand. And because she couldn't help it, when she got to the stop sign at the corner, she glanced in the rearview mirror. Nick was still standing in the middle of the lane.

He saluted her.

Damn!

SAVE SUNDAY FOR HIM? Just like that? She wouldn't do it. He was arrogant, arbitrary and pushy. She counted off the days, hours and minutes until Sunday, building up steam to tell him off.

On Saturday morning she bought herself a swimsuit, a smashing pair of white shorts, and a tube top so revealing she didn't have the courage to wear it without an overshirt.

A picnic did sound like a good idea. She'd take Bethany to the beach. She shopped Albertson's for little cartons of seafood salad, potato salad, chicken salad, and the deli for a selection of sliced turkey, ham and roast beef. Late in the afternoon she and Bethany and Claudine walked over to La Parisienne. Willa bought pastries and loaves of fresh-baked breads.

"You having a party?" Claudine asked.

"I'm just stocking up," Willa said.

At 9:32 a.m. Sunday morning Willa was ready to tell Nick to take a hike.

Sandwiches of every possible combination were prepared and overflowed the small cooler that had traveled with her from Kansas. Her tote was stuffed with towels, a sand bucket with shovel, and sunscreen. Her camera was loaded with fresh film.

Bethany was dressed. She wore her swimsuit beneath her rompers. Good idea, Willa reasoned and went to rearrange her own attire. Slinky black maillot first, shorts next, and then the white shirt she planned to wear later over the tube top, if she found the nerve. She tucked the tube top into her bag.

When Willa came out of the upstairs bathroom Nick was in the kitchen hoisting the cooler.

"Stop," she called down over the railing and rushed down the steps. "How did you get in?"

"Bethany opened the door. I sent her to the car to keep Roddy company." He tracked her from head to toe and exhaled. "You look good enough to eat."

Roddy? Willa felt a flood of confusion. "Save your charm for where it will do you the most good. Bethany and I are going to the beach."

"You're angry. What'd I do?"

"I'm not in the least angry. You know I can't go off with you while you have Roddy. It's against the rules."

"What rules?"

"Client privacy."

"Keta is my client, not Roddy," he said, patience running thin. "Roddy is my Little Brother. And I promise not to discuss the Worthington case with either you or him."

"You just did. Anyway, I don't know the first thing about sailing."

"I'll teach you."

"No, thank you."

"Okay. Go tell Bethany she can't go."

"No way. You're not going to make me the villain," said Willa, wondering how she was going to get out of this and come out on top. "You started it all."

"I started—?" Nick stared at her. The shoe dropped. "We're not arguing about Roddy and going sailing. You're hanging on to some mistaken idea about me and Keta. I'm not interested in her. Not in the way you think."

"I believe you."

"Wonderful. Lock up and get in the car."

"I am curious. Did you get into Big Brother to assuage your guilt?"

Nick threw up his hands in exasperation. "What guilt?"

"Well, you don't parent your daughter. You did say you have a daughter..." A stab of instant regret shot through Willa's conscience. The comment stretched between them like a wire, alive with current, taut, ready to snap. Dear Lord, what had she done? Nick's enthusiasm seemed to have vanished, the light in his eyes dimmed. She'd crossed a boundary that Nick held close and dear. She'd gone too far.

"Nick, I'm sorry. I shouldn't have said that."

"You really know how to throw a punch out of left field, don't you?" He sounded so disappointed in her that Willa wept inwardly.

Roddy and Bethany appeared on the threshold. "What's taking you so long, Mommy? We're ready to go. This is Roddy. He doesn't have a daddy, like me. He says we might see alligators. And the last time Nick took him sailing, a porpoise followed the boat."

Willa looked from the children to Nick. His expression was unreadable. "We're just coming," she said, and hoped it was so.

Nick hesitated. Then he bent and picked up the cooler.

It wasn't until they reached the yacht club that the pocket of tension between them eased. His sloop was named the *Matanzas Bay Runner*. Willa pretended a glibness she didn't feel. She couldn't. She was awed. The mast towered above a white and brass sleekness.

"Like it?" Nick asked as the children scrambled aboard.

"I don't know much about boats, but I think yours is magnificent." She touched his arm, felt his muscles tense beneath her palm. "I wish I hadn't said what I did back at the cottage. I was out of line. I can't think of any excuse except that I wasn't thinking straight. I hurt your feelings."

A long silence ensued. Finally he broke it. He gave a wry grin. "I have a couple of ideas on how you can make it up to me."

"Not walking a plank, I hope," she joked, sick with relief. She had been forgiven.

"That's not at all what I have in mind," he said. Together they unloaded his car and stored supplies below deck. Nick went aft to gather in the mooring lines.

He used engine power to navigate the North River channel until the boat cleared the May Street drawbridge. Willa stood on the bow with the children. The sun was bright, the sky was blue, the wind swept away her worries.

They raised sail before they navigated St. Augustine Inlet, the passage into the Atlantic. She helped Roddy and Bethany into life jackets then went to stand at the helm near Nick.

"I hope I don't get seasick."

"You won't have time."

To her delight and dismay, Willa discovered he wasn't kidding. He put her through her paces at the helm and mast. It was luff, pinch and claw to windward; tack downwind, wind abaft the beam, sail with the wind aft. Then it was hard alee! give her more rudder! larboard! starboard! and helm aweather! After two hours of spread sails, top mast studding, Genoa jibs, outer jibs, mizzen sails and spinnakers, Willa collapsed on the deck. "I'm soaked with sweat. Take me home. This fun is too much like work!"

Nick grinned. "Just to prove to you that I'm sensitive, considerate and good-hearted, what about a slow, calm sail down the Matanzas River?"

She stared at her palms. Nylon riggings had sped through her hands at every maneuver. Blisters were forming. "How many sails have to go up and down and around for a slow, calm sail?"

"You won't have to stretch a muscle," he said. "See this panel? In a pinch I can raise and lower them all with a flick of a switch."

Willa didn't speak to him again until the sloop was riding at anchor near the Municipal Yacht Pier. Landward, the ancient city of St. Augustine spread out before them. Avenida Menendez and the Old Market Square swarmed with tourists and natives alike. The redtiled roof of Flagler College was just visible. Aft was a spectacular view of the Bridge of Lions, flags flying. Beyond the bridge loomed the Castillo de San Marcos surrounded by a moat and the remnants of the old city walls. Willa pushed her sunglasses atop her head and sighed. "This is more like it."

Nick brought up the coolers from below decks and with the picnic Willa had prepared and the basket Keta Worthington had sent along for Roddy—and Nick, Willa was certain—they shared an array of food that would feed a dozen hungry linebackers.

Nick joked and teased both Roddy and Bethany. He showed no favoritism. He put his arms around them, listened to their replies, and complimented them both on their seamanship. They ate it up.

Nick went up several notches in Willa's eyes. If there had once been an affair between Nick and Susan Elliott, she surmised that its dissolution had not been Nick's fault. Still, the disparity in their ages tormented her. Nick should have known better. Like her Dad should've known better than to marry a woman younger than his own daughter. Loneliness made for strange bedfellows, she knew. But she couldn't excuse it. It hurt.

She took off her shirt, exposing her swimsuit, and rubbed lotion on her shoulders and arms. Then she closed her eyes, leaned back against a locker and lifted her face toward the sun.

She came awake with a slight start. Nick's lips were pressed to her ear. "Snoozing in my presence?" he whispered. "Does that mean you're comfortable with me or just bored?"

Willa's eyes darted left and right. "Where're the kids?"

"Hanging fishing lines over the bow rails. You don't think I'm nitwit enough to attempt making love to you in front of them do you?"

"That never crossed my mind."

"It hasn't? I'm crushed."

She gazed at his sun-bronzed face, the lambent and watchful eyes, the dark beard stubble that gave him a rakish and sexy look. "Just how many women have you charmed naked on this boat?"

"Would you believe hundreds. Just for practice, though, so when the right woman came along—" He watched the way a line formed between her eyes, indexing her emotions. "Whoops. Wrong answer."

"You can speak the truth with me," she said in a deep, honeyed voice.

He laughed. "I wouldn't dare. I can see the icicles forming."

He withdrew his arm from around her and sat shoulder to shoulder with her, stretching his long legs out beside hers.

"Hundreds, Nick. Really?"

He looked at her out the corner of his eyes. "You're certain you want the truth?"

She moistened her lips. "Of course I'd rather have the truth. Lies have a way of coming back to haunt a friendship."

"Friendship?"

"Aren't we friends?"

"What about 'more than friends'?"

Her heart took a leap. She was silent for a long moment. "That's shaky ground. I don't know."

"What would make you know?"

Honesty between us about your relationship with Susan Elliott, she thought. "Time, I suppose."

Nick was stung. He wanted Willa to be madly in love with him. She ought to be suffering the same airy, woozy sensations he was. He exhaled. "Zero," he said. "No naked women or fooling around on this boat. It lodged in my mind somehow it'd be bad luck. I'd run into the dock, or tie up and not watch where I was stepping and sink into the bay between the hull and the pier...or be below deck when the anchor started dragging and we'd hit a buoy."

Willa's heart dipped and soared. "It sounds to me as if you made a practical decision."

Nick crossed his legs to camouflage the effect her nearness had upon him. "Doesn't seem so practical right this minute," he said wryly.

She had to ask: "Have you ever invited Roddy's mother to sail with you?"

"Nope. If she wants a father figure, she'll have to go out and find her own."

"She's very attractive."

"So are you." He had a thought. She was a widow. Maybe that was getting in the way of Willa falling headlong in love with him. "Tell me about your husband."

Willa started. "Peter? What about him?"

"Was he the love of your life?"

"I loved him. He was warm and funny and a dedicated scientist."

"Does his memory get in the way of anything?"

"What a peculiar question. I'd have to say, no. If you mean other relationships—there haven't been any." Until now, she thought, and she couldn't blame its lack of progress on Peter.

"Nick! Nick!" Bethany yelled. "I got a fish! Hurry, before it gets away!"

He clamored to his feet and stretched his hands to Willa. "Up and at 'em, mate. Sea duty beckons."

He pulled her to her feet, and then into his arms. The embrace was brief, but it set every fiber in Willa's body trembling. The sensations lingered with her the remainder of the afternoon.

How she would handle the situation if Nick ever admitted he was Bethany's father, she didn't know.

Forget it! she chastised herself.

Today was for loving, if only from a distance.

Chapter Nine

"I don't want to go to school today. I want to stay home. Claudine and Clytie can watch me."

Bemused, Willa coaxed, "Out of that bed, miss."

Bethany put her head under the covers. Willa tugged them down. "Come on. What's with you? You love school."

"Not anymore. I won't go. I can't go. I have a stomachache and a headache and a ringworm. Miss Weston doesn't let kids with ringworms in class. Cindy told me."

"Show me this ringworm."

"I can't. It crawled off somewhere."

"Okay. We'll do this the hard way." While Bethany lay on the bed as stiff as a board, Willa dressed her. "Your cereal is on the table downstairs. Go eat, or I'll prove to you I believe in spanking naughty little girls."

Balking all the way, Bethany flounced down the stairs. "You don't love me 'cause I'm adopted. You're not my real mommy, and daddy wasn't my real daddy and that's why I don't have a grandma or grampa. I'm not anybody's real little kid."

Unnerved, Willa's breath caught audibly in her throat. "You are my daughter. You're the most special person in the world to me."

"Before I was in the hospital was I in your stomach?"

Willa moved to sit in a chair and sagged. Dear God. She'd left explanations too late. "No, you were never in my stomach."

Bethany put down her spoon and looked at her mother. "Then I'm not your real little girl."

Willa needed a moment, if only to gather her thoughts. "Tell me where you got this idea that just because you're adopted, you're not my very own little girl."

"Cindy told me. She's in the second grade. She's my helper in summer school because she's advanced like me. She knows all about being adopted because her baby brother is adopted. He didn't get in her mother's stomach, either. They got him from the hospital. He was an orphan nobody wanted and Cindy's mother brought him home out of the kindness of her heart."

Willa knew a direct quote when she heard it. But she didn't know of any way to stave off an explanation without leaving Bethany confused and hurt. "You've always known I got you from the hospital. We've talked about it many times."

"But now we're coloring a family tree with all these little birds on limbs for brothers and sisters and mommies and daddies," Bethany explained. "Then we paste a ribbon from mommies and daddies to the kids. But adopted kids don't get a ribbon. Cindy said so. So I can't put Grandma Dawson on my tree, or Grampa Dawson, either. Adopted kids just have pretend mommies and grandparents. I don't have any birds on my tree. Cindy said adopted kids have to be buzzards, not cute little robins or bluebirds. I'm not going to school and be a buzzard.''

Willa's heart sank. How useless it was to struggle against Fate, she thought, utterly miserable. Sibling jealousy from far afield had undone her timetable, wrenched her from her emotional comfort zone. The risk she had to take now lay before her like a precipice. She was going to have to step off the edge and hope she landed on her feet. Hope that she was not going to do damage to Bethany—or herself.

"You're going to school," she said with a forced determination. "And you're going to be a bluebird or a robin."

"How?"

"Let me think about it a minute," she said, buying some time. She had to alert John and Claudine. "Finish your breakfast. I'll be right back."

Before she knocked on Claudine's door, Willa hesitated, radiating the uncertainty she was suffering. But wasn't this moment the very reason she had traveled to St. Augustine? She had freely made the decision to give Bethany her true heritage. So why did she now feel it was like giving away a piece of herself?

She should've seen it coming. The day spent sailing with Nick had caused her to keep her head in the clouds all week. If she had been paying more attention to Bethany...

Clytie opened the door. "What's wrong?" she said, alarmed. "You're as pale as milksop. Bethany's hurt!"

"No... Are John and Claudine up yet?"

"In the Florida room."

Willa gave greetings short shrift. "I'm going to tell Bethany who you are this morning," she said before she lost her nerve. She related Bethany's tale to the startled Elliotts.

"That dreadful child," Claudine exclaimed of Cindy. "Miss Weston ought to expel the little horror."

"If it were only that easy. I'm scared for Bethany's sake. I don't know how she'll absorb so much at once. I should've known things couldn't just meander along."

Claudine's expression became pensive. "I know you've been reluctant to tell her. Is it something John and I have done? Or not done?" She looked at her husband.

Willa took the plunge. "I really wanted to know more about Susan, is all. If only we knew who Bethany's father..."

John's eyes grew sad. "We don't have the slightest idea of who he was, Willa. You might ask Nick. I've always sensed he's kept something from us out of kindness to our sensibilities. But if you think it's so important..."

Only for my sake, Willa thought, and knew that was true. She couldn't put a hold on Bethany's happiness and future because her own might not be so rosy.

Claudine began to tremble. "I'm scared. Suppose Bethany doesn't want us for grandparents?"

Clytie, clearly as emotional as everyone else, snorted. "Sounds to me like Bethany would be happy with a bag lady if she could put her on a family tree."

Willa thought the lump growing in her throat would choke her. "I'd better get back to the cottage. I'll bring Bethany over after I've told her."

Claudine looked down at herself. "I'd better get out of this dressing robe. I want to look my best for...for whatever happens. You should, too, dear," she said to her husband. "Perhaps you should wear that pocket watch of your father's. It looks grandfatherly."

"I haven't finished my breakfast."

Clytie snatched his plate off the table. "Now you have."

Bethany had her version of events within two seconds of Willa's stumbling explanation.

"But that means I'm not the one who's adopted, Mommy. You are!"

"You could say that," said Willa, feeling as if she truly was orphaned.

"I was a real baby in Susan Elliott's stomach?"

"Yes, you were."

"And poor Susan died." Bethany put on a sad expression.

Willa was being as noncommittal as possible, trying not to influence Bethany's thoughts. But selfishly, she had only used "birth mother" once, preferring instead to refer to Susan by her first name.

Bethany traced the sketch Willa had drawn showing her connection to the Elliotts and Susan. On a line bisecting Susan's, Willa had put in her own name.

Bethany couldn't read the news clippings in the scrapbook about herself and Susan Elliott, but she accepted that she and Susan were the focus of the articles.

She was thrilled with the photos of herself as an infant hooked up to machines.

"Where's my real daddy?"

"No one knows. He's a mystery."

"Could we put me in a newspaper again? Maybe Nick could find him, too."

"That's something to think about," said Willa cautiously. "You would have to discuss that with John and Claudine. But it might hurt their feelings."

"You mean Grampa and Grandma Elliott," Bethany corrected. She pulled the diagram of her heritage in front of her again and studied it. Then she turned the pages in the scrapbook until she came to the adoption papers and birth certificates.

Willa waited.

The child looked up at her mother with her immense brown eyes. "You're my real Mommy now. That's what it says on the papers?"

"That's what is says."

"And you want me to be your little girl forever and ever?"

"Positively. I couldn't live without you."

Bethany flipped back through the scrapbook again until she came to a photo that had always been particularly heart-wrenching for Willa to look at. It showed more tubes and wires than baby. "Did it hurt me when the doctors saved my life and put all those needles in me?"

"Dreadfully."

"Did I cry and cry or was I a brave little baby?"

"Both."

"Can I take this picture to school and show Cindy?"

"I guess so. If you take care of it."

Bethany got up from the table. "I have to go talk to Grandma and Grampa Elliott now."

They gathered in the family room. John sat in his favorite chair, Claudine and Willa at opposite ends of the sofa. Clytie hovered. Bethany stood near the arm of the sofa and draped her arm around Claudine.

"Did you know I'm your granddaughter?" she asked solemnly.

Claudine nodded. "We did, but we had to wait for your mother to tell you."

"Have you ever been a grandma before?"

"No."

Bethany smiled. "That's okay. I can tell you what grandmas have to do. You have to come to my birthday party and bring me a present all wrapped up with lots of ribbons. I want a red velvet dress with tiny little hearts on it. At Christmas you're supposed to give me a toy. Grampa, too," she said, turning her eyes on John. "On Valentine's Day I get a big box of candy in a red box with lace on it. Chocolate. An' for Easter grandmas are supposed to buy their little kids a big basket with a fuzzy white rabbit."

Mortified, Willa dropped her chin into her hand. "Bethany. You little mercenary."

"I'm not finished."

"Yes, you are."

"Oh, let her go on," Claudine pleaded.

Willa shot her daughter The Look.

"And when Mommy gets mad at me, I get to come live with you," Bethany put in quickly. "An' when you get really, really old, I'll take care of you and Grampa." She glanced at Clytie. "What are you to me?"

Clytie beamed. "I'm your auntie. That sounds good to me. Sure does. Auntie Clytie."

John made a strangling noise in his throat.

Bethany crossed the room to him and gave him the same treatment she'd given Claudine. "Grampas are supposed to read stories, and take their little kids to the movies and to the beach and for ice creams and send notes with hugs and kisses on the bottom. If you have some paper, I'll show you how. Mommy said I get to keep Grandma Dawson as my guardian angel. She's already in heaven, but when you get to heaven you can be my guardian angel, too." She smiled. "If you forget how to be a grampa, you can ask me. Wanna see a picture of me when I was a baby?"

"That's enough," Willa said, getting to her feet. "I'm late for work and you for school."

"I want Grandma and Grampa to take me to school."

"We'll do it," Claudine said delightedly before Willa could protest.

"She has an ulterior motive," Willa warned.

Claudine's eyes gleamed. "If its name is Cindy, so do I."

"I'll get the car," said John.

"I'll just grab my purse," said Clytie.

John stopped in his tracks. "You're not invited."

"You'd deprive the woman who changed your diapers of the pleasure of seeing her only niece off to school? John Elliott. For shame."

Bethany giggled. "Grampa, did Auntie Clytie really change your diapers?"

THE STAFF MEETING droned on into the late afternoon. Willa paid scant attention. She was still drained and dazed from the morning's events. She had given up a piece of her heart and nothing seemed to fill the void.

Bethany, Claudine, John and Clytie were reveling in their new relationships. She was the outsider. She was miserable. And she felt guilty for feeling miserable.

The caseworker opposite her began presenting his problem clients. The man was very good with the elderly and children, but he was the office skirt chaser. His name was William Joseph, but everyone called him Joe. Willa avoided him as much as was possible. She listened halfheartedly. He kept glancing at her as if expecting her input so that she was obliged to pay attention.

"The mother came to us in January," he said. "She's in her seventies. Seems every time she visits her daughter for Christmas, they argue and she comes home threatening suicide. The daughter was so concerned she accompanied the mother back to Florida. After several days it was as if the spat never happened. Her mother was fine.''

"Where's the daughter live?" asked another counselor.

"Maine, in the house she grew up in."

"Maybe the mother has bad memories of that house."

Joe shook his head. "Not to listen to her. She's a widow, but she and her daughter both say her husband was a gentle, shy soul."

"Maybe she just doesn't like the weather in Maine during December," said the supervisor of caseworkers jokingly. "I wouldn't. Not after getting used to the mild winters we get here in St. Augustine."

"Chalk her behavior up to SADS," mumbled one of the staff.

"I'll look into it," said Joe. He glanced at Willa and winked. "You free for dinner?"

"No, I'm not," she said, a stiff edge in her tone.

The office receptionist peeked around the door. "Telephone for you, Willa. One of your clients. She's a little bit excited."

The supervisor nodded, excusing Willa. In the boxlike office she shared with a colleague, Willa answered the call. Keta Worthington's voice was high-pitched, exuding panic.

"I thought you said you were going to help me?" she wailed.

"I am. I have been," said Willa. "I turned in a report that favored you. I recommended against removing Roddy from your home."

"It hasn't done any good."

"Why? What's happened?"

"A deputy just came by. I've been subpoenaed!"

"I know that's scary, but it's a normal procedure."

"It means I still have to go to court!"

"I wish you didn't have to, but I came on your case late, Keta. Otherwise, we could've had more input with the social worker and asked for it to be dismissed. Please don't worry. Roddy passed his physical with flying colors. That counts for a lot."

"That's what Nick said."

Willa's fingers tightened on the receiver. "You've talked to him?"

"Last night. He stopped by to pitch a little ball with Roddy."

"He doesn't know about the subpoena?"

"I called his office and left word. He's in court today."

"I'll have a talk with him myself," Willa heard herself saying. "I'm not supposed to—"

"But you went sailing with him. You and your little girl. Roddy said so."

"I—that was personal."

"Oh."

Willa heard the dismay in Keta's voice. "I'm sorry, Keta. I know—" But then she couldn't think of the right words; or any words.

"He was never interested in me. I guess I knew it all along. I was just hoping—y'know. He's so good with Roddy."

"Roddy is easy to be good with, Keta. That's your doing. He's a charming, healthy little boy. You can be proud of that."

"I might lose him. It's all up to the judge."

"You'll have two friends in court. Me and Nick. Try not to worry."

"Shouldn't I prepare Roddy for the worst? Just in case?"

If Keta had asked her that yesterday, Willa knew she would've said, no—don't discuss it with him. But in light of what had happened with Bethany only that morning, she could not dish out such advice so glibly. There were some things in her job that psychology textbooks never addressed. "It's two weeks before your court day, isn't it? Why don't you sleep on it, then we can talk about it some more. But, Keta, you're a good mother. That comes through. If you decide you want to discuss the situation with Roddy, I know you'll find the right words."

A sad sigh came through the wire. "I thought all along I was doing my best. Maybe I'll wait a few days before I say anything. I'm just having a bad morning."

"Keta—keep in touch. If you need to talk—"

"Thanks, but I guess I'll be all right."

IT WAS A BEAUTIFUL, mellow summer night. The yard was illuminated by the faint light of late June stars and a rising moon.

Claudine sighed with a happy vitality so palpable it reached across and touched Willa. "After today I could forgive anybody anything! I told you didn't I? I spent all day in school with Bethany. Miss Weston put me to work."

"I think you've mentioned that about forty-two times," said Willa, laughing.

"Oh, dear. I'm going to be one of those grand-mothers who bores the pants off anyone who'll listen."

"You're not boring. I'm glad you had such a terrific day. Bethany enjoyed herself immensely."

"Well, we did put Cindy to rout. Heaven's but that child is bright. I think she's getting back at me. She's teaching me how to work the computer. She literally beamed every time I made an error.''

''You're going to volunteer teach then?''

''One day a week, until something better comes along.''

''Claudine!'' Willa shifted in the lawn chair, leaning into the other woman's space. ''Are you considering going to work?''

''Actually I am. Yes. Doing what, I don't know, but something will come to me.''

''You've discussed this with John?''

''No, but I'll get around him somehow.''

''I believe you will.''

''You're not just saying that?''

''I think you're just beginning to realize your strengths, Claudine. You can accomplish whatever you want.''

The older woman was quiet for a moment. ''That's one of the nicest things anyone has ever said to me. Or about me. I'm so glad we found you, Willa—and Bethany. I hope, wherever Susan might be, that she knows what joy her child is bringing to us. Oh—I'm sorry. That was thoughtless of me. Bethany is what she is today because of you. I mustn't forget that.''

''I like to think that but in so many ways she's an Elliott through and through.''

''I hope we don't ruin her like we did Susan.''

Willa came alert. ''What makes you say that?''

''Because we indulged her so. I watch you with Bethany and then I look back on how we acted with Susan. So often we just smoothed things over—or avoided touchy subjects altogether. There were times when she was so much like Natalie I wanted to throttle her.''

Willa thought of her list of unanswered questions. "I've given some thought to Natalie," she said cautiously.

"What kind of thought?"

"Professional thought. Three-fourths of all agoraphobics are women. The way you described Natalie's behavior—well, it fits. As long as a spouse or a friend or a parent is present, the agoraphobic is okay. You—"

"I really don't know what an agoraphobic is," said Claudine, alarm tipping her voice.

"It's a fear of open places. Or a fear of symptoms. There's a long list of symptoms, but most agoraphobics suffer anxiety, hyperventilation, a sense of unreality, or isolation. While John senior was alive, Natalie continued to function, but after he died, from what you say, she didn't."

"She was emotionally disturbed?"

Willa shook her head. "No. It's just a phobic disorder."

"Could Susan have been—?"

"I don't think so."

"But you do think there was something wrong with Susan?"

"Claudine, there had to be. I know you. I've seen how kind you are, how kind John is. He's stiff-necked, maybe, but kind nevertheless. Clytie is a part of your household, too. But there again, Clytie is spicy, but still a good influence."

Clarity struck Claudine. "You're worried that whatever problems Susan suffered will surface again in Bethany."

Willa exhaled. "I'm trying not to worry. I'd just like to be prepared—for whatever. Do you remember what happened the day Susan left?"

Claudine closed her eyes, visualizing. "She wanted to go to Daytona for Spring Break. All of her friends were going. But the weather was so bad that year. We said, no. She argued with me, with John, with Clytie, with Nick. She refused to come down to supper. She left sometime during the night. We never saw her again."

"If this is too painful for you—"

"I'm not thinking of myself. And I don't want to be second-guessing Bethany's behavior all of our lives."

"I don't, either. When exactly was Spring Break that year?"

"It was early that year, the end of March. We'd had an awful winter, lots of storms off the Atlantic—"

Willa was doing some mental mathematics. Bethany had been premature, having been born in early November. But that still left a window of opportunity for Susan and Nick. Perhaps Susan had not realized she was pregnant when she left—or perhaps— "Did Susan go to Daytona?"

"Oh, yes. She used her credit cards. Nick found out where she had stayed, where she bought gas. He went down there. But by that time break was over and the kids had gone back to school. The following month bills came in from North Carolina, Tennessee, Arkansas. Then they stopped. We never did find her car. How she lived and on what, we never learned."

Or Nick never told you, Willa thought. But she couldn't fault him for that. For a moment, she gazed up at the star-studded sky. "I'm afraid I've taken away some of today's joy for you by talking of Susan."

Claudine gave an elegant snort. "You're wrong about that! I loved today. Bethany is an absolute delight." She swatted at a mosquito. "Oh, no, the bugs have found me. I'd better go up to the house." She gave Willa a gentle hug. "I'm probably going to suffer buckets of guilt for saying this, Willa, I loved Susan dearly, but I do like you so much more."

Willa smiled. Claudine's comment was touching. "I have the advantage of maturity, y'know. I probably gave my own mother fits back when I was Susan's age."

"That's another thing I like about you—your tact."

Willa watched until Claudine reached the back porch, then she folded the lawn chairs and stacked them by her own back door.

The house was quiet. She tiptoed upstairs. Bethany, soundly asleep, was curled up with stuffed toys and favorite dolls.

Things were working out, Willa thought. All the hurt and recriminations that she had endured from Peter's parents and her stepmother were fading. Bethany had her grandparents; her continuity.

But what did Willa have? Seeing her daughter happy and secure meant a lot.

But . . . It wasn't enough. She wanted something for herself. She stopped at the bottom step. Oh, well, isn't that the thing to do? she chastised herself. Wallow in self-pity. Find fault with having a roof over your head, a job, food to eat, money in your pocket.

Her purse lay on the telephone table. She picked it up and rooted for the list she'd made. It was crumpled and scruffy.

Agoraphobics weren't mentally disturbed. Just people who suffered severe anxiety attacks. She put a line through Natalie's name. Claudine was less timid than she had first thought. Perhaps not timid at all, just in a rut. She put a line through Claudine's name. John was taciturn but loosening up more each day, especially with Bethany. She scratched his name from the list.

Susan was still a question mark.

Nick—arrogant, egotistical, devoted to Elliotts, she read. Fond of Susan?

Fond of me? she wondered. How fond?

Admit it, she told herself. Nick is the something else you want.

Okay, she went on in her one-sided conversation. So do something nice for yourself. Pick up the phone and call him. Just wanting to hear his voice didn't mean jumping headlong into bed or marriage. It was just being friendly.

She placed her hand on the receiver for a long moment.

Then she went upstairs to shower and wash her hair.

Chapter Ten

Her first reaction on seeing him was a surge of pure pleasure—instinctive, so great that it took all breath away. Her second reaction was mortification. To answer the door she had thrown on a threadbare chenille robe. Her hair was dripping wet. She looked a disaster. "Haven't you ever heard of phoning ahead?"

"I knocked. When you didn't answer I went up to the house. I was going to phone from there, but Claudine said Bethany was asleep. I was just trying to be considerate." He looked her over from head to toe, grinned and asked the obvious. "Did I get you out of a shower?"

"No, I was playing in a sandbox."

"Sarcasm suits you. Are you going to let me in or not?"

"I ought to say—not."

She left him standing there and raced upstairs to towel dry her hair and slip into a pair of slacks and shirt.

Returning downstairs she discovered him pouring chilled champagne into jelly glasses. He looked up and gave a low whistle. "Very nice."

"Don't make fun of me."

"Loosen up. I'm hinting that I'd like to make fun with you."

"I've had my fill of skirt chasers today, thank you."

Nick fixed her with a slate-colored stare. "Some guy is putting the make on you? Who? I'll defend your honor. I'll throttle him—"

"I can take care of myself."

"I hate women who can take care of themselves. They never let me feel—"

"Macho?"

"You're smirking."

"I'm not. What's the champagne for? You win a big case?"

"We're celebrating John and Claudine's new status as grandparents. John called me." He handed her a glass. "Toast to you. I'm proud of you. That was a good thing you did, telling Bethany."

His approval cloaked her warmly, as if she were wearing the finest silks and furs. "It was a forced decision."

"So is this," he said, coming around the kitchen counter. He pulled her to him and pressed his lips to her brow. She was flesh and soft and smelling of soap and shampoo. It was heady stuff. Nick felt his stomach somersault. He wanted more than anything to feel her suppleness yield beneath his body.

"Nick . . ." said Willa, all the air seeping from her lungs. "If we keep this up, we're going to be in big trouble."

His arms tightened so that the length of her was aligned against his body; the activity in his loins unmistakable for what it was. "I *like* trouble. I'm *trained* for trouble."

Her face was at his shoulder, her lips just brushing his neck. "I'm not ready for this," she half lied. Physically she was ready, emotionally she was still unsure.

His hands trailed down her spine. He could feel her trembling beneath his fingers. "You're ready," he murmured. "But I won't push."

She disengaged herself from his encircling arms. "I thought we were having champagne."

"We are. But you make things happen inside me—"

The female in her couldn't resist. "I could tell."

"Ouch." He passed her a jelly glass. "Toast. To a special lady—you."

"I'm not supposed to drink my own toast."

"You will this one. I make my own rules. Besides, this stuff cost me forty-two bucks. Drink."

"Wait. Let me make a toast, too." She tapped his glass with her own. "To you, my new friend."

He gazed at her, mute for a heartbeat. "Friend? That's all I am?"

She wet her lips. "Don't we have to start somewhere?"

"Start?" he croaked. "I'm at the finishing line. You didn't hear the gun go off?"

"I don't think it's good form to argue over toasts."

"Who taught you to back and fill? You shoulda been a lawyer."

"I've been watching you."

"Toast accepted," he said.

Glasses emptied, Nick refilled them. He moved to the sofa. Willa trailed, but curled up nearby in the chair.

Eyeing the distance she put between them, Nick sighed heavily. "Okay. Let's talk business."

"What business would we have now?"

"I'd like to hint at something evocative, but you'd throw me out."

"I might. Then again, I might not."

He leaned forward, expression suddenly intense and hopeful. "Are we flirting?"

"It's the champagne," she said with an easy smile, knowing that loving him was no longer a remote and unconsidered possibility, but a warm and immediate fact. The only problem was, she couldn't tell him.

"Honorable man that I am, I won't take advantage of that."

"Oh, shoot."

"On the other hand, maybe I'm not that honorable. Come sit over here."

"Too dangerous. Tell me about this business we have."

"How? Dangerous?"

"Nick . . ."

He smiled ruefully. "Okay. I want you to evaluate a couple for me, and talk to their daughter. They've filed for divorce, but something smells fishy in Denmark— only I can't figure it. I need some professional input. It's right up your alley."

"I can't. I'm not licensed to practice on my own."

"You could do it as a courtesy. There's no rule against professional courtesies is there? As long as you don't get paid—in dollars that is. I can think of any manner of remuneration—"

"You have a one-track mind."

"I admit it. How about this? You come over here and sit in my lap or I'm crawling into yours—"

"Don't be silly," she said with some asperity.

"That way my eyes will stay above your neck. That blouse you're wearing is awfully thin. I don't think I ought to mince words, do you?"

Willa jumped up, but she wasn't nearly as angry as she ought to be. "You've been looking down my blouse since we met, Nick Cavenaugh. Out!"

He grabbed her wrist and she found herself giving in to the temptation to join him on the sofa.

He curled his arms around her and locked them, hugging her back to his chest. "Much better," he breathed, fighting the urge to allow his hands to travel. Pressing his cheek to her still-damp hair, he inhaled the scent of her and sighed. "Where was I?"

"You were leaving." Being tucked into his arms, feeling his strength encircling her was wonderful. She belonged in his arms. Her body told her so. She could imagine an entire future in his arms. For a second she was afraid to stir for fear of the dream dissolving and cold reality taking its place. But slowly it was borne upon her that there remained a truth she had yet to learn about him. Its name was Susan. Yet, allowing his arms to stay around her, snuggling up to his chest, she knew she had burned her boats and there was not a mortal thing she could do now to change what she felt in her heart.

"I'm having a terrible time concentrating," he said.

She spoke into the air. "You were speaking of professional courtesies."

"Ah. You're off tomorrow aren't you? Can you come in to my office? Say about eleven. See these folks that can't seem to make their marriage work, then I'll take you to lunch or, we could horse around—"

"Lunch sounds nice."

"You've never seen my place."

"Lunch."

"It's right on the beach."

"A stroll on the beach sounds nice."

Nick's heart leaped.

"After I pick up Bethany from school, maybe we'll drive over."

"Funny. I don't recall inviting the whole family."

Willa moved away abruptly, catching Nick by surprise so that she escaped his arms. She looked at him with an expression of dismay. "You don't like Bethany?"

"I do like Bethany. But I like her mother, too. I like her mother a lot. It's not like you don't have a baby-sitter. Claudine—"

"I didn't come here just to dump my daughter on the Elliotts—"

"Did I say that? Why're you so prickly?"

Willa plunged without thinking. "Because I think you know something about Susan and Bethany that you're not telling."

"Like what?"

Stimulated by the champagne Willa became reckless. "Like the name of Bethany's biological father."

Nick sat dead still, his face growing tight. "Willa, don't dredge that up." His voice was even, very cold.

The champagne she'd drunk could not overcome the sinking sensation—like drowning—in her stomach. She realized that his coolness belied a certain knowledge and that he meant to keep that knowledge his own. "You know, don't you? I have a right to know."

He shook his head. "We discussed this before. Susan is dead," he said, his voice flat. "There's been enough pain all around—"

"Wouldn't the truth free…everyone from that pain?"

"I don't think so."

"You don't trust me enough to tell me."

He heaved himself off the sofa, making motions to leave. Willa knew a sensation of panic. Her curiosity about Bethany's paternity was moving toward obsession. Unless she was very careful, it was going to slip out of control. Suddenly she discovered herself reluctant to be told the truth. Nick was right, no good could come of that—now. But how to make amends?

"May I expect you in my office tomorrow?" he said, giving her an inch, but only just.

She felt defeated. She had ruined the evening for him, for herself. "I—all right," she agreed, telling herself it was an opportunity to see him, to smooth things over.

"Eleven o'clock. Afterward, if you feel like lunch..." his voice trailed off, as if withdrawing that invitation. Then he went away and left her, closing the door behind him.

RIGHT ON TIME," said Nick's secretary, Harriet Volte, looking up to scrutinize Willa. "He said you would be."

Willa tolerated the scrutiny uneasily and knew at once that Harriet Volte was efficient, intelligent and unflappable. The kind of person you wanted as a friend when your back was against the wall. Harriet was sharp of eye and nose, white-haired, and had the longest, most elegant hands Willa had ever seen. Not even the blunt, unpolished nailtips detracted from their elegance.

"He's not here, is he?" Willa said, her heart sinking. She had taken special care with her dress and cosmetics. Taking a page from John's book so to speak, she had prepared a speech of few words to apologize. Now she wouldn't even get to do that. It put her at sixes and sevens.

"He's in conference with the Wiltons," she said, nodding toward Nick's private office. "We've put the daughter in the law library. She's waiting for you there. Her name is Juliana. She's a pistol. You'll like her."

"But—"

Harriet thrust a manila folder into Willa's hands. "Make your notes and stuff them in here. I'll type them up for Nick later."

"Just like that? No preparation?"

"Nick wants an unbiased opinion. He won't get that if you're briefed."

"Mrs. Volte, you never gave me a chance to introduce myself. How do you know I'm Willa Manning and not some—"

"I've seen your photograph... Nick talks of you— constantly, I might add. Frankly I'm sick to death of listening to him. And since I know you as Willa, you can do likewise. Harriet."

"Harriet. Thank you." She tensed. "What does Nick say about me?"

Harriet rolled her eyes. "You're beautiful...you have these legs... you're smart, and about two or three hundred other things I don't have time to put an ear to. Anyway, welcome to St. Augustine."

Willa stared at the secretary. "People don't often like you on first meeting, do they?"

Harriet laughed. "Nope, but I like it that way. It keeps them from getting in my space and interrupting my work. Nick is the most impatient man I've ever worked for." She smiled pointedly. "The best-paying, too." She gestured toward the door of the law library. "Let me know when you're finished. I'll alert Nick."

Willa took that to mean Nick was avoiding her. She put a good face on it for Harriet's benefit and nodded. Still...he thought her beautiful... She entered the library wearing a smile.

The child glanced up from a book held in her lap. She had large, young-old eyes that seemed to take up her whole face.

"You're Mrs. Manning?" she asked.

"Yes, and you're Juliana?"

"Could we get down to it? I don't know how long we have."

Willa sat down across from the child. "How old are you?"

"Eleven. Whose side are you on?"

"I'm supposed to be objective."

"I need somebody on my side. I need somebody to listen to me for a change. Mr. Cavenaugh said you would."

"I think I'm a good listener."

Juliana sighed heavily. "This isn't the first time Mom and Dad have filed for divorce. They'll never go through with it. They always use me as the excuse not to go to court and finalize it."

Willa raised an eyebrow. "Then what happens?"

"They go back home. They don't live together, did you know that? Mom has her house and Dad has his. They're next door to each other... I'm always being packed up and sent across one yard or another. It's frustrating. I'm working on science projects, writing computer programs ... I need peace and quiet."

"Writing computer programs?"

"Yes. Medical programs. I'm in the tenth grade. I'm trying to hold off finishing high school until I've grown breasts. I don't want to be the only flat-chested college freshman at the University of Florida. Having a brain like mine is freaky enough. Am I going too fast for you?"

"Don't worry. I'm keeping up, but just barely."

"Listen, Mom and Dad really love each other, but they're so immature, they don't know how to show it. So they end up being selfish, hateful, and self-centered. They're their own children...if that makes sense to you."

"It makes perfect sense," said Willa, leaning back. "Tell me, what do you want? What would make you happy?"

"I want to move in with my grandmother. She lives across the street from us. She doesn't allow Mom and Dad over at the same time, though ... so that's their excuse why I can't live with Gram. There's another thing, my parents haven't yet grasped just how smart I am. Gram understands me. I mean, I'm still a kid, so I like cookies and hugs and being tucked into bed at night.

"But I know things. Mom thinks my brain won't start functioning until I start my period. And I don't think that will be for a while yet. My grandmother didn't start until she was seventeen, my mother when she was fifteen, so I don't think I'm genetically programmed to start for a while."

The sounds of a sudden commotion in the outer office filtered through the closed door. "That'll be my folks," said Juliana with a shrug of resignation. She watched the door a moment. When it didn't fly open she looked back at Willa.

"Maybe you've had a reprieve," Willa said to the child. "Tell me about your dad and yourself."

Juliana kept a peripheral eye on the closed door. "I'm doing some medical assays, that means controlled experiments—"

"I know, my husband used to be a biophysicist."

"Used to be?"

"He died."

Juliana was quiet a moment, thinking. "His energy still exists, y'know. The body rots but the energy field continues. I'm going to study that one day."

Willa didn't want to dwell on that. "About your dad," she coaxed.

"I'm studying about the sex life of aquatic arthropods. Dad thinks what I'm working on is inappropriate for a girl."

She leaned forward suddenly, her face tense, her eyes glittering. "I love my mom and dad, Mrs. Manning, but I don't have any illusions about them. They're children. They're never going to change—and they're never going to divorce, either. They've been through a half-dozen attorneys in this town already. First they get mad at each other, next they hire a lawyer, then they find something to get mad at the lawyer about. They focus their anger on him for a while then turn on each other again and the cycle begins all over.... My parents are addicted to turmoil. They thrive on it.

"I don't. And I can't live with them like this. I want to live with my grandmother. She's willing, but she just can't cope with both my parents at the same time." The girl leaned back suddenly and dropped her arms to the sides of the chair. "Can you help me?"

Willa nibbled her lip, thinking. "I'll try. Realistically it'll take either your parents' cooperation or a court order, not to mention your grandmother's acquiescence."

Juliana dropped her chin into her hands. "Could Gram hire Mr. Cavenaugh on my behalf? I have to save myself—somehow."

The library door flew open.

A blonde with plain features, but skin the color of honey signaled to Juliana. "We're leaving." She aimed a chill look at Willa. "We didn't get our full hour, so don't even consider billing us."

"See what I mean?" Juliana cast out the side of her mouth.

"I'll talk to Mr. Cavenaugh for you," Willa replied sotto voce. She offered a smile to the parents, but too late. They were already in the hall, Juliana following and shaking her head.

Then Nick was standing on the threshold, his face drained of color. Willa's heart caught. She leaped up.

"Has something terrible happened?"

"I don't know." He was dazed. "My daughter's here."

Willa knew she hadn't heard him right. The session with Juliana had confused her. She hadn't yet gotten back on track. "Who?"

"My daughter...after all these years. I mentioned her once."

So many variables were racing through Willa's mind, they rendered her speechless.

His *daughter*. Bethany? What would Bethany be doing...*years*? The conversation they'd had last night had piqued his conscience... He was going to tell her...

"She's in my office," Nick was saying, "phoning her mother. I insisted. She's run away from home."

"She's phoning her mother?" Willa's legs felt wobbly. She collapsed in the nearest chair with a soft thud. "You have a daughter who has a mother who's *alive*?"

Nick nodded. "Can you believe it? Right out of the blue she walks into my office—"

"She's run away from home?"

"She flew from Milan, to London, to Jacksonville and took a bus to St. Augustine. All by herself. And found me."

"But that means...that has to mean..." Willa felt a glorious sensation throughout her body. Her heart seemed to swell beyond the confines of her chest. "Nick! That's...why—how *wonderful!* Your daughter is here!"

"Wonderful?" He leaned against the doorjamb as if something were blurring the outlines of thought.

"I can't get through. The operator is going to keep trying."

The voice was musical with a slight European accent. Nick turned. Willa followed his gaze.

She found herself staring at a slenderly built, willowy teenager clad in faded jeans and several loose overshirts. The layered look, Willa thought, but held the notion only a second, because the girl was so obviously Nick's daughter.

She had his dark hair, it fell to her waist; immense gray eyes with brows that were identical to her father's. Hers was a feminine variation of Nick's face. Willa looked at the hands. Long, lean fingers, nails blunt and bitten down to the quick.

"I'm Willa Manning," she said. "A friend of your father's. Call me Willa." She thrust out her hand.

After a slight hesitation, a glance at Nick, the girl accepted Willa's hand. "I'm Amanda D'Amato. But I'm changing my name to Cavenaugh."

The sound of his name galvanized Nick. He retrieved the telephone in the room from a wall nook and put it on the table. "Try your mother again."

"I won't go back," said Amanda, and there was steel in her lilting voice. "I won't. No matter what you say, what she says."

"Nick," Willa intervened. "Let's sit here and talk for a moment. Perhaps we should discuss what Amanda needs to say to her mother." She turned to the girl. "Who is your mother?"

"Countess Alfredo D'Amato. Alfredo adopted me when he married Mother." She gazed at Nick with something akin to hate in her eyes. "Why didn't you marry Mother? Why did you abandon us?"

Nick refocused his thoughts on the reality of the moment. "Sit down," he said, pulling out a chair for her and one for himself opposite his daughter. "I've rehearsed in my mind a thousand times what I'd say to you if we ever met." He turned to Willa. "I'd like to have you here, but you don't have to stay if you'd rather not."

Put that way an army of Viking warriors couldn't have budged her, but she was prepared to leave if Amanda objected. "If Amanda doesn't mind, I'll stay."

Amanda shrugged noncommittally and turned her attention to her father. Nick stared at his daughter and his eyes seemed to reach toward some haunted memory. "What has your mother told you about me?" he asked.

"She says you ruined her life. She and Alfredo argue about you."

Patches of scarlet gleamed in the pallor of Nick's cheeks. "Years ago," he said measuring his words. "Your mother and I fell in love—or at least I fell in love with her. We went together to her parents to tell them she was having a baby. They refused. The next thing I knew, Stella was whisked away to Europe. She cabled me when you were born. I borrowed the money from my godfather to go to her, and you. I wasn't permitted to see her or you. Stella was moved from the clinic in Switzerland to Milan. Soon after you were born she married D'Amato. The event made the social columns here. When I saw them, I wrote to her, asking to see you. What I got back was a letter from an attorney that said my name was not on your birth certificate and that D'Amato had adopted you. I was ordered to stay out of your life and Stella's."

"You could've persisted," Amanda accused.

Regret filled Nick's face. "I wanted to. I should have. But I was young, penniless and still in law school."

"I've had a horrible life because of you! Alfredo didn't want me, Mother didn't want me—" She dumped the contents of her purse on the table. "This is all I have from them—" She scattered her passport and credit cards over the table melodramatically.

Nick crumbled. "I'm sorry."

Willa ached for both of them.

Harriet came into the room. Her expression was no less surprised and troubled than Nick's. "The international operator is on the line. Your call—"

Nick snatched up the telephone. "Stella? It's Nicholas Cavenaugh—" He took the receiver away from his ear and stared at it. Fifteen years of stored-up vitrol and hysteria poured out.

"You ruined my life!" Stella was yelling. "How dare you call! You sent that stupid letter, Nick. You didn't think I actually told the man I married the truth about our affair, did you—"

There was a stark expression on Nick's face. "Amanda is here—with me," he injected.

"Amanda!" There was a heartbeat of silence, then: "So she's with you! Good. Keep her. She's your daughter. You cope with her. She does nothing but pout, cause trouble and run away from school. I wash my hands of her!"

Nick and Amanda both appeared so stricken at the harsh words, Willa wanted to take both into her arms and comfort them. But her instinct told her this was Nick's show. Unless invited, she had to stay out of it.

The telephone receiver weighed heavily in Nick's hand. Stella had hung up. Nick replaced the receiver. "She'll change her mind," he said.

Amanda shook her head. "She won't," she said with a maturity and sophistication beyond her years. "You heard her. She's rid of me. It's what she's always wanted. She only put a good face on about it while Grandma and Grandpapa were alive."

"They died?"

"When I was nine. Are your parents alive? Do they know about me?"

Nick closed his eyes. "They're alive. They don't know about you."

"You've kept me a secret. You're ashamed of me, too?" The girl seemed to curl inside herself. Watching Amanda's body language, Willa surmised that withdrawal was the teenager's defense mechanism. She made a mental note to talk to Nick about it at some more suitable time.

"I'm not ashamed of you. I didn't want to hurt them or you." He tried a smile and failed miserably. "You've been traveling for two days. You must be tired. I'll take you home. We have a lot a years to catch up on."

Nick was talking sense but Willa noticed his eyes retained their bewildered look. "If you need to talk after you get Amanda settled, feel free to call me," she said.

Nick nodded. With a word to Harriet to cancel his afternoon appointments, Nick took his daughter home.

The instant they were out the door Harriet came into the law library. "How about that for 'what goes around comes around'?"

"It's wonderful, isn't it?" Willa replied, radiating happiness.

Harriet pursed her lips. "I missed something."

Chapter Eleven

Nick looked shredded. Willa gave him a tentative smile. "Things didn't go well?"

He took a sip of his drink, then grinned sheepishly. "I feel like I've been gut-punched. Amanda's a Cavenaugh through and through. Could you tell?"

"Anyone can. She's beautiful."

"You'd think..." He paused, then began again. "I have a lot to make up to her. For the past five years she's been shunted off to boarding schools and camp. She's only allowed home at Christmas and then she eats with the staff in the kitchen. Not much of a life for a kid, is it?"

"You can't carry the blame for that on your shoulders. Life has a way of getting in the way of the best intentions."

"That's the psychologist in you talking?"

"The experienced parent in me."

They were sitting at the rail on the deck at Panama Hattie's, a local beachfront watering hole. The sun was going down, the breeze off the Atlantic refreshing. Unseeing, Nick gazed at the bathers and surfers leaving the beaches en masse. They were hiking up and down sidewalks, dragging towels, plastic floats and surfboards.

"I cabled my parents," he said. "But who knows how long it'll take to reach them."

"Are you worried about what they'll think?"

His eyes pinned her. "I'm more worried about what you think."

"It's wonderful, Nick. You have your daughter. It's something you wanted."

"I'm not soliciting compliments."

"I know that."

He shook his head. "I don't get this. Your reaction seems all wrong. We...like each other... We're involved...or at least, we're trying to be. Aren't we?"

Willa's spirits soared. "Yes."

"So why aren't you curious? Why aren't you asking dozens of questions? It's like you're relieved of... of...something. I just can't put my finger on it."

"How do you want me to react? I'm happy for you."

"That's just it—you're happy all out of proportion. A girl shows up in my office, claims to be my daughter—"

"Claims?"

"Is. I'm not disputing that. But it's obvious that I had an affair sixteen years ago that resulted in her birth—and all you can say is, wonderful? Aren't you angry?"

"Angry?" Willa laughed softly. "Oh, Nick. If only you'd known what I have been thinking—"

"Now's the time to clue me in."

"It's meaningless now."

She averted her face, seeming to take great interest in some activity on the fishing pier in the distance.

"Not to me it isn't. You were curious as hell about Keta Worthington. You never miss an opportunity to discuss—" Nick stopped. Clarity struck. "Willa, look at me." The tone of his voice was odd. "What were you thinking?"

"I told you. It was silly."

"Susan." He said the name and it lay between them like tainted fish.

Willa felt her face grow warm. She made a small gesture with her hand, as if brushing away some small irritant.

But Nick was nodding his head. "Dear God. You thought—" He choked, stunned by his own realization. "All this time... You thought that Susan and I... that Bethany—"

A sliver of dread gripped Willa. "You refused to talk about Susan. I asked you about her. I wanted to know for Bethany's sake. But you always clammed up. If you weren't... what was I to think?"

"Not that."

"Don't you see? Whoever Bethany's parents were didn't matter except that I wanted to track the genetics..."

"Genetics?" He jerked his head heavenward in disbelief. "That's bull! I get it now. I had you pegged, didn't I? Only I figured you were here to scalp John and Claudine. Hah! It was me. You wanted to establish paternity, didn't you? Then what? Were you going to haul me into court for child support?"

"That's not even possible."

"Anything is possible! I learned a lesson from the school of hard knocks today. When you have a child, you take your chances. They grow up to be good or bad. You just do the best you can. So why can't you be like every other parent, Willa? Being an adoptive mother doesn't give you special privileges."

She cringed. "That's cruel. You've been a father for all of eight hours—you think that makes you an expert?"

"However Amanda is, I'm accepting her."

"Nick can we stop this? Everything we're saying to each other is coming out deadly. Meant to hurt."

Strain altered his features so that the bones had new prominence. "Don't defend myself, you mean? You'd like that, wouldn't you? You're not going to see me digging around in Amanda's past to find out what quirks may show up in her future. Think about it. Maybe what you want is a perfect kid. They don't exist."

"Then why be so secretive about Susan?" she wailed softly. "Why?"

"Because she was promiscuous," he said gravely, his anger barely in check. "Because one day I came home from the office and found her in the cottage with a man in my bed. She was sick, Willa. Sick! John and Claudine had their hands full with her. Nothing anyone did helped. I couldn't make myself sleep in that bed again. I bought my own place. When she left and I began trying to find her, I followed a trail of motel rooms and men. I knew she would end up dead. I felt it. And that was enough for John and Claudine to bear. They didn't then, and don't now, need to know the gruesome details."

"But I do!" Willa felt as if she'd been run over by a train. But she couldn't just sit there tamely and listen to this. "What was wrong with Susan?"

"I don't know. Nobody ever put a name to it." He slid off the bar stool. "But jumping to conclusions doesn't make for happy landings, does it?"

"Nick. Please. It was just a *thought*. Deep down I was never certain. I didn't want to believe it."

"Why didn't you just come right out and ask?"

"Well! Where would that have gotten me? Look at how you're behaving at my only thinking it!"

"My behavior is well justified. If there's anything I've learned in my career it's that a woman will make a false accusation without the first thought of how it might affect her poor victim."

Willa bristled. "We aren't talking about rape, here."

"Close enough." A shell of hardness was settling on him with every word he spoke. "How could you think that I'd mess around with a child half my age!" A spike of hurt plunged deep into his soul. "I thought you had a better opinion of me than that. The rose-colored glasses are off, friend. You're the kind of woman who thinks the worst without any foundation in fact. You really had me fooled." He took a deep breath in an effort to maintain an emotional balance. "I have to leave. Amanda will be waking up soon."

"Wait," Willa called softly, aware that other patrons had been staring or eavesdropping. Nick turned, putting her under a cold scrutiny with not a scrap of caring visible in his eyes.

"For what? Another stab in the back?" Or my heart, he thought, hurt beyond measure.

"Put yourself in my shoes, Nick—just for a minute."

He shook his head. "No way."

Willa tried to quell the terrible sensation she felt of impending disaster. But she had to know. "Then it's finished between us?" she asked in a small whisper, which was only a filament of sound.

"Finished?" His voice was filled with irony. "On your end there was never a beginning."

"Isn't it exciting about Amanda?" said Claudine, her hands busy arranging a bouquet of pink and lavender alstermerias. She turned the vase around, studying the way the tiny lilylike flowers lifted and spread. "What do you think? I don't want an arrangement so high we can't talk over it."

"It's lovely," said Willa. Then: "Claudine, I don't suppose you'd excuse me from supper tonight?"

The older woman looked up. "Why? Are you ill?"

"No, just a little tired."

"Oh, but I'm sure Nick is counting on you being here. He's a bit taken with you. To tell you the truth, I like the idea that you and he..." Claudine smiled. "Nick's never had anyone of his own. Nathan and Margot adore him, but they've sacrificed themselves and Nick for their work. John's father doted on him, but—"

"Nick had Stella," Willa said, sounding more waspish than she had intended. She had said nothing to any of the Elliotts about her break with Nick. She couldn't. She feared collapsing into tears.

"An all too brief affair of the heart. And I can assure you that Stella's was never involved. But of course we couldn't tell Nick."

"So you knew about Amanda."

"Peripherally. Some months after her parents whisked her away, he dashed off to Europe and came home frustrated and bedraggled. John senior told us to mind our own business. We did." She smiled at Willa coaxingly. "Listen, Clytie and I will keep an eye on Bethany. She's got her nose in the dollhouse anyway. Why don't you run along and take a nap?"

Trapped by her own excuse, Willa retreated to the cottage, ostensibly to nap. Napping was out of the question. She was too tense.

She had to drop the hope of discovering Bethany's paternity. But the nagging sense plagued her, that whatever had motivated Susan to destroy herself was latent in Bethany's tiny body, just waiting to emerge and cause disaster.

Nor could she stop thinking about Nick. Every time she thought she'd managed to erase him from her consciousness, thoughts of his face and body moved in to shadow her mind.

She told herself she was content with her lot, she didn't need to become attached to some man.

Armed with that thought she arrived to supper only a few minutes late. Bethany was "helping" Clytie in the kitchen. Willa checked Bethany's face and hands and found them presentable. She offered Clytie her own assistance but was shooed into the family room.

John was pouring wine. "We thought you'd overslept," he said.

"Amanda is a young Nick all over again," said Claudine, smiling at the girl.

"She is," Willa said. She did not swing her gaze to Nick but kept them on Amanda. The teenager looked lovely. She'd spent time on the beach over the past few days. Her skin glowed with health and tan. "Are you settled in?" she asked pleasantly.

Amanda's eyes darted to Nick. "I guess."

Willa picked up on the teenager's uncertainty. She had the impression that Amanda had long ago stopped trusting adults and it followed that they had long since given up trusting her. "It'll take you a while. After all, you're used to a different culture, different customs."

"I want to get a job. I could meet kids my age that way."

"That sounds like a wonderful idea."

"Nick won't let me."

"Oh." Willa made herself glance at him. He was sitting in one of the great old armchairs. He met her eyes briefly, nodded, then turned away to engage John in conversation.

Willa felt as if she'd just had her heart removed without benefit of anesthetic.

"Grampa won't let Grandma work, either," said Bethany. "But she's gonna anyway, aren't you Grandma? Grampa's a relic of another age," she added, repeating a comment she'd overheard.

"Oh, dear," said Claudine.

Bethany went to John and leaned on the arm of his chair in an air of innocence. "You're lots of things aren't you, Grampa?"

"I won't have the suffragette banner waved in this house," he said sternly.

"That means you're smug," said Bethany. "Aunt Clytie, what comes after smug? I forgot."

"Sanctimonious," Clytie deadpanned.

"More wine anybody?" Claudine said.

Nick laughed. John glared at him.

Willa chastised Bethany. "You're not supposed to repeat everything you hear."

"Nobody said it was a secret."

"We'll discuss this later."

The discussion swung back to Amanda, and for the remainder of the evening, the teenager with her lilting voice was the focus of an admiring audience.

Willa allowed the conversation to flow around her. No one noticed that she and Nick were only as civil as strained manners dictated. Throughout the meal Willa was addled by his nearness, the sound of his voice, his laughter in response to Amanda or Clytie or Bethany. Pleading an early morning, she made a motion to leave as soon as dessert had been served.

"Oh, but we haven't even discussed the Fourth," said Claudine. "Nick's taking us out on his boat so we can watch the fireworks from the bay. We haven't done that in years.''

"I may have to be on call," Willa said. Her supervisor had been pressing the staff for volunteers to work the holiday. She'd put her name up first thing in the morning, she decided.

"I want to watch the fireworks from Nick's boat," said Bethany.

Claudine assured her that she wouldn't be left out. Nick said nothing. But as Willa coaxed a protesting Bethany away from the table, he pushed back his chair.

"I'll walk you and Bethany to the cottage," he said.

She didn't ask him in. At the cottage door she sent Bethany off to get into her pajamas, then turned to face him. Neither of them said anything. Willa couldn't bear the silence.

"You won't have to put up with me on the Fourth. I'll work."

"The sloop is big enough for you to stay at one end and me the other," he said dryly. "I'd rather John and Claudine weren't brought into this."

"They won't be," she said silkily. "Was there something else?"

"I just wanted to thank you for the report you did on Juliana and her parents."

"The child's got an IQ off the charts. More than that, she uses it. Are you going to help her?"

"Well, we can't force them to allow Juliana to move in with her grandmother. But we might encourage them to consider it an alternative. I'd like you to be there when I talk with her parents."

"I couldn't."

"Thinking only of yourself again?"

"That's not fair."

"Very little in life is fair."

"It makes you feel good that I made a mistake, doesn't it?"

Nick wanted to make a statement, a declaration that would illustrate that, if nothing else, he was trustworthy. But he didn't know where it'd get him or how much of his ego it would leave intact. The only maneuver left to him was to attack. "You're being irrational. Let's work this damned thing out, okay?"

"To what end?"

"I'm having second thoughts," he admitted, watching her to see how she reacted. Stone-faced. Damn. "Could we leave it at that for the moment?"

"All right."

He wanted to take her into his arms, crush her lithe body to his and lose himself in her softness. Standing so close to her was weakening the resolve that had sustained him the past week. He shoved his hands into his pockets. "I'll call you."

"Famous last lines."

"Mommy?" Bethany pleaded. "Are you coming to read to me?"

"Right away, sweetie." She turned to Nick. "Good night."

"Make that lousy night," he said bitterly.

Willa slipped inside, joining Bethany.

The door closed on him, Nick rocked on his heels. For a guy who likes to play it safe, he told himself, he was taking one hell of a risk.

He gazed for a moment at the great old house in which his daughter awaited his return. He sighed heavily. Fatherhood wasn't as easy as he'd imagined. Amanda had a mind of her own, ideas of her own and they didn't dovetail with his mind, his ideas. Cultures and customs be damned; Amanda was pigheaded. Willa was pig-headed.

He was caught between the two.

FROM HER UPSTAIRS WINDOW Willa watched Nick walk across to the Elliotts' house. His broad shoulders were slumped. She had a ludicrous urge to call him back, throw herself into his arms...

"Did you kiss Nick good night?" Bethany asked.

Willa spun around. "No! Listen you, eavesdropping and spying are not ladylike."

"I'm not a lady, I'm a little girl. Grandma told Clytie that Nick likes you. If he married you, he could be my stepdaddy. Then Amanda could be my sister an' I could learn to say words like she does."

"You want too much."

"I just want a whole family. I'm the only kid in school without a daddy."

"That's not true."

"It feels true."

"Move over, I want to snuggle."

"No. I've got all my dolls in bed with me. They're already asleep."

Willa went alone and lonely into her own bed.

Chapter Twelve

Willa decided she owed Nick an apology. He had tried to make amends in the best way he knew how and she had rebuffed him. In anybody's book that was cutting off her nose to spite her face. She took a detour on her way home from work and stopped by his office.

"Well! Speak of the devil," exclaimed Harriet as Willa entered Nick's office. "I was just trying to reach you."

"Is Nick available then? I just need a few minutes."

"He was called home."

"Oh. Trouble?"

"Let me put it this way, dear Papa has bitten off more than he can chew."

A little wind went out of Willa's sails. She sighed. "Haven't we all? What were you calling me about?"

"Nick has set up an appointment with the Wiltons for Thursday, the day after the Fourth. He wants to know if you can be here about two-thirty."

"I told him, no."

"Apparently he misunderstood."

"Impossible."

"That describes Nick to a T. Two-thirty it is." Harriet noted it on her desk calendar.

Willa frowned. "You're as bad as he is."

"I know. It rubs off. Would you believe I used to be a sedate, wimpy little grandmother?"

"And now you can handle a battalion of angry marines with a switch."

Harriet laughed. "See? Nick's rubbed off on you, too." A roll of thunder punctuated her comment. "Bye now. Don't get wet."

On that unsatisfactory note, Willa departed. She arrived home just as the storm broke, sending down sheets of gray water.

It was Claudine's day at school with Bethany. They weren't yet home. At loose ends, she made herself a pot of tea and sat at the kitchen counter in the deepening gloom, watching the rain beat against the kitchen windows.

She almost didn't hear the telephone above the thunder.

"It's Claudine. I'm still at school with Bethany. It's raining too hard for us to make a dash for the car. I just didn't want you to worry."

"Are John and Clytie home?"

"No, Clytie went with John into Jacksonville. She's shopping. John's at a director's meeting of some sort. We're on our own for supper. Shall I stop by O'Steen's. They have terrific seafood takeouts."

"None for me. You and Bethany enjoy." A clap of thunder and a bolt of lightning caused a wave of static on the line that jarred the eardrums.

Claudine squeaked. "Oh! I'm hanging up!"

Willa stood in the gloom feeling more miserable by the moment. She went around the cottage switching on lights until a cozy glow permeated every nook.

The lights flickered. A gust of wind caught on the doors and windows, rattling them in their frames. It was a few seconds before she realized there was a steady rhythm to the rattling. She yanked open the kitchen door.

"Amanda!" The girl was wet through, her knit shirt clung to her, outlining small round breasts. Water dripped off shaggy cutoffs onto her legs and down into her tennis shoes. "Heavens! Come in." Willa glanced beyond the teenager with hope in her heart. "Is your dad here?"

"No. I've left him."

"Left him? Wait, we'll talk in a minute. You're shivering. Let's get you into dry clothes."

Amanda was willing to be led upstairs and shooed into the bathroom. Willa found a bulky terry robe she seldom wore and passed it to the girl. "I was just having some tea. Does that suit?"

"Hot chocolate sounds better," came the lilting, muffled reply.

Downstairs Willa dialed Nick's home number. No answer. Wondering how best to handle Amanda, she heated milk and stirred in chocolate mix. Chocolate instead of tea. The girl had no trouble being politely assertive. But how was she with Nick? Smug? Constrained? Self-centered? Angry?

Lightning crackled, the lights dimmed, thunder pounded, the door flew open and Nick stumbled into the kitchen.

He regained his balance. "I fell over her damned bicycle so I know she's here!" Fury racked his voice. "Don't try to hide her."

"Hide—?" Willa's chest constricted with anger.

Amanda leaned over the upstairs balcony. "You can't make me go back with you," she yelled. "You can't!"

"Like hell!"

"Stop it! Both of you!"

Nick and Amanda gaped.

"All right. Just stay calm." Willa carried the hot chocolate to the foot of the stairs. Amanda came down to take it but then retreated midway up the staircase and sat down. "You're welcome," Willa said pointedly.

"Thank you," Amanda mumbled.

"What for you?" she asked, rejoining Nick. "Coffee, hot chocolate, or tea? The tea is steeping."

"Nothing, thanks. I'll just take Amanda and go."

"No, you won't," a voice came from the steps.

Willa spun about. "Amanda, shut up."

"Don't talk to her like that."

"This is my house. I won't be caught in the middle of your petty squabbles."

"Petty?" Nick raged. "You know what she did? She filled my house up with boys! Surfers, beach bums!"

"We were on the beach. It started to rain. I just asked them in. We weren't doing anything."

Willa handed Nick a kitchen towel. "Dry off. You're dripping all over the floor."

"They drank all my beer." His words were muffled as he ran the towel over his head and face. "My house-keeper quit. Amanda never picks up after herself . . . there are clothes from one end of the house to the other . . . dirty dishes piled in the sink every day—"

"Fatherhood is a whole lot different from bachelor-hood, isn't it?"

He wadded up the towel and tossed it onto the counter. "Gloat, why don't you?"

"Nick, you're an unreformed male chauvinist. It's just no one has ever caught you at it before."

"I'm her father! I only want what's best for her."

"He asked me if I was still a virgin!" Amanda yelled. She started to cry.

Willa cringed. "Nick! How could you?"

He sank onto a kitchen stool and sighed wearily. "All those boys in the house— Damn it. It just slipped out."

"You mean you made assumptions."

"I was...mad."

Willa lowered her voice. "I made an assumption about you and Susan—remember? How did that make you feel?"

"Awful, and you know it."

"I rest my case." She moved around him to the stove. "I'll make a pot of coffee."

Nick watched her a moment then went to speak to Amanda. Willa stayed in the kitchen alcove. He was back just as the coffee had finished perking.

He shook his head. "She's stubborn."

"Gets it from your side of the family," Willa said dryly.

"I deserve every lousy name you can think to call me."

"True." After a moment, she poured the coffee, slid a cup toward him.

"She wants to stay here with you," Nick said glumly. "I'm a failure as a father."

"You'll improve. It takes time. And common sense."

"It takes uncommon sense, if you ask me. I don't see how people raise kids without losing their sanity."

"You'll adjust."

His eyes followed her as she poured tea for herself and took a sip. He lowered his voice. "You're beautiful."

Willa kept very still. "Thank you."

"If it wasn't raining I'd ask you to walk me to my car, maybe sit in the back seat for a while."

"I haven't had an offer like that in years," she replied lightly.

"You don't mind if Amanda bunks down with you for a few days? Until she cools off?"

"It'll be okay. If she doesn't mind the sofa."

"I'd sleep on a marble slab if it meant I didn't have to go back to his house!"

"I didn't invite you," Nick directed to the stairs. "You came on your own."

"You're just like Alfredo and Mother. You care less about me than your precious servant."

"I do care about you, damn it!"

"Nick," Willa suggested, "maybe you ought to leave. Arguing like this won't get you anywhere—either of you. Anyway, you're functioning on an adrenaline high. You need to back off, be objective."

"I am objective."

"Go home."

"My place is a wreck."

"It can be cleaned. Get some rest. You look as if you could use it."

Her jerked his head toward Amanda. "I do. She keeps the television on until all hours of the night."

"I'll talk to her."

He devoured Willa with his eyes for a heartbeat and groaned, "Ah, hell..."

"My sentiments equal yours," Willa said.

"You're making it tough for me to leave." He moved to the door, opened it and looked out. "It's still raining."

Willa wanted to pry herself from behind the counter and go to him, but Amanda's presence inhibited her. She took a deep breath.

Nick shook his head. A shadow crossed his face as he glanced toward the stairs and Amanda. "We'll talk later—among other things.'' Then he was out the door and running across the yard to the Elliotts' driveway.

Willa watched him through the kitchen window until the rain hid him. Among other things. She discovered herself more than willing to explore thoughts of those ''other things.''

''He's gone?''

Willa snapped out of her reverie. ''Yes. Want a sandwich? I was just going to make myself one.''

''The food here is so different.''

''Are you homesick?''

''No—never.'' Amanda plopped onto the stool Nick had vacated. ''Maybe for the language. But when I get English better, I think I won't even miss that.''

''Your English is excellent.''

''Excellent enough for me to have a job?''

''I think so. But there may be some legal snags. You're a visitor—''

''I have American citizenship. My mother is American, as were my grandparents. They registered my birth with the embassy in Switzerland. When Alfredo adopted me, they refused to allow him to subsume my American citizenship.''

''Then you only need apply for a social-security card. Nick will help you with that. But if you want a job to meet other teens, why don't we see what alternatives are available? I may know someone who can help.''

Amanda closed her eyes and tilted her head back. Her neck was long and elegant. She was going to make a striking woman, Willa knew. ''I'm glad I came to you. You soften Nick. He'll do what you say.''

Willa laughed. ''Don't count on that.''

''His idea of being a father is rules and more rules. He just wants to buy me things. I dreamed many times about what it would be like to have a real family, a real father, a mother who cares for me." Amanda smiled wanly. "I don't want things. I want to be doted on—like Bethany."

"You will be. You have to get to know each other first. Here, let me make you another cup of hot chocolate, then I'll tell you a story—about Bethany."

"I HATE IT that Nick is having problems with Amanda," said Claudine.

"They'll work it out. It's just they've both been imagining perfection. If we're going to go through those clothes you mentioned—"

Claudine led the way upstairs. At Susan's bedroom, she hesitated, her face drawn. "We seldom go in here anymore. It's too painful."

"Claudine, please. You don't have to. All Amanda needs is a pair of shorts and a shirt or two to last until Nick brings some of her things over."

"I should've cleaned out Susan's things once we knew that she was . . . I couldn't make myself do it."

A musty, unused smell assaulted Willa. She gazed about the room. It was dark. The small lamp at the bedside did little to eliminate shadows. The walls were paneled in dark wood, the furniture heavy and draped in brown.

"You see why I wanted to brighten it up on her sixteenth birthday," Claudine said. "We put up wall hangings, but Susan tore them down. It's like a cave in here."

"Or a womb," Willa said, thinking of how Susan must have suffered. How confused she must've been—and how out of control.

"What an odd observation. But I think you're right. Susan did a lot of her living in here. It used to be Natalie's room."

Willa opened her mouth to speak, but the look on Claudine's face stopped her. Claudine went to a closet, switched on the light inside. "There are dresses in here Susan never wore. Lovely, frilly things. I imagine they're out of style now."

Willa riffled through them. She chose two sundresses, and out of a chest of drawers, a pair of tan Bermuda shorts and a knit shirt. "These will do."

"You're certain?" Claudine shivered. "I'm going to have this room painted. White or yellow."

"I approve wholeheartedly," Willa said. The room was giving her the shivers, too.

"Speaking of approval..." Claudine cleared her throat. "You know last Saturday when I went to the ladies' exchange luncheon? They had a fashion show. Some of the models were my age."

"And?"

"Well, the moderator approached me afterward. She said I had photogenic bones in my face and asked would I be interested in modeling."

"You could do it!"

"Not so much enthusiasm yet. I'd have to take a course."

"Well?"

"John's against it. He said it would be flaunting my body, unseemly for a woman my age."

"Flaunting?" Willa laughed. "Work on him."

"With what?"

"Your unseemly body."

"Willa!"

"He's not that old. And neither are you." Willa paused. "Maybe that's what's worrying him."

"I don't think so. Age *has* taken a toll, you know."

"He's worried you'll outgrow him. That you'll find some new and exciting life and leave him behind."

"At my age?"

"Fears don't age, Claudine. They just thicken."

"You may be right. His waist certainly has."

"I've got to get back to the cottage before the skies open up again. Or these clothes will be as wet as those Amanda arrived in. Oh, and can you pick Bethany up from school tomorrow? I have errands to run."

"My pleasure. What about Amanda?"

"She's got her bike. She's going to cycle around the old city, take in the sights."

"Well, tell her to come up to the house for lunch."

"Thanks. I'll pass the invitation along."

On the back porch Claudine put her arms around Willa. "I'm so glad you came to us. I don't feel so empty anymore."

Willa looked into the older woman's eyes. "Neither do I."

Chapter Thirteen

Joanne Green looked around the hospital cafeteria and laughed. "This wasn't what I had in mind when we agreed to lunch."

"I'm sorry, but I've only a few minutes between home visits."

"The center is keeping you busy?"

"Not a spare minute. But I'm learning a lot."

Joanne frowned. "You're not thinking of staying on with them permanently?"

"Never. I'd be on a collision course with burnout within a year."

Joanne relaxed. "I knew I chose right."

"I need another favor," Willa said, and told the personnel director about Amanda.

"Cavenaugh?" mused Joanne. "Nick Cavenaugh has a daughter? Bless my soul."

Willa was disconcerted. "You know Nick?"

"He's only one of the most eligible bachelors in St. Augustine." Joanne watched Willa's cheeks redden. "Don't tell me. He's no longer eligible. You've hooked him."

"No."

"But he's dangling."

Willa gave an embarrassed laugh. "No." But Joanne had tweaked the green-eyed monster within her. "You know Nick well?"

"He probated my dad's will and still looks after the estate for my mother. And when Nick's parents visit they always come over and speak to our nursing students. They really inspire."

"Small world."

"And getting smaller. As for Amanda, we'd be glad to have her join our candy stripers. She'll meet kids her own age. In no time at all she'll feel like one of St. Augustine's own. Have her sign up."

"I'll bring her over myself after the holiday."

"Planning on going to the fireworks tomorrow night?"

"Nick's bringing his boat around to the city pier. We're going to watch from the bay."

Smiling, Joanne arched an eyebrow. "Nice."

IT WAS MORE THAN NICE, Willa thought, observing the activity in Matanzas Bay. On either side of the Bridge of Lions, only the channel was free of the anchored fleet of sloops, sailboats and yachts. It was becoming dusk and running lights were beginning to blink on. Flags rippled softly in the rain-washed breeze. A lively Ray Charles tune carried across the water from one of the other boats. Willa felt the beat of the piano in her bones.

"You look fabulous standing there," Nick said, moving up beside her. "I'm glad you decided to come. You saved me the trouble of shanghaiing you."

"Being shanghaied looks pretty good to me right this minute."

"Uh-oh. Amanda is giving you a hard time."

"Nope. She's even learning how to keep house. Bethany is teaching her."

"Then what's the frown for?"

"I've found Amanda a job—"

"She doesn't need to work. I'll take care of her."

"Now you sound like John. It's a volunteer slot with the candy stripers at the hospital. She needs to be with kids her own age. It'll give her something to feel good about."

"Does she need to feel good?"

"About herself, yes. Everyone does."

Nick looked down at the smooth surface of the water then up to the sky where a magic canopy of stars was beginning to light up against a velvet sky. "I want to be her father. I want to do all the things a father is supposed to. I can't seem to get it right, at least not in her opinion."

"She's almost an adult. You've been treating her like an infant."

"She reminds me of how Susan was."

Willa turned and glared at him. "You said it yourself, Susan was sick. Amanda is not sick."

"Amanda likes boys too much."

"She's just looking for affection wherever she can get it."

"You're saying I should be more affectionate?"

"Yes."

"Willa, I have a small box of a house. She runs around in it practically naked! How can I be affectionate with a teenage nymph?"

"Buy a bigger house! Demonstrate appropriate behavior."

"Okay."

"Okay? Just like that?"

His hand trailed up her spine and then down again to circle her waist. "What about this for appropriate behavior?"

Willa's defenses were melting. "You're trying to change the subject."

"I want to be alone with you, off on an island somewhere. So when we fight we can make up for hours on end."

"Do you know what you and I should do?"

"Get into the dinghy and make love under the stars?"

"We should say goodbye. We should get out of each other's life."

Nick was looking at her incredulously. "You're crazy. We're made for each other."

"You don't know me at all and you should be paying attention to your daughter."

"I tried, but she's got the binoculars glued to her eyes watching for boys."

"You don't know that."

"She told me. 'See that one, Nick. He's got cute buns.'" He mimicked Amanda's lilt perfectly.

"Then you should be spending time with Roddy."

"He's teaching Bethany how to tie knots." He held up his hand to forestall her stalling. "John and Claudine are perfectly content sitting on the aft deck, and Clytie is in the galley laying out our supper. You're stuck with me."

Stuck. That was it. That was why Willa was making an about-face. Amanda, Bethany...two kids—he was thinking marriage. But marriage brought all kinds of responsibilities, especially a marriage that started out with two ready-made children. "You're scared," he accused.

"You don't know what you're talking about."

He pulled her down on the deck. "Yes, I do," he whispered lest what he said carried to all and sundry across the water. "Let's talk about us."

He lowered his head and put his mouth on hers. His tongue searched entry, found it and thrust deep. Willa closed her eyes, accepting his caresses. She could feel the heat building inside her. Her arms went around him, her hands caressed his neck.

He began to nibble on her earlobe. "I need you," he said softly, intensely. "Like I've never needed a woman in my life. I've lost five pounds since I met you. I'm pining away."

"It doesn't feel like you're pining away," she murmured, feeling him swollen and throbbing against her thigh.

"What are you doing on top of my mommy?"

Nick jerked. "Nothing. She had something in her eye."

Willa cleared her throat. "What is it, sweetie?"

"Clytie says come eat. She says she's not goin' to be stuck in the galley when the fireworks start." She turned and made her way back to the aft. "I just saw Nick kissing my mommy," came clearly on the breeze to Willa and Nick.

He groaned. "Cut her tongue out."

Willa laughed, but softly. "You go aft first, I'll follow in a minute."

"In my condition? Think again."

By the time Nick joined them for the alfresco supper, the fireworks had begun. Pom-poms and fizgigs and pinwheels burst overhead accompanied by the ooohs and aaahs of the spectators. A shower of cinders and tailings scattered and fell into the water with a hiss and the reek of cordite hung in the air. The last firework was a grand display of the American flag in all its splendor. When it faded there was a swell of applause from the boats and the crowds ashore.

"This has been one of the nicest evenings I've spent outdoors in years," announced Claudine.

"Do I hafta go home now?" asked Roddy.

Nick clapped him on the shoulder. "You do, sport. But suppose you help me batten down the ship and I'll let you man the tiller on the dinghy while we ferry these land-lubbers ashore?"

"All right!"

Amanda stood next to Willa as Nick helped Claudine and Clytie down into the small craft. "Why can't he be that way with me?"

She put her arm around the teenager and squeezed gently. "He will be, he just hasn't found the right approach."

It took two trips to get them all to the city pier. Nick and Roddy walked the five blocks with them through the historical district. Street lamps lit their way along the narrow cobblestoned lanes. Roddy and Bethany ran ahead, which gave them time to inspect dark nooks and crannies for who knew what.

"How are you going to get Roddy home?" Willa asked, knowing Nick had left his car at the yacht club.

"I was hoping you'd offer to give us a lift."

"I need to get Bethany bedded down."

"Can't Amanda do that? She's old enough."

"I—"

"I can do it," offered Amanda.

"Maybe if Clytie—"

"I'll check for boogeymen and locked doors, but then I'm off to bed," Clytie shot over her shoulder. "I'm beat."

"John and I can sit with Amanda and Bethany," added Claudine. But Willa was watching Amanda's face. The girl's expression had stiffened.

"Oh, I think Amanda can manage Bethany on her own," Willa heard herself saying. She hung back a few seconds until the others were a yard or two ahead of her and Nick. "When you say good-night to Amanda, give her a hug," she whispered to him.

He gave her a baleful glance. "She'll bite my head off."

"If she does, I'll administer first aid."

"Suppose I require mouth-to-mouth resuscitation?"

Willa's chin went up a degree. "Let's catch up to the others, why don't we?"

She struck out ahead of him.

Smiling to himself, Nick sauntered along behind watching the fluid way Willa moved. The promise of sensuality in her was so potent it was almost tangible. And once they'd dropped Roddy off, he'd have her to himself. He was daring the devil. But it didn't matter. She may have bruised it a bit, but his heart was still in one piece.

"AMANDA," Willa said as she ushered Roddy and Bethany into the cottage, "your dad wants a word with you outside."

The teenager wrinkled her nose. "That sounds like the matron ordering me into her office for discipline."

"It's not an order. He's in a good mood. Go." She glanced over her should and caught Nick's eye. "A hug," she mouthed silently.

Nick rolled his eyes, but once Amanda was near him, he gingerly put his arm across her shoulders. "Let's talk a minute," he said.

Amanda eyed him warily. "About what?"

"About us." Amanda was holding herself rigid beneath his arm. He wanted to shake her, loosen her up.

"I'm too much trouble. You want to send me back to Milan."

"I don't want to send you anywhere. I want you with me. I want to spend time with you, to get to know you—the real you. We need to learn to be comfortable in each other's space. So how would you like to go out on a date with your dad? Saturday night?"

"A date?"

"Sure . . . we'll go to dinner, then the movies."

"That's funny. Going on a date with my own father . . ."

"You're ashamed to be seen with me. I'm ugly. I'm too fat, too old-fashioned. I wear suspenders—"

Amanda giggled. "You know you're not."

"Do we have a date?"

"Just by ourselves?"

"Just you and me."

"Okay. But I'll need a dress. I want to look my best. I've never had a date."

"Never?"

Amanda shook her head. "Will we go to a very grown-up place?"

"Very grown-up." He pulled her to him and kissed her on her brow. Amanda flushed.

"Perhaps I should think about coming home?" she said cautiously.

"Let's work out the details on Saturday."

"You're not angry that I came? That I—"

"Amanda, I'm so glad you found me I'm beside myself."

She sniffed. "You don't always act like it."

He grinned. "I'm improving. Admit it."

"Maybe a little."

He patted her shoulder. "Go on inside. Tell Willa and Roddy to hop to it."

"You're in love with Willa?"

Nick lost his voice. "I—uh . . ."

Amanda laughed. She gave Nick a quick, shy peck on the cheek and slipped away.

He watched her as she passed through the kitchen and disappeared up the stairs. I did that right, he thought, surprised. He felt good all over.

"You're wearing a cat-who-ate-the-canary smirk," Willa told him a moment later.

"I'll drive," he said, holding out his hand for the car keys. Willa gave them over. In the car he started the engine and began to back out. Willa tapped him on the shoulder.

"Don't you think we ought to wait for Roddy? He's using the bathroom."

"What? Oh. Sure."

Willa grinned. "Being a parent does have its moments, doesn't it?"

By the time they arrived at Keta Worthington's, Roddy was sound asleep between them. Nick carried him in. Keta looked strained.

"We go to court on Friday. You haven't forgotten?"

"I'll be there," Willa assured her.

"I don't want to lose my son."

"Keta—you won't. You're doing everything right."

"I'm still scared."

"I know. It is scary. Please, think positive."

"I just took his shoes off," Nick said, emerging from Roddy's bedroom.

"I know it's late, but can the two of you stay for tea?"

Declining, Nick took Willa's elbow and ushered her out.

"We could've stayed for a cup of tea," Willa protested once out of Keta's hearing. "You were almost rude to her."

"And you are telling her she wouldn't lose custody of Roddy, building what might be a false hope. I deal in realities."

"I don't think she'll lose custody of Roddy. How can the judge—"

"He can call it any way he sees it. Keta is accused of not feeding her kid."

"But she does!"

"Judge Henley is a meat-and-potatoes man."

"Judge Henley? Isn't he the one the courthouse staff is having a birthday luncheon for?"

"Right. On Friday."

"But, he's—" She stopped.

"He's what?"

"Never mind."

"Suits me. I don't want to talk business."

"What do you want to talk about?"

"Nothing. I have other things on my mind."

Willa's stomach began to flutter with uncommon activity. "Is it permissible for me to ask where we're going?"

"We're going to the beach?"

"In the middle of the night?"

"I'm going to drive this rattletrap right down to the water's edge and we're going to get out, roll up our pants legs and wade in the surf in the moonlight."

"Why, Nick. That's romantic."

The moon was out, the canopy of stars brilliant, the waves lapping lazily ashore. Nick stared mutely. Dozens of others had had the same idea as he. Cars were bull-dozing up and down the packed sand. Couples strolled past hand in hand. Children raced back and forth waving sparklers.

"So much for my romantic evening," he said glumly.

Willa slid over next to him. "We can make of it what we will," she heard herself saying, her voice so faint Nick had to lean forward to hear.

He put his arm around her. She felt the weight of bone, the breadth of his hand span in the firm pressure he exerted. He bent his head and touched his lips to hers. He felt her breasts rising and falling against his chest. Moving from her lips he expelled a long sigh. "I'm crazy about you, Willa. I just want to eat you up. I want—"

The sound of the surf, the smell of the sea, and Nick's arms around her acted as an aphrodisiac. Willa could feel desire surging, filling her, and an undercurrent of excitement sprang palpably to life. Light-headed, she put her hand on his thigh. "Kiss me again, Nick. Hold me...."

IT WAS NINE O'CLOCK in the morning and Willa sat, sipping herbal tea in Keta's kitchen. Roddy was outside, weeding the garden. "That's my idea," she said. "Think you can pull it off?" She needn't have asked. The line of determination was so firmly etched around Keta's mouth it appeared set in stone.

"I'll produce so many mouth-watering, cholesterol-free, meatless concoctions Judge Henley won't know what hit him."

"It could backfire y'know," Willa warned. "We might both be hung by our toes for impeding justice or something. And not a word to Nick." She opened her purse and took out an envelope of cash. "Here's what the courthouse staff collected. Remember, when you deliver everything, you're Worthington Catering Services.''

Keta's determined mouth melted into a thin grin. ''That has a nice ring to it.''

''If you need any help, I can come over tonight when I get off work.''

Keta came around the table and put her arms awkwardly around Willa. ''I can do it. I won't fail you, or Roddy.''

''The probate clerk's name is Gena. You see her. She'll show you where to set up.''

Keta moved to the door and looked out at Roddy. ''I'm trembling, but now I really have hope.''

Willa smiled. ''It's the single most important ingredient in life. I've got to run. I've got clients backed up to my kazoo and I've got to be in Nick's office by two-thirty.''

''I hope when he discovers what we've done, you won't be in Dutch.''

A warmth seeped into Willa. She and Nick had not succumbed entirely to wayward passion on the beach, but they had come awfully close. The possibility of what might yet happen—had to happen—was meant to happen, stayed foremost in her mind. ''If the hearing goes in your favor we won't have to worry about Nick.''

''What if it doesn't?''

Willa arched a brow in mock despair. ''Then I'll worry.''

Chapter Fourteen

She arrived at Nick's office with thirty seconds to spare. Harriet didn't bother to look up from her typing. She just lifted her hand and waved Willa into Nick's private sanctum.

Mr. and Mrs. Wilton were sitting in chairs before his desk. They did not look happy. Near a bank of windows sat Juliana and an elderly, sweet-faced woman whom Willa surmised was the grandmother.

"Ah," Nick said. "Here's Mrs. Manning." He indicated a chair placed strategically off to one side of his desk. It was positioned to face the agitated couple.

Behind them, Juliana caught Willa's eyes and lifted both her hands. She had her fingers crossed. Without moving her hands from her lap, Willa reciprocated.

"We don't have any idea why you've insisted we come in," said Mrs. Wilton.

"Too true," growled her husband. "We decided against using your services, Cavenaugh. We don't seem to be on the same wavelength here."

Nick's expression was cold to the point of ice. "Oh, I think we're on the same wavelength, Wilton. I've discovered from several of my colleagues that you've approached them in the same manner you approached me. Not a single one of them has been able to collect a fee.''

"They didn't do anything to earn it!'' snapped Mrs. Wilton.

Nick glared at the two of them. "We'll get to that in a moment. What we're dealing with this afternoon are allegations of child abuse.''

"What!'' Mr. Wilton leaped from his chair.

"That's your mother's doing!'' shouted his wife, turning to snarl her lip at the woman.

"Sit down,'' Nick ordered, authority present on every syllable.

Mr. Wilton puffed up, but he sat. "I have never in my life hit Juliana.''

"We're speaking of mental abuse. That's Mrs. Manning's specialty and why she's here. If you recall, she interviewed Juliana as a courtesy to me. You two use Juliana as a pawn in your squabbles. Juliana doesn't like that. It's distracting to her. It makes her unhappy. She can't study. You don't allow her to have friends over—''

"We like our privacy,'' Mrs. Wilton interrupted.

"Good. Because Juliana would prefer to live with her grandmother.''

"We can't allow that,'' Mr. Wilton said.

"She's *our* daughter,'' his wife agreed.

"You two don't live under the same roof. Whose home would you prefer she lived in?''

"Mine!'' said Mr. Wilton.

"All you keep in your fridge is beer,'' his wife announced, sarcasm evident. "Juliana would starve to death. She's better off with me.''

"But you don't cook, Mama,'' Juliana said from the back of the room. "I eat at Grandma's every day.''

Nick turned to Willa. "What would the County do in a situation like this?"

She swallowed. She had no rights whatsoever in this situation, except as an ordinary citizen. "Well, once a formal complaint is filed, and that can be done anonymously by any one of us, even Juliana, there would be an investigation."

"Investigation of what?" asked Mrs. Wilton. Her tone was a little less bold.

"The way in which you live. How you care for Juliana—"

"She takes care of herself."

"Eleven-year-olds are not supposed to take care of themselves. They require love, guidance, food, clothing, positive affirmation and stability."

Nick suddenly leaned forward, piercing the Wiltons with his gaze. "The two of you are spoiled, ineffectual, immature adults. Juliana has more common sense and intellect then the both of you put together. I think a juvenile court judge would find in her favor." He reached for the telephone.

The Wiltons panicked. "Wait!" they chorused.

"What for?" Nick asked innocently. "We're at an impasse."

Mr. Wilton's eyes darted from Nick to Willa. "Surely we can work this out?"

Nick allowed his lips to curve upward in a bare smile. "If you have any ideas, I'm willing to listen."

"It's simple. We'll let Juliana move across the street and stay with Mother."

"I won't agree to that," said Mrs. Wilton with a toss of her blond curls.

Her husband turned on her. "Yes, you will—if you want to stay married to me. I don't want my good name dragged through Juvenile Court."

"We came here for a divorce in the first place," Mrs. Wilton spit out.

"You want it? You got it. I'll hire Cavenaugh as my attorney. You get your own."

Mrs. Wilton tossed off a shrug. "You don't mean it. You're bluffing—as usual."

"Try me. I'm tired of being made the scapegoat. I'll go through with it." He sounded as if he meant it.

Mrs. Wilton crumbled. "If Juliana wants to live across the street, it's all right by me. I'm tired of her filling up the fridge with her experiments anyway."

Juliana raced forward, hugging first her dad, then her mother. "Thank you! Thank you!" She smiled at Willa, and out of view of her parents, gave Willa the victory sign. "C'mon, Gram, let's go get my room ready."

The Wiltons, too, got up to leave.

"Just a minute," Nick called to them.

In unison, they turned back.

"Leave a check for five hundred dollars with my secretary, please. For services rendered. And both of you sign it."

A moment later the office door was closed. Nick swiveled in his chair to face Willa. "Come sit in my lap and let me do nice things to you."

"My job could be on the line for participating in what we just did."

"Wrong. You had every right, and according to the laws in this state, the obligation."

"You're good at what you do. I'll give you that."

"Only good? What about nice? Sexy? Extraordinary?"

"You left out arrogant."

He reached out and pulled her into his lap. "I was saving arrogant." His hand slipped beneath her blouse to cup her breast while he nuzzled her neck. He made a throaty inarticulate sound.

"Stop that," Willa said weakly while tiny, thundering sensations began to sweep over her. "Suppose somebody walks in?"

"The whole world can walk in for all I care."

"Well, here's the whole world," said Harriet brightly, standing on the threshold.

"Cripes!" Nick yelped.

"It's not what you think, Harriet," Willa said.

"Whatever it is," she said pithily, "here's that check from the Wiltons." Her gaze swept first Willa then Nick. "Why don't you invest part of it—in a motel room?"

"The reason I hired you, Harriet, is you have a solution to everything."

"I know that."

She laughed, pivoted and exited the office.

Willa straightened her clothes. "I have to get back to work. I still have to see Mrs. Wheatly."

"You'd leave me like this, in the middle of passion? When I was just getting a feel for you?"

Willa flashed him one of her more flamboyant smiles and kissed him demurely on the forehead. "Some of us are destined to suffer more than others."

"There'll come a time when I'll make you eat those words."

She turned to leave. "I'm breathless with anticipation."

"Good. Put me down for Sunday."

Her step faltered. "Not before?"

"Well, I'll see you in court tomorrow afternoon. Other than that, I'm booked. Busy attorney that I am."

"You're up to something."

"No more than you."

"What would I be up to?" Her voice was hardly more than the chirp of a sparrow.

The intercom buzzed. "Duty calls," announced Harriet. "Mr. Cameron is here."

Willa made a hasty exit with a breezy wave of her hand. And all the way to Mrs. Wheatly's she wondered if Nick had gotten wind of the newly created Worthington Catering Services.

"I WISH ALL THE OLD LADIES you see at work sent me fudge," said Bethany.

"All of them don't cook like Mrs. Wheatly. And, even if they did, I'm not supposed to accept it."

"Then I think we should eat all the evidence," said Amanda, reaching across the counter.

Willa whisked the plate from under her hand. "After supper. No, make that after supper dishes—which you two can wash."

The girls sent up a collective moan.

Clytie knocked to announce her presence, and came through the door. "What'd you say to Claudine?" she asked of Willa.

"Nothing. I haven't seen her today. Why?"

"She's rooting through the attic for who-knows-what and won't say boo about what she's searching for." Clytie climbed up on a stool and crossed her little stick legs. "Invite me to supper."

"Consider yourself invited. Claudine is an open book, so what's the mystery?"

"I thought you might know. When I offered to help her find whatever it is she's looking for, she snapped at me and clammed up."

"What does John say?"

"Say? He's scared to open his mouth. Claudine's behaving all out of character."

"Maybe she's just getting into character. She wants to take that modeling course."

"That's another thing. The discussions she and John are having about that are not fit for human ears."

"I hope she brings him around."

"She'll have to change a century of Elliott thinking to manage that."

"But, Clytie—you went to work. John senior didn't stop you."

"Ah! But I'm an Elliott by osmosis. I've never been married to one. Besides, I never made the mistake of asking could I do something. I just went and did it." Clytie turned to Amanda. "How's your daddy?"

"Oh, he's fine. We're going out to dinner together Saturday night. Just the two of us."

"I want to go," said Bethany.

"You can't."

"But I want to."

"Bethany," Willa cautioned. "Amanda and her dad want some time together. Nick wants to get to know Amanda better."

"He knew me first!"

"That has nothing to do with it."

"That's not fair!" Puffed up, Bethany stalked upstairs where she leaned over the railing. "Don't anybody talk to me! I'm mad."

Clytie arched a brow. "Boy, have I heard that line more times than I can count."

"From whom?" Willa asked.

"Susan."

Pain washed over Willa's features.

Clytie rushed to apologize. "I wasn't thinking straight. Claudine's got me rattled."

"It's not that. It's... Amanda, go start Bethany's bathwater."

"Before we eat?"

"Shoo." Willa turned back to Clytie. "Did Susan ever see a doctor?"

"Of course."

"I mean ... for mental illness?"

"Are you kidding? The Elliotts do not suffer any mental dysfunctions whatsoever. So speaketh the master of the house."

"But she might've been ill."

"Willa ... Susan was spoiled, self-centered and a very private person. She was with us, but outside of us. When she was happy, she was a delight to be around. When she wasn't, she made our lives miserable."

"But didn't anyone ever wonder about her mood swings?"

"What mood swings? She was a teenager. Teens think they know everything, don't they?"

"We know all the modern things," said Amanda, coming out of the bathroom and passing through the kitchen.

Willa frowned. "I know a teenager who had better stop eavesdropping."

Amanda sniffed haughtily. "Nick wouldn't like it if he knew you spoke to me like that."

"See?" said Clytie. "Sweet as pie one minute and frog droppings the next."

Willa drew in a quavering breath, then exhaled slowly. Give it up, she told herself. Whatever Susan's problem, it had not manifested itself in Bethany.

Yet.

She shook off the afterthought. "Which do you prefer, Clytie? Hamburgers or spaghetti."

"Spaghetti. With lots of garlic."

Willa grinned impishly. "What! No heavy date tonight?"

"No. What about you?"

Willa shook her head.

"Ain't it awful when our men ignore us?" Clytie commiserated.

"Mine is up to something sly."

"And mine is so old he can't get up to anything."

Willa laughed. "Lots of garlic, it is," she said.

SHE COULD NOT STAY AWAY from the courthouse until two-thirty. Too much was at stake. Not only Keta's custody of Roddy, but her relationship with Nick—in the event that anything went wrong. There was a line of people in the probate office. She couldn't catch Gena's eye. Outside the office in the hall she was snared by the HRS caseworker who had initiated the proceedings against Keta. Willa's heart sank. The woman had a hard edge and a cynical attitude.

"Your report to Juvenile Court puts us in a bad light," she accused.

"I was told to be objective. I was. I am. And the child is in good health. The doctor verified it."

"The mother is weird, a vegetarian—"

"We don't follow blueprints when it comes to motherhood," Willa lashed out. "A woman has a right to raise her child as she sees fit."

"Not if it's harmful to the child."

"You know what I think? I think you don't have a leg to stand on. I think you haven't been able to verify a single instance of Keta Worthington not feeding her son."

"Your supervisor is going to hear from me."

Willa stared at the woman in dismay. "You want the judge to remove Roddy from his mother, don't you? You actually want it."

"I only want what's best for the boy."

"No, you don't. You want what's best for you. You just want to close out a file."

"You're new here. You better get with the program if you want to survive."

"Survive?" Willa's eyes narrowed to slits. "I know more about survival than you could guess. You're a bully. Please do call my supervisor. Then perhaps he'll call yours." She pivoted on her heel and bumped into Nick.

"Whoa. What's—"

"Not a word, Nick. Not a single word."

"Where's Keta? We're due in chambers in less than a minute."

"Here!" she said, rushing up with Roddy in tow. She opened her mouth to speak to Willa, but Nick took her by the elbow and whisked mother and son into the elevator. He held the door. "Coming?"

The HRS caseworker, face set, brushed past Willa. She had no choice but to follow. It was a silent, tense ride up. Keta had her eyes closed. Praying, Willa knew. The caseworker was first off the elevator. Wordless, Keta thrust a paper into Willa's hand.

They were barley seated at their respective tables in the small courtroom when the judge entered. The bailiff ordered them all to rise, be seated. Then, wearing a bored expression, he moved to the side of the room.

Unobtrusively Willa smoothed out the note Keta had passed to her. The judge spoke. "I've read the files and reports. Little boys should not have to live without hot-dogs and hamburgers—"

"Your Honor," Nick said, "There are a number of children who are allergic to the preservatives and hormones in beef and pork."

"And is Roddy Worthington one of those who's allergic?"

"No. But his mother would rather he did not eat a food that she, and many others find harmful."

"I've eaten beef and pork my entire life," said the judge. "It hasn't done me any harm."

Willa spoke out. "But aren't you on a low-cholesterol diet that restricts meat of all kinds? Hasn't a lifetime of indulging in meat fats caused—"

"Aren't you sitting at the wrong table, Mrs. Manning? Defense is seated on your left."

Willa could feel the malice emanating from her colleague in waves. She gave the judge her most winning smile. "The County pays my salary, Your Honor. I'm obligated—"

"Good. One of your obligations is not to interrupt."

Willa stood. "Then may I have your permission to speak?"

"One minute. Then we'll hear from HRS."

Face flaming, Willa asked, "How was your birthday luncheon?"

"Superlative. But, Mrs. Manning, we do try not to bring personal situations into the courtroom. Now let's get on with it."

"Your Honor, if Mrs. Worthington allowed her son to eat the foods you ate at your luncheon, would you consider that she fed her child well?"

"I don't see what that has to do with this case, but, yes—"

Willa glanced quickly at the note. "Let's see, there was mock cheese cake with fresh strawberries in a honey glaze...a spinach-and-shrimp quiche made with whole-wheat flour and egg whites...oat-bran-and-date muffins...again—made with honey, not granulated sugar and a crabmeat bisque made with spices and evaporated skimmed milk, a huge fruit salad and tossed salad with—"

The judge leaned forward. "Stop. Mrs. Manning we are not here to discuss what I eat, but what Mrs. Worthington feeds her son."

"That's just it, Your Honor. Those are the foods Keta Worthington feeds Roddy. Your Honor, Mrs. Worthington catered your birthday luncheon. Vegetarian diets and low-cholesterol diets are very similar. You see, one of the benefits of being a vegetarian is that one learns to prepare food without using animal fats. Or at least, holding them to a minimum—with respect to protein."

For perhaps a second the judge looked perplexed. He rearranged some papers, then glanced up. "I'll see the boy in my chambers," he said.

The bailiff moved to Roddy. When he and the judge left the courtroom, Willa sensed a donnybrook coming on—from Nick and HRS.

"You engineered this entire—" declared her table-mate, voice angry.

Nick grabbed Willa's arm, pulling her out of earshot. "You little fool—you could've—"

"Aren't you jumping to conclusions? The judge hasn't made his decision."

"You made him look the fool."

"I didn't. I was only educating him. Like Keta educated me."

"It's my fault," said Keta. "I—"

Willa jerked her arm loose from Nick. "It isn't. We both knew the risks involved. We both—"

"All rise!"

"We're going to talk about this," Nick promised. He guided a teary Keta back to the defense table.

Judge Henley banged his gavel. "I find in favor of Mrs. Worthington. Court dismissed." He banged the gavel once again. "Mrs. Worthington, I'll see you in my chambers for a moment."

Keta was too stunned to object. The bailiff took her elbow. Every ounce of adrenaline Willa possessed drained from her body. She collapsed in the chair. She felt her eyes getting hot. "It worked."

The flaring antagonism of her colleague fanned into flames. "This is the last time you'll ever be in a courtroom with me or anyone from HRS," she rasped.

Quietly, as calmly as she could manage, Willa said. "Good. I don't like working with people who don't do their jobs well. Had you done as thorough an investigation as HRS requires, none of us would've been here."

The woman snapped her briefcase closed and stomped out.

Willa faced a thin-lipped Nick. "Well, it's your turn." She held out her arm. "Take a bite out of my hide, if it'll make you feel better."

"You could've told me what you were up to. Unofficially we were on the same side. That means no secrets. If you had gotten into trouble with your premise, Keta and Roddy would've lost—not you."

His probing gaze and anger held her rigid. "We knew the risks—"

"Willa, you took advantage of Keta's desperation."

She closed her eyes. "I'm sorry."

Keta emerged from Judge Henley's chambers with Roddy in hand. Her eyes were alight, her face free of shadows and fright. "He gave me his home address," she gushed. "His wife wants the recipes for everything!"

"We were lucky—" Willa began.

The bailiff signaled. "Mrs. Manning, Judge Henley wants to speak with you."

"Me?" She glanced from Keta to Nick, concerned.

"I wouldn't keep the man waiting if I were you," Nick said.

Willa went.

Judge Henley sat behind a great expanse of a desk. His expression was stern. He did not invite her to sit. Willa had the very real sense that she was being called on the carpet.

"Mrs. Manning, are you an attorney?"

"No, Your Honor."

"But, you like to practice law?"

"No, Your Honor, I—"

"Old dogs like myself aren't particularly fond of new tricks."

"I'm sorry."

"I'm glad to hear it. However, it's always been my policy that 'sorry' ought to pack a punch. Therefore, I'm assessing you court costs."

"But—"

"Have a nice day, Mrs. Manning."

Chapter Fifteen

"Are you sure you don't mind, Clytie? I hate to saddle you with Bethany on a Saturday."

"It won't tie me down. A few of my old cronies and I are going fishing. She can tag along. What about Amanda?"

"She'll be occupied all afternoon shopping. Nick gave her the money for a new dress."

"What possessed you to volunteer to work on a Saturday, anyway?"

"Court costs, and time-and-a-half pay," Willa said dryly.

"Judge Henley is a friend of John's. You should've mentioned that."

"Oh, sure. Then I'd've been hanged from the rafters for bribery. Look, I've got to run. I agreed to be in the office by nine. Bethany's watching cartoons and Amanda is still asleep. Oh, I meant to ask. Are John and Claudine getting along better?"

"The same. Claudine's got a wild hair and John means to pluck it."

Willa paused on the porch step. Summer dew lay thick on the carpet of grass. Claudine's flowers were lifting their heads into the early-morning sun. "I hope I didn't start something else I'll regret."

"Claudine has hinted for years that she wanted to work. The seed was already there. All you did was help it to sprout. But no matter the outcome, this time at least you won't have to pay court costs."

"Nick hasn't said two kind words to me back-to-back since that escapade. I'd hate to have Claudine and John disappointed with me, too."

"Just go on your merry path. Life has its own way of smoothing out the rough edges."

"Clytie, you sometimes make very good sense."

Clytie's eyes sparkled. "I know."

Willa went off to work, smiling. Clytie was right. Life did have a way of smoothing out the rough edges. Two months ago, she mused thoughtfully, she'd had no idea of the direction her life would take. Now she had a job, a place of her own, new friends, and Bethany had grandparents who adored her.

And she was in love.

At the office all was quiet, the telephones still for a change. She was the only staff person there. She used the time to catch up on paperwork, and daydream about Nick. Perhaps after he brought Amanda home that night, he'd stay for a while. Privacy in the cottage was at a premium. Still, just being near him caused a yearning in her heart.

"Well! My luck's improving."

Willa jerked out of her reverie to find the office Casanova eyeing her. His expression was amused. "I didn't hear you come in."

"My dear, you were so deep in thought, a herd of elephants could've marched through without discovery."

His amusement seemed coy. "You were thinking of a man."

"I might've been."

"Me, right?"

"Wrong. What're you doing here?"

"I worked an emergency last night. I'm just in to drop off the paperwork. But I have time for coffee."

"I don't."

"Touchy, aren't we?"

"Yes. What was your emergency? Do I need to follow up?"

The man shrugged off his Lothario persona and became the professional. "One of my fourteen-year-olds curled himself into the fetal position in the hallway of his home and refused to straighten out. His parents got him to the hospital. He was released this morning."

"Drug-induced paranoia?" she asked, feeling her stomach tighten. Dealing with teen drug and alcohol abuse was not her specialty. And her heart went out so, to the victims, that she was never very effective.

Joe shook his head. "This kid has never been on drugs. We've been treating him for depression. It's not easy being a kid these days. But I knew he was going to break. He'd been holed up in his room since we had that rain earlier in the week."

Willa came alert. In with the rain, out with the sun, Clytie had once said. "How does that factor in?"

Joe-the-Casanova smiled. "Wanna talk about it over coffee?"

"Yes!"

He was suddenly flustered.

Willa moved from behind her desk to the coffee machine. "I'll get it." She put the paper cup before him. He took a sip and Willa noticed for the first time the tiredness in his eyes, the slump of his shoulders.

"I really needed that," he said, and his whole carefully manufactured image of playboy dissolved. "You know my case, the old lady from Maine who has terrible visits there with her daughter?"

"I remember the case."

"Well, I think she has seasonal affective disorder syndrome. The kid has the same symptoms, but the docs say he's too young."

Willa sat forward in her chair. "Explain it to me."

"A person susceptible to SADS lacks seratonin and the right complement of norepinephrine in the brain. Those two chemicals are necessary for the brain's neurotransmitters to work. Simply put, if your neurotransmitters are suppressed, you don't feel good about yourself. You become mentally unstable."

"But why call it a seasonal affective disorder?"

"Because it is seasonal. It has to do with ultraviolet light—sunshine. The way it was explained to me is that light feeds into the eye, the eye distributes the light into the brain, which triggers the production of seratonin—"

"So if you don't get enough sunlight—"

"Exactly."

Willa sensed the theory falling apart. "But this is Florida—the sun shines here almost every day!"

Joe was shaking his head. "If you have a predisposition to SADS, cloudy, overcast days can do you in. And we do have our share of those."

It rained all during Spring Break.

"When the sun comes out, a SADS victim begins to get better. Or rather when the SADS victim gets himself into the sunshine, he improves, the symptoms disappear... unless he's hidden himself in a dark room and pulled the drapes."

Susan's room was like a cave.

"The government has done studies on this in the arctic. Guys who'd worked fine together in say, California or Texas, and then were shipped to weather stations or bases in Alaska during winter, suddenly became neurotic, quirky, refusing to work with one another. When my little old lady visits Maine during a mild winter, the visit with her daughter is fine. But during severe winters, lots of snow and no sun—the visit is a wipeout."

"But you don't think young adults are susceptible?"

Susan was eighteen.

"The doctors don't. But I think that's mostly because they haven't looked for it. Like this kid I'm working with now. He's just entering puberty, which is a shaky time. He's confused. His behavior isn't normal. But it's put down to his becoming a teen or he's accused of being on drugs."

Growing pains.

Joe gave a small self-deprecating laugh. "Ever notice how people complain when it's cloudy or raining? I'm beginning to think everybody has a touch of SADS. But most of us must have an ability to store up seratonin or we'd all be basket cases within a few hours of the sun going behind a cloud."

Susan had steadily traveled north and northwest. The winter that she'd been found on the streets had been one of the worst in Kansas history. Joe was making so much sense, Willa trembled. "Is it genetic?"

He shrugged. "I don't know."

"Who would?"

"Nobody yet, I don't think. It hasn't attracted researchers like schizophrenia and manic-depressive psychosis. But the parents of the boy are just as levelheaded as they can be—rain or shine. As is the daughter of my elderly client."

Willa took a sip of lukewarm coffee to wet her dry mouth. "Is there a cure?"

"Maybe not a cure—but there's a prevention—ultra-violet light panels. They mimic the sun. You just plug 'em in, set the timer and rain or shine outside, the light comes on mimicking sunrise and you get your dose of sera-tonin before you even get out of bed. That's why I think my fourteen-year-old case has SADS. A few hours under those strong hospital lights and he was in shape to go home. I'm going to suggest to his parents they have a light panel constructed."

Willa's eyes suddenly felt as if they were swimming in their sockets. She moved around the desk and kissed Joe-the-Casanova on his cheek. "You have a friend for life."

He blushed furiously. Feeling it creep up his neck, he moaned glumly, "Damn. I just ruined my macho repu-tation."

Willa laughed. "I'll never tell."

SHE WAS BURSTING to tell everyone. Nick, Clytie, Clau-dine and John. She called Nick, but the phone went un-answered. At home she discovered he'd already picked up Amanda. Clytie and Bethany had yet to return from the fishing expedition. Willa went up to the house and knocked long and loud on the Elliotts' back door.

Claudine finally answered, but opened the door only a crack and peeped through. "Willa."

"I've got some news, Claudine..." She glimpsed a bit of gray fabric wrapped around Claudine's shoulders. "I'm sorry. Did I get you out of the shower?"

"No..."

Willa sniffed. "What *is* that smell?"

Claudine uttered the sound of every consonant in the alphabet without shaping a word.

Willa leaned forward, alarmed. "Claudine, are you ill?

"It's the horse blanket."

"What is?"

"The smell."

Horse blanket? John making an honest woman of...
"But—"

"I'm taking your advice," Claudine said, her color high. "And actually, I'm right in the middle of it."

The door snapped shut, the lock tumbled.

For a stunned few seconds, Willa stared at the door. Clarity struck. "Oh!"

She walked back to the cottage grinning, and silently wished Claudine luck and love.

Ten minutes later, Clytie arrived bearing a wet, tanned, and sand-encrusted Bethany. "Mommy! I caught a fish! I caught the biggest. An' it pulled me in the water an' Bubba had to dive in and save my life!"

"Don't panic," Clytie cautioned. "We were fishing from the beach. She didn't fall off a pier or anything."

"But Bubba saved my life!" Bethany insisted, unwilling to allow any lessening of so exciting an occurrence. "He said so. An' then, cause I was wet already, Clytie let me go swimming."

Willa scooped up Bethany and nuzzled her neck. "I love you," she murmured over and over. Bethany tolerated the affection for only a moment.

"I got to go tell Grampa about my fish."

"First, you get a bath. Then we'll see."

Clytie hovered, concerned. "She's making it sound a lot more dangerous than—"

Willa nodded. "I know."

"She did land the biggest drum fish, though. It was still hooked when we retrieved the pole." Clytie tossed a paper sack into the sink. "And here it is. Happy cooking."

"Wait. Is it cleaned?"

"You can have that honor. I've got a half dozen of my own to do. And I'm off to do just that. Bubba's waiting." She rolled her eyes. "Salt air, sea, and me have got him stirred up. I can't afford to waste another minute in chitchat."

"Clytie, I've never cleaned a fish."

"It's easy. Cut off the head, gut it and scale it. Bye."

"Clytie—"

But she was out the door.

"Don't cut the head off my fish! I want to show it to Grampa. Nick cut the head off my first fish and made it littler."

Willa put the fish, bag and all, in the freezer. "You can show it to Grampa tomorrow. He's busy right now."

"What's he doin'?"

"Grown-up things. No more questions."

Bathed and fed, Bethany wound down and was soon asleep.

Willa occupied her time straightening the cottage, flipping through the newspaper, glancing at the clock. Nick would have Amanda home any minute. She turned on the television and curled up on the sofa.

She awakened with a start. Amanda was shaking her shoulder. "I'm home."

"Hello! Did you have a good time?" She looked beyond the girl. "Where's your dad?"

"Gone. He said to say he'll see you tomorrow."

Willa sank back among the cushions. "Tomorrow."

"I had a marvelous time." Amanda's voice was dreamy. "You should've seen him, Willa. He was so tall. He wore a white suit and a shirt unbuttoned down to here... So European."

Willa came wide-awake. "Nick?"

"No—the boy at the yacht club. That's where we went for dinner. His parents came over to have a drink with Nick and he came, too. I think he likes me. He's going to telephone me."

"What about Nick?"

"Oh, Willa, Nick's my father. He's *supposed* to like me."

Willa emitted a melancholy sigh. "Somehow it just hasn't been my day all week long."

"OPEN YOUR EYES, Mommy," Bethany said, tugging on her mother's eyelids for emphasis.

"Stop that, you goose," Willa said drowsily.

"Grandma says for us to come to breakfast."

"Grandma says? Did she call?"

"No. I showed Grampa my fish and she said—"

Willa glanced at the clock. Seven-forty-five. "This morning? You scamp. You left the house without telling me?"

"You were asleep," Bethany said with five-year-old logic. "Grampa adores my fish. And he's so glad I didn't drown. And I'm the nicest granddaughter he could have. He's going to read me the funnies and after church he's taking me to Potter's Wax Museum and Ripley's Believe It or Not and he's gonna buy me a Chinese yo-yo, and for my birthday he's gonna buy me a bicycle with training wheels so I don't scuff my knees or break my head open—"

Willa tried to visualize this flood of words out of the taciturn John. She couldn't. "And where was your grandmother while Grampa was saying all this?"

"Sitting in Grampa's lap, but he made her get up 'cause she was mashing his legs flat. She's not little like I am."

BREAKFAST was Claudine's best effort; eggs scrambled into oblivion, warmed over croissants, cream cheese and jam. John sat at the kitchen table following her with his eyes.

"Claudine has convinced me," he said to Willa, "that taking the modeling course will set a good example for Bethany. The child should have more than one role model. Don't you agree?"

"Oh, I do."

"That's not to say you haven't been, my dear. You've done a splendid job with Bethany. And as her grandfather, I feel I, too, should take a more active role."

"Having you and Claudine in Bethany's life was my motive for coming here," Willa said.

"This is not a yes dear, no dear, three bags full dear, kind of thing. I won't have you women running roughshod over me. I'm staying well within my principles."

"You're one of the most principled men I know," Willa told him.

He took a last sip of coffee and excused himself to have a cigar.

Bethany trailed after him. "First, read me the funnies, Grampa. You promised."

"After I have a smoke," he said.

"Before," Bethany insisted.

"You're too bossy." The words came faintly back to Claudine and Willa. They heard the rattle of the news-

paper and exchanged smiles. So much for John's principles, Willa thought.

"You're wearing your professional look, Willa."

"It's not professional. It's dumbstruck. John actually
came into the kitchen, sat down and—"

"We've indulged in quite a few actualities these past
two days." Her face went pink. "I hadn't realized how
sentimental John really is."

"Sentimental as in horse blankets?"

"I'm trying not to be embarrassed saying this. I got
caught up in being Natalie's daughter-in-law, keeping the
peace, being Susan's mother, then I got caught up in her
problems and her disappearance. John was just too polite to...to push himself on me. I forgot to cleave to him.
The forgetting became a habit."

"You told him all of this?" Willa asked admiringly.

"I did. And he told me things. He's been carrying
around so much guilt about the influence his mother may
have had on Susan and her behavior—"

Willa stopped her. "I have a theory about Susan's behavior, Claudine. It fits. It fits her like a glove...."

Ten minutes later, Claudine cried, "Oh, Willa! If only
we had known!"

"But that's just it. Ten years ago, few professionals
knew about SADS. And even today, it's extremely difficult to diagnose, especially in teens. I've been so concerned about Bethany. Now..."

"That's one of the reasons you decided to come here,
isn't it? To find out about Susan's background, and
ours?"

"Do you hate me for that?"

"No, I think I would've done the same. But we're past
all that, aren't we?"

"We are." She glanced at her watch. "It's also past nine-thirty. I've—"

"Oh!" Claudine's hand flew to her mouth. "I forgot to give you a message from Nick. He said he'd pick you up at ten. John and I are to keep an eye on Bethany and Amanda—"

"Ten? I look a wreck!"

Clytie was just coming up the steps as Willa raced down them. "Don't tell me things aren't back to normal yet."

"See for yourself," Willa called back over her shoulder.

"I've been doing that my whole life," Clytie said and walked into the kitchen. She surveyed the pans on the stove, the dishes on the table, her strategically placed stools all out of order. Claudine at the sink. "This is my kitchen."

"And mine, Clytie Elliott. Now sit down and tell me what you've been doing the whole night long."

"Snuggling," said Clytie.

"Really? Me, too."

"You've lost your mind, Claudine."

"No, I haven't. I've just started using it."

Clytie sniffed. "What's that smell?"

"Horse blanket," said Claudine, her hands in the dishwater. "No..." She lifted the silver-and-black thing out of the soapy water. "Dead fish."

Chapter Sixteen

Willa was so happy to see Nick she would've been content to curl up and spend the rest of her life in one of his pockets. On the other hand, he had given her barely thirty minutes of himself all week. To her horror the litany of complaints just seemed to roll off her tongue of its own accord.

"How nice to see you, Nick."

He wore pleated white slacks, a white shirt, sleeves rolled to forearm with buttons undone to reveal an expanse of dark curly hair through which she had the urge to run her fingers. She held the urge in check.

"What's the sarcasm for?"

"Why should I be sarcastic? You haven't called, you rushed me out of your office after the Wilton thing. When I came out of Judge Henley's chambers, you'd disappeared, you dropped Amanda off without a word to me—"

"I told you hold Sunday—"

"You didn't say what time! I've barely had a moment to get ready because—"

He lifted an eyebrow. "You're aching to be in my arms."

Her chin went up. "Think again."

Amanda rose from the sofa. "Could you take your bickering elsewhere? I'm trying to sleep."

"We're just leaving," Nick said, taking hold of Willa's arm and ushering her out the door and into his car.

"Don't I have any say in this?" she said, unwilling yet to give an inch.

Nick settled himself behind the wheel. "Nope. Just sit there stiffed-neck and as argumentative as you like. Only keep your mouth shut."

"I won't."

He parked at the city pier.

"We're going sailing? I'm not dressed for sailing."

He tracked her for a moment with his eyes. Her dark chin-length hair hung in a soft inviting frame around her face. He could see faintly the straps of her slip through the beige silk blouse. Her breasts rose and fell with a telling rhythm. "You can undress down to whatever makes you comfortable."

Her heart sped up. "You'd like that wouldn't you?"

"What'd you expect. Lawyers make abysmal saints. We're as prurient as the next guy."

She took off her shoes.

Once he'd secured the dinghy, he handed Willa aboard and started the engines. He did not raise sail, but motored downriver. Willa sat on a locker that stored a spare canvas, legs crossed, watching him skillfully maneuver the boat midchannel.

Behind the boat, the dinghy bobbed in a lacy wake. The air was pristine, the expanse of blue sky dotted with puffy white clouds. Now and again a gull squawked, punctuating the sound of the throbbing engines. Willa was finding it difficult to maintain her anger.

Nick looked back at her. "Want to take the helm?"

"I might as well. It's boring just sitting here."

He stepped aside. She took his place. He put his arms around her, living ropes that molded himself to her. The dormant passion within her came so alive it seemed to spasm.

"Still boring?" Nick said, pressing his lips to the curve of her ear.

"Slightly less," she said, managing to keep a scrap of pride or anger intact, but only just.

"I'm going to make love to you, Willa."

There were no ifs, ands or buts in his tone, no cross-purposes. It was a simply stated fact. She found herself responding. Her gaze swung inward to tangled memory and desire; the channel markers blurred. Time suspended.

His arms enclosed her, his hands covered hers on the wheel, guiding hers until eventually they steered out of the channel. Switching off the engine, he allowed momentum to carry them alongside a pier jutting some yards out from a bank of wildly tangled palmetto fronds and ancient wind-bent trees draped with moss. He left her clutching the wheel dumbly to run a line through mooring swivels fore and aft, then he came back to her and took her hands from the wheel.

"Now is the time to say, no."

She must've conveyed her answer with her eyes or some gesture of acquiescence because he helped her over the boat rail and onto the gray-planked pier. She thought the moment called for something profound and dramatic to be said, but what came was:

"We aren't staying aboard the boat?"

"Performing acrobatics in a two-foot wide bunk is not my idea of romance."

"And the boat might sink?" she said, recalling his superstition about naked women. *Naked.*

With every forward step toward the canopy of trees, Willa felt increasingly awkward. The trees suddenly gave way to an enormous open deck that was attached to a house. She paused in midstep. "Who lives here?"

"Nobody." He went ahead to unlock a set of double French doors and threw them open. A lovely blast of cool air swept over Willa as she stepped through.

"The air conditioner is on."

"I think of everything. Want a quick tour?"

The family room was huge and vaulted and faced the river, but the remainder of the house seemed to go on forever with a step up here into a windowed cubbyhole, a turn into a bath, closets tucked there, a kitchen its own ell, which somehow twisted back on itself so that one had a view of the river. All was unfurnished until Nick led her down a wide hall and threw open a door to a dim cavern of a room.

"Master bedroom," he said, as if announcing royalty.

It held but a single piece of furniture. A bed.

He crossed the room and pulled the drapes away from the windows. A small gray lizard warming itself in a patch of sunlight on the outside sill started, then leaped into the dense shrub and shade beyond.

"What do you think?" Nick asked, returning to her side.

"I don't know if I could find my way back to the front door."

"You won't have to—not for hours."

"But what's the meaning...?"

"Meaning? Dear heart...here's the meaning..." He began unbuttoning her blouse and slowly pushed it back off her shoulders. Her heart knocked frantically.

His breath caught at the sight of her creamy shoulders, only lightly tanned, at the gentle swell of her breasts above the lacy inset of her slip.

"Is this meaning enough for you?" His voice was hoarse with the growing heat of passion. He pressed his lips to the hollow in her throat.

Did he carry her to the bed or did they walk? Willa could not be sure; only that she was there upon it, her skin under his hands, her body under his, separate entities, but only for moments.

Her arms and legs were around him, silky and sleek, binding him to her.

He was thrusting into her, seemingly beyond the limits of endurance...then...the finite moment of ecstasy as he made her finally and forever a part of himself.

He looked down into her eyes, and saw into their blueness, into the alluring depths; reaffirming his decision to live there.

"I've needed you since you first walked into my office shrouded in prim cotton from neck to knee."

Willa was desperate for something to say, but her mind was still recording the act of love, the incredible energy they had each given to it.

He lifted himself up a little and looked down at her—breasts upthrust, nipples swollen, he could count her ribs, the hollow curve of her belly, and below where they were joined.

And even as she struggled to find some word to let him know her joy, her acceptance, he began to move again, finding a rhythm, thrusting and holding...until her own heartbeat matched his....

PROPPED ON AN ELBOW and looking at her, Nick trailed a fingeritp from throat hollow to nipple to navel. "Hungry? The fridge is stocked."

"I am a little. But I wouldn't dare get off this bed. My legs wouldn't hold me. And even if they would, I probably couldn't find my way to the kitchen."

"Familiarity will take care of that."

"Familiarity?"

"If you lived here."

"But I don't."

"You could. You and Bethany, me and Amanda."

Willa's eyes grew large.

"I took your advice, I bought a bigger house."

"This house?"

"I sold my place on the beach and my boat. I hand it over to the new owners in the morning."

"Nick! Your boat? You love your boat."

"I love you more. You're going to spare me that awful ordeal of having to go down on my knees, aren't you?"

"Am I to consider that a proposal of marriage?"

"Please do."

"How are we going to furnish the house?"

"Beachfront property is ungodly expensive. But so are boats like mine. There's a bit left over for furniture."

"How many bedrooms are there? I lost track."

"Five. Ours, one for Bethany, one for Amanda, guest room, one extra."

Nursery, Willa thought. She sat up. "Let's go through the house again."

"May I take it that you're agreeing to become Mrs. Nicholas H. Cavenaugh?"

She lay back down. "What's the *H* stand for?"

"Henry."

"Henry!"

He pinned her to the bed. "I'm a nice Henry."

"Yes, you are."

"And you love me."

"I adore you. I want to look at the kitchen. Was there a window over the—"

"There are windows all over the damned place."

Willa turned toward him. "I get it, you want my undivided attention."

"Brilliant deduction."

"Nick—about my job. I like working—"

"You'd take off for a honeymoon?"

"Oh. Of course."

"And maybe a few days when my parents are here?"

"Your parents. You're making me nervous. When are they coming?"

"Day after tomorrow. I thought we could get married—say, next Saturday."

"Saturday. Six days from *now*? Let me up! I have a thousand things to do."

He held her tightly and tickled her ear with his tongue. "Sure you do."

"We have to tell everybody, we have to talk to the girls, make certain it's okay with them—"

"Hold it. We're not asking *anybody's* permission."

"If you say so. I have to have a new dress, so will Bethany and Amanda. We can't possibly have company without furniture..."

"We. I like the sound of that. I've never been a 'we.'"

"Don't put your tongue in my ear like that. It's distracting."

He trailed his mouth down to her breasts and sucked on her nipple.

"Oh... That's even more dis—"

His hand slid lightly across her belly... and lower.

"Nick . . ." she moaned, barely audible.

"Do I have your undivided attention?"

"You have it," she whispered and gave herself up to loving him.

HARLEQUIN
American Romance®

COMING NEXT MONTH

#345 AMERICAN PIE by Margaret St. George

Spirited and ambitious, Polish immigrant Lucie Kolska arrives in New York on the eve of the twentieth century. Proud and daring, Dublin native Jamie Kelly dreams of feasting on his slice of the pie. But to make it, Lucie and Jamie must cast off the baggage of their old ideas before they can embrace the best of what America has to offer: hope for the future and a love that is as brilliant as the promise of the American Dream. Don't miss the first book in the "Century of American Romance"—a nostalgic look back at the lives and loves of the twentieth century.

#346 RANCHO DIABLO by Anne Stuart

Isabelle Romney couldn't escape her memories of Rancho Diablo—and the man who'd stolen her birthright. Luke Cassidy had been first in her father's heart—and for better or worse, Luke was first in hers. Isabelle swore she'd never again be vulnerable to Luke. But to do that, she had to make one last trip home....

#347 BELOVED DREAMER by Anne Henry

She'd never forgotten him. Twenty years before, Chad Morgan had asked Julie Harper to join him in a dream. Although she'd married someone else, she never forgot her first love. Now, at her high school reunion, Chad's face was the most welcome. She wondered what she would do if Chad asked her again. Would she sacrifice everything for the sake of love?

#348 PHANTOM ANGEL by Kathy Clark

The man Melora Delaney was bringing back from Vietnam had lost his youth and his memory. As a psychologist, she couldn't restore Bo's lost years, but she could help him begin life again. Melora planned two months of intensive work with her patient. When the time came—and it would—would she be able to let him go!

Take 4 bestselling love stories FREE

Plus get a FREE surprise gift!

HARLEQUIN'S "BIG WIN"
SWEEPSTAKES RULES & REGULATIONS
NO PURCHASE NECESSARY TO ENTER OR RECEIVE A PRIZE

1. To enter and join the Reader Service, scratch off the metallic strips on all your BIG WIN tickets #1–#6. This will reveal the values for each sweepstakes entry number, the number of free book(s) you will receive, and your free bonus gift as part of our Reader Service. If you do not wish to take advantage of our Reader Service, but wish to enter the Sweepstakes only, scratch off the metallic strips on your BIG WIN tickets #1–#4. Return your entire sheet of tickets intact. Incomplete and/or inaccurate entries are ineligible for that section or sections of prizes. Not responsible for mutilated or unreadable entries or inadvertent printing errors. Mechanically reproduced entries are null and void.

2. Whether you take advantage of this offer or not, your Sweepstakes numbers will be compared against a list of winning numbers generated at random by the computer. In the event that all prizes are not claimed by March 31, 1992, a random drawing will be held from all qualified entries received from March 30, 1990 to March 31, 1992, to award all unclaimed prizes. All cash prizes (Grand to Sixth), will be mailed to the winners and are payable by cheque in U.S. funds. Seventh prize to be shipped to winners via third-class mail. These prizes are in addition to any free, surprise or mystery gifts that might be offered. Versions of this sweepstakes with different prizes of approximate equal value may appear in other mailings or at retail outlets by Torstar Corp. and its affiliates.

3. The following prizes are awarded in this sweepstakes: ★ Grand Prize (1) $1,000,000; First Prize (1) $25,000; Second Prize (1) $10,000; Third Prize (5) $5,000; Fourth Prize (10) $1,000; Fifth Prize (100) $250; Sixth Prize (2500) $10; ★ ★ Seventh Prize (6000) $12.95 ARV.

   ★ This Sweepstakes contains a Grand Prize offering of $1,000,000 annuity. Winner will receive $33,333.33 a year for 30 years without interest totalling $1,000,000.

   ★ ★ Seventh Prize: A fully illustrated hardcover book published by Torstar Corp. Approximate value of the book is $12.95.

   Entrants may cancel the Reader Service at any time without cost or obligation to buy (see details in center insert card).

4. This promotion is being conducted under the supervision of Marden-Kane, Inc., an independent judging organization. By entering this Sweepstakes, each entrant accepts and agrees to be bound by these rules and the decisions of the judges, which shall be final and binding. Odds of winning in the random drawing are dependent upon the total number of entries received. Taxes, if any, are the sole responsibility of the winners. Prizes are nontransferable. All entries must be received by no later than 12:00 NOON, on March 31, 1992. The drawing for all unclaimed sweepstakes prizes will take place May 30, 1992, at 12:00 NOON, at the offices of Marden-Kane, Inc., Lake Success, New York.

5. This offer is open to residents of the U.S., the United Kingdom, France and Canada, 18 years or older except employees and their immediate family members of Torstar Corp., its affiliates, subsidiaries, Marden-Kane, Inc., and all other agencies and persons connected with conducting this Sweepstakes. All Federal, State and local laws apply. Void wherever prohibited or restricted by law. Any litigation respecting the conduct and awarding of a prize in this publicity contest may be submitted to the Régie des loteries et courses du Québec.

6. Winners will be notified by mail and may be required to execute an affidavit of eligibility and release which must be returned within 14 days after notification or, an alternative winner will be selected. Canadian winners will be required to correctly answer an arithmetical skill-testing question administered by mail which must be returned within a limited time. Winners consent to the use of their names, photographs and/or likenesses for advertising and publicity in conjunction with this and similar promotions without additional compensation.

7. For a list of our major winners, send a stamped, self-addressed envelope to: WINNERS LIST c/o MARDEN-KANE, INC., P.O. BOX 701, SAYREVILLE, NJ 08871. Winners Lists will be fulfilled after the May 30, 1992 drawing date.

If Sweepstakes entry form is missing, please print your name and address on a 3" × 5" piece of plain paper and send to:

In the U.S.
Harlequin's "BIG WIN" Sweepstakes
901 Fuhrmann Blvd.
P.O. Box 1867
Buffalo, NY 14269-1867

In Canada
Harlequin's "BIG WIN" Sweepstakes
P.O. Box 609
Fort Erie, Ontario
L2A 5X3

© 1989 Harlequin Enterprises Limited   Printed in the U.S.A.

LTY-H590